A FATAL RENDEZVOUS IN MAYFAIR

PREVIOUSLY PUBLISHED AS 'LOVING LILY'

LONDON LADIES IN PERIL

BEVERLEY OAKLEY

A FATAL RENDEZVOUS IN MAYFAIR

CHAPTER 1

Lily had become deaf to the screeching.

The din of the madhouse and the stench of unwashed bodies no longer brought her hands to her ears or the bile to the back of her throat.

Every day was more of the same.

Except today.

She blinked, shock making her slow to pick up her spoon and wolf down whatever sustenance she could before someone else did.

For today, a faint tendril of steam rose up from the tin bowl that had been thrust in front of her.

The food was hot.

Or, at least, it was not as cold as the stone floor she was sometimes made to sleep on as punishment.

"Eat up, girl, if yer know wot's good fer yer!"

A passing warden slapped the back of her head, and quickly, Lily dug her spoon into the thin gruel, shovelling it into her mouth as quickly as she could.

But the warden was not yet done. "Yer reckon our food ain't good enough for Lady High-'n-Mighty?"

Lily shook her head; though as mistress of Bradden Hall, she'd have declared the weevil-ridden victuals unfit for the servants. And the dogs.

But it had been two years since Lily had been mistress of anything, much less her own destiny.

"The Lord will have thee for thine…gooseberry pie!"

Shouting her latest favourite lines as she tried to evade one of the servants, Mad Maria passed by in a waft of stale body odour, some vestige of golden hair still bright beneath the filth. "Is thy a gooseberry that will grace the Lord's gooseberry pie?" The young woman doubled back to stand in front of Lily and cocked her head, her expression trusting and curious.

"Yes, Maria, now sit down and eat your gruel before you starve to death." Lily waved the girl away before snatching back her plate as her neighbour tried to take advantage of the unguarded moment. The nuns would as likely let Lily starve as they would Maria, whose family would doubtless rejoice at being relieved of the burden and stain of insanity.

When a cockroach staggered out of the mess in front of her, Lily didn't even recoil. She'd lost too much flesh off her bones to concern herself with such niceties as vermin-free victuals.

Scraping up the last of the porridge, she pushed her plate aside, whereupon it was greedily snatched up by her neighbour who began to lick it clean.

"Madame Bradden, you have a visitor."

Instantly, the twenty-five women in the noisy refectory stopped eating, spoons suspended in midair, some with mouths hanging open—in the case of the truly insane. A good half of the women merely turned polite enquiring gazes towards Lily.

In two years, no one had ever visited Madame Bradden.

Lily put her hand to her heart. It was beating so rapidly

she couldn't focus on the novice who'd delivered the information.

Someone had come to visit her? Pushing back a strand of lank, greasy hair that had escaped from beneath her grimy hessian cap, she looked down at her nail-bitten hands as her excitement drained away.

Her visitor was of no account. Unless Robert had sanctioned her release, a visitor was here either to gloat, or was someone she'd hoped would never have learned of her circumstances.

She rose.

"Mother Superior's office."

"Mother Superior's office." Lily whispered it in the reverential tones such a statement deserved. Punishment for only the gravest of misdemeanours were meted out in Mother Superior's office.

But 'someone' suggested a stranger.

A stranger. Someone from the outside.

Teddy?

At this thought, her heart beat more furiously as she followed the novice down dark and damp twisting stone corridors until they reached an arched doorway. Lily stepped into the panelled, comfortable interior, and remembered the first time she'd stood in this room.

With Teddy.

Dear Teddy, who had declared his horror and torment at what Robert was demanding of them both.

He'd promised to lay down his life if that was what was required to rescue her from this place. Tears had streamed from his eyes as the nuns had torn Lily from his embrace.

No, Teddy would not let her down if he could help it.

Her husband, Robert, however—

"Lady Bradden?"

Lily inclined her head slightly and glanced between Sister

Bernadette seated behind her large mahogany desk, and a tall, spare gentleman who was in the process of seating himself as Lily lowered herself onto a spindly chair opposite.

His brown hair and side-whiskers were fashionably coiffed, but his suit was cheap. His skin was sallow, and his nose was long and sharp. Like his eyes, which regarded her with obvious distaste. Lily didn't recognise him.

"She goes by Madame Bradden, not Lady Bradden, Mr Montpelier," said Sister Bernadette, shuffling some papers on her desk as if she were looking for something, "having lost the moral right to be his lordship's wife." Like Mr Montpelier, Sister Bernadette's nostrils twitched.

Not that their collective distaste should come as a surprise. Lily couldn't remember the last time she'd been given clean clothes.

"So, Madame Bradden, it appears you will be leaving us." Having found the letter she'd obviously been looking for, Sister Bernadette sent Lily an impassive half-smile while Lily hid her surprise. It was rare that an inmate left the maison other than via the morgue.

"Apparently, a more conducive environment for your care awaits you back in England." Sister Bernadette raised a sceptical eyebrow. "I will not scruple to say that it is my belief that the affliction which sent you to us is correlated with the dissipated ways you embraced in your mother country; however, your husband has written that you are to return."

"My husband—?

"—has not forgiven you, and nor will he." Sister Bernadette's eyes narrowed and Lily turned towards Mr Montpelier who muttered, "I am to bear you back to England on tomorrow's packet."

Lily glanced about her, suddenly visited by the suspicion that Robert's intention was simply to lodge her in a different facility, perhaps having been coerced by a more kindly member of his family.

Then, remembering there were none of those, she pressed her lips together and thought of Teddy once more. Yes, her own Teddy—or rather, Dr Theodore Swithins, Robert's friend before he and Lily had become lovers—who might still have sufficient sway to persuade Robert that his cruelty towards his wife went beyond barbarous.

"Lord Bradden has employed warders to ensure you are properly supervised, he writes." Sister Bernadette sent Lily a warning look. "As he must, for there is no telling when the taint of insanity will rear its ugly head with no mercy for those innocents who may be slumbering in their beds before they are consumed by the madwoman's fire."

Mr Montpelier looked alarmed. "How often has Madame Bradden displayed the…insanity which caused her to be incarcerated here?"

Lily noticed that though his fingers were long and elegant, he did not have the hands of a gentleman. The tips were stained and calloused. Whether he spoke like a gentleman was impossible to tell for his French was halting.

"She was a wild cat when she was first brought to us." Sister Bernadette looked sorrowful. "Yes, a wild cat, believing the walls were breathing and the furniture savage creatures she must slay."

"And, more recently? This last year? How… deep…is her insanity?" Mr Montpelier had barely looked at her. Lily hid her shame.

Until a few years ago, she'd considered herself the sanest of people, though she would concede that pride and vanity had once been among her vices. Two years ago, the last time she'd laid eyes on a man he'd looked at her with raw desire.

She'd been used to admiration—from both men and women.

But not Robert. He'd never desired her. She still wondered why he'd married her.

Her stomach clenched as she listened to the pair discuss the clinical details surrounding her incarceration—Madame Bradden's sudden attacks of fear and frenzy. Lord, they'd terrified Lily too, but she'd never done anyone any harm. And each one had lasted only hours, leaving her wracked and depleted. But no less herself in the morning.

Now Robert was taking her back? He had relented?

Oh God, what other punishment did he have in store for her?

"She has displayed no insanity this past year, no." Sister Bernadette sounded proud. "Not, in fact, since she came here. We work hard in this house to beat the devil out of our inmates, though it is well known that insanity cannot be cured. I hope Lord Bradden has a sturdy lock on the door of the suite in which madame will be incarcerated. And I hope he has thought long and hard about the merits of undertaking her care, himself. Dealing with the feeble-minded and criminally insane is our specialty."

Mr Montpelier rose. "I believe he conveyed everything necessary in his letter," he said, nodding at the missive that lay on the table in front of Sister Bernadette. "The carriage is waiting outside. We will leave once Madame Bradden has packed her things and, I hope, will make good progress so we can catch the dawn packet tomorrow."

"Madame is ready to depart now," Sister Bernadette said, flicking her a look that Lily would have described as gloating had she not known what a sainted being Mother Superior's right-hand tormenter really was. "Our inmates are allowed no possessions."

CHAPTER 2

Lily sat, shivering with hope and fear, opposite Mr Montpelier in the carriage as it jolted gently down the hill away from her place of incarceration.

She'd been given a brief opportunity to wash her face and hands, but she doubted she'd ever feel truly clean. Like the dirt and grit from the coal mines that polluted the air of the local village, she could never wash away the sin that had caused her fall from grace.

Not that Robert had lived a spotless life.

But then, he was a man. He didn't need to be free from sin to remain a pillar of polite society.

"When does my husband expect me?" she asked, breaking the silence as they passed through the cobbled streets of the smoky Belgian village in the lee of the hill upon which nestled the *maison*. Then, more bravely, "Please tell me if he has forgiven me?" For this man opposite her must be in possession of information that would help Lily craft the artful petition she'd rehearsed for two years to be granted her freedom. Robert might be bringing her home, but he'd not install her as his lawful wife; of that she was very sure.

He cast her a look that conveyed both irritation and disgust. "Your husband is not a forgiving man."

"Then…it *is* someone else who has secured my freedom?" She couldn't contain the excitement in her tone.

Mr Montpelier studied her a long moment before he looked away. Clearly, he was not the kind to humour her. Finally, he replied, "Your former lover is married now, with a child, and has, to the best of my knowledge, made no enquiries regarding your welfare."

Lily tried not to reveal the extent of her wounding. The dismissive tone was as painful as the information. So, Teddy was not behind her removal. She was being brought back to the country of her birth where she'd spent the first twenty-three years of her life, to be reviled and incarcerated, simply in a different environment.

"Dr Swithins is not worth your tears." Mr Montpelier's tone was unsympathetic.

"He promised to secure my release."

"He said what you needed to hear to make you go quietly with him. Channel your finer feelings where they are due, Madame Bradden."

"And where are they due? Who has concerned themselves with my welfare since my husband took me as his wife and then beat me and suppressed my will?" Emotion threatened to overcome her as she leaned forward, tense and tearful. "Is it at his pleasure that I am being brought back to him? Does his conscience smite him that not once in two years have I shown the degeneracy of character that was the basis of him committing me to an asylum for the insane?" Her flare of anger was tempered by his look. Lily pressed her lips together, suddenly afraid. She must heed her words if she were not to be sent directly back from whence she came.

"Your husband has not spoken your name in two years.

You are dead to him." Mr Montpelier looked bored. "It was a marriage that was pressed upon him, but yielded him nothing but shame and misery. Not even the heir he required."

"That was not entirely my fault." Lily muttered. "Nor am I the vain, self-centred creature my husband painted me." She said this as proudly as she could, though the response was predictable as he raked her with disdainful eyes, starting from the top of her hideous flannel cap, travelling down her emaciated body in its grey flannel tunic to her shabby boots.

"You have little to feed your vanity, it is true, Madame Bradden."

Lily stared miserably down at her hands clasped demurely in her lap, the nails ripped and dirty. "For five years, I tried to be the wife he wanted me to be." She looked up. "It is difficult to respond to harsh dealings and cold contempt with an abundance of good humour and…fidelity."

"You traded your modest standing in society in order to deport yourself in silk and satin and jewels. Your husband spared no expense, I believe."

"My father bartered me to a man I'd met but once. From the age of ten, I lived quietly with my aunt, then seven years later, having barely seen my father during that time, he told me I was to be married. It was a business transaction that suited them both, and I was the showpiece for my husband's wealth. That is not the same as bartering my modest standing in order to deport myself in satin and jewels, though I've no doubt it's what my detractors will tell you," she softly.

"Marriage is a contract, Madame Bradden. Even at the tender age at which you married, you'd have been well-schooled in what your side of the bargain required of you."

"My husband has clearly revealed a great deal about our

marriage, Mr Montpelier." Lily's aversion to the cold-faced man opposite her grew.

"He has said nothing to me about you, or your marriage, Madame Bradden. This is what the gossips say." He put his elbows on his knees and leaned forward. "You appear as fond of your husband as he is of you. Do you really want to be returned to his tender care?"

Lily leaned back against the squabs and closed her eyes. "What choice do I have?"

"I'm offering you one."

Her first response was to put her hand to her breast in a show of outraged modesty that caused him to laugh for the first time.

It was not a respectful laugh. "Let me spare your concerns on that front, madame. You may have been a beauty, once, and indeed my endeavours in rescuing you from the *maison* are based on the hope that a good dousing and a month of nourishing food may restore you. But right now, you are a filthy, vermin-ridden creature who holds absolutely no appeal for me or for any other red or blue-blooded male, I shouldn't think."

It was the longest speech he had made, and Lily observed that although he phrased his sentences like a gentleman, a coarseness to certain words proclaimed him the charlatan he must be, she now realised, if he had made this journey unbeknownst to her husband.

"There are few ways a woman can earn her keep other than on her back, yet I have a proposition that will safeguard whatever modesty or virtue you claim to possess. It is easy enough to return you to the *maison*." He made a sweeping gesture of the passing countryside—muddy and bleak. "However, I wished to gauge for myself, during our journey, that you had the mental faculties needed to fulfil the new role I have in mind for you, should you accept my terms."

Lily considered him in this new light—abductor and charlatan. "Your terms?" For if he was not taking her back to Robert, he was indeed kidnapping her. "I must agree to your terms to gain my freedom?" Terms that did not include the bartering of her body. It sounded too enticing to be real. "What are your terms?" Despite the impression she'd given of outraged modesty, she couldn't think of anything she would *not* do to secure her freedom.

No, that was not true. She would not barter her body. She'd taken a lover once, and she was still paying for that mistake.

"Patience, Madame Bradden. I would not overload your feeble brain with too much information. You have been over-come by enough novelty already today."

"I cannot agree to any terms if I do not know what you are offering me."

He gave another of his slight, dismissive shrugs. "I can return you to your husband, or you can agree to work for me. Women are ungovernable creatures ruled solely by their emotions, and yours have clearly got the better of you too many times for your own good. No, you will be told what is required of you in good time to be properly equipped for your role. Disappointingly, I will have to wait for you to gain some flesh, and a bloom to burnish your sallow, filthy skin before you bear any resemblance to the woman you once were. But I am patient. After a few weeks of nourishment and training, I trust you will be ready to put our little plan into practice. And did I mention that there would be rewards for both of us?"

Now Lily truly did tremble. She was to be used for someone else's ends, yet he would tell her neither whose ends nor what her role was?

She glanced uneasily over her shoulder at the disappearing asylum, a tiny speck on the hill, and then at her boots. Her stomach growled audibly.

"What say you to a saddle of beef and a bottle of claret when we reach our lodgings? Something substantial to sustain us before the crossing tomorrow."

Food.

Mr Montpelier knew how easy it would be to make her sing to his tune.

Her stomach growled again. But what did that matter when she'd sell her soul for a saddle of beef and a bottle of claret? A few more months at the *maison,* and she suspected that in her currently weakened and ill-nourished state, she'd be dead from any number of the diseases that swept through on a regular basis.

"I say that the prospect of such a meal sounds delightful!"

Her tinkling response landed badly when received with his usual dour contempt. "The street urchin trying to sound like a lady." He looked amused as he narrowed his eyes. "That's what they will make of you." Then he sobered, and added, "Those who don't know who, and what, you truly are."

Lily met his stare, unafraid. She would agree to Mr Montpelier's terms because he was returning her to England. Not to her husband. In a day or two, she would be back in the land of her birth.

Once in London, amidst the press of traffic, it would be easy to do what she now intended must be her only course. She would flee the carriage and, on foot if necessary, make her way to where her aunt lived in Norfolk. Aunt Kerridge would keep Lily safe until Lily found a means to support herself.

It was even possible Robert did not know she was missing.

"A saddle of beef and a bottle of claret," she sighed,

dreamily, stretching and closing her eyes as a feeling of contented satisfaction enveloped her. Mr Montpelier thought he was so clever, abducting her so he could make her do his bidding.

But he'd met his match.

"I'd agree to anything," she added, "for a saddle of beef and a bottle of claret."

CHAPTER 3

Hamish McTavish tapped his fingers on his knee, quietly impatient at the delay caused by the cooper's wagon blocking Bond Street. The driver had jumped down to inspect the wheel, and now the horses were getting restless.

As was his sister, though that was nothing new. Lucy had been complaining about something for the past few minutes, but Hamish had been too busy thinking of his forthcoming interview with Sir Lionel to pay her any mind.

Until she thrust an object onto his lap, demanding, "I tell you, it's shoddy work, Hamish, and I shall demand my money back. Already the flowers are detaching from my new bonnet—"

"Good luck with that," he muttered, casting a dispassionate look at the floral confection resting on his thigh, then at his sister's pretty, indignant face. "Papa thought it looked mighty becoming, and that's saying something. You do realise the girl who made it is lucky to earn enough to put one square meal on the table from her labours?"

Lucy sighed, taking the bonnet back and thoughtfully

fingering one of the silk blooms, before thrusting it back at him with the exhortation that he must see the stitching that was come undone, adding, "Papa only praised me in the hope of bending my will so I'll yield and return home to live with him; which you know I will never do! And you always get so fired up about the poor and unfortunate, yet you never publish a word about injustice in your magazines. Anyone would think you were just like Papa." She said this almost sorrowfully, and Hamish had to temper the hot retort that sprung to his lips. Little could get him riled up, but a barb like that, especially coming from his sister, needed to be treated with kid gloves. Though perhaps not quite as expensive as the ones his sister adored.

"Which you know I am not," he managed calmly, wrapping the reins about his wrist to prevent him flicking them in agitation when the horses were still at a standstill. Hamish was considering whether to enlarge upon his offence at being compared with his father when the incompetence of the carriage driver in front decided him that his assistance might expedite matters and get the traffic moving once more.

Jumping down from the seat, one long ribbon of his sister's bonnet became caught in his cufflink, and he stopped to extricate it in order to return the piece of millinery to his sister.

What happened next caught him totally off-guard; for one moment, he was aware of a flurry of grey, and when he turned, Lucy was screaming, pointing at a figure that was now running across the road, the trailing pink ribbons suggesting that his sister's unsatisfactory bonnet had just found a new home.

"Catch her! Don't worry about me!" Lucy exhorted him, still pointing at the figure of the beggar woman who'd just evaded death from beneath the wheel of a cooper's wagon coming from the opposite direction.

The dirty bundle of rags was in the process of picking herself up from the cobblestones before making a run for a group gathered beneath a shop awning, where she no doubt hoped to evade notice.

Ducking and weaving between the carriages, Hamish tore off in pursuit. For all Lucy's complaints, the bonnet had cost a pretty penny, but above all, he considered society was in a parlous state if law-abiding people waiting in carriages were not safe from such assaults on their liberty to go about their business.

He stopped to let a dray go by, still keeping in sight the woman whom he saw ducking and weaving amongst the throng of shoppers. He might have lost her had a stretch of empty road not cleared up, and he was able to dart down a side street where he saw her in the distance.

Lucy would either wait or make her own way home, for she'd made clear her priorities: the return of her bonnet. And although he'd decry he was as unlike his harsh and puritanical father as it was possible to be, Hamish was nevertheless concerned about upholding law and order. It would set a poor precedent if he couldn't arrest a brazen thief in the middle of the day; and a delinquent young woman, at that.

Yet, the brazen thief appeared to have outwitted him. Frustrated, he stood on the corner and shaded his eyes, scanning the cobbled street until, in the distance, he saw that the person had obviously been crouching in the shadows, pressed against a wall, before, perhaps perceiving it was safe, darting back into view, pausing, then dashing up a short flight of stairs and into a four-square dwelling, whose door had just opened. A couple of ladies were now stepping out onto the pavement.

He would have been surprised at their lack of concern at

being passed by a clearly desperate creature had he not drawn close enough to recognise the establishment as Madame Chambon's notorious House of Assignation. Stories of desperation—and vice and villainy—were common enough here, he supposed, and although this was the last place Hamish would willingly step into, the street was now empty, and he had an excuse that was valid enough reason to satisfy his curiosity, though he told himself that mere curiosity had nothing to do with entering.

If the thief was one of Madame Chambon's girls, then she should be brought to justice.

But as he stopped in the vestibule, breathing rather fast as he gazed about the sumptuous surroundings—which he put down to exertion only—he recollected that Madame Chambon's girls were renowned for being as refined and well-dressed as any duchess. Their beauty, poise, and wit made them highly sought after by the discerning male establishment looking for diversions their wives could not provide.

No, this creature was an urchin. She most definitely was not one of Madame's girls.

"Sir, how can we help you?"

The purr belonged to a young woman of considerable beauty and in accents that would have done any duchess, or person with pretensions to gentility, proud. For a moment, he could only stare. The light from the high window highlighted the sheen on her glossy dark ringlets, which were arranged in the elaborate curls and twists so fashionable at the time. Her gown would have had Lucy in raptures, except that the low cut of the bodice so early in the afternoon was just one indication of the woman's calling.

She really was a beauty, was his first thought.

Then what brought these creatures so low? he wondered as he realised, with embarrassment, that he'd obviously been mistaken for one of the clientele.

"My sister's bonnet was stolen just now, and the thief who snatched it ran into this establishment."

The young woman raised her brows and widened her eyes as if the news was distressing to her personally. Then she smiled and put her hand on his arm. "A brazen crime like that can't go unpunished. Can I offer you something while I despatch someone to search the premises?" She pressed a little closer, and he was assailed by the scent of violets. When he looked into her eyes, he saw that her own eyes were the colour of violets, as well. She was, he thought, the most beautiful woman he'd ever seen.

He glanced away, ashamed of the wave of raw desire that washed over him, reminding him that he really was so much more like the hot-blooded, tempestuous youth who'd left England in disgust at serving his father's empire six years before, than the cold and reserved adult he must, these days, pretend to be for the world.

He fought the impulse to humour the young woman with at least a smile, instead saying stiffly, "That would be appreciated." And then, because he had to make it clear, in case she was under any misapprehension, adding, "I am here only to secure the return of my sister's bonnet."

"I imagine a disgruntled sister would be highly vexatious to one's afternoon plans, sir. Let me show you into the sitting room where you can wait while I make enquiries." The young woman took his arm and led him through an entranceway hung with heavy red velvet curtains, into a room which, thankfully, was empty. Pausing on the threshold, she sent him an appraising smile, then added, "Perhaps another time."

"I doubt it, madam; no offence intended," he murmured as he lowered himself onto a plush gold-tasselled settee and stared about him. The room was tastefully decorated, a portrait of the queen above the mantelpiece, several Turners

—prints, of course—on the walls. It could have been the room of repose of any respectable person of his acquaintance.

The house was surprisingly quiet. No other customers were about, thank goodness. He hadn't thought of that. A chronic embarrassment it would have been—to both parties —had there been. Not that he expected he would have been recognised. He did not frequent houses of ill repute, and he supposed he was not likely to associate with those who did; though he'd discovered that even people one thought one knew well could surprise one.

He frowned at an elegant porcelain vase on the sideboard filled with hothouse blooms of the variety his Aunt Madeleine favoured, his cheeks suddenly flaming up at the thought of conjuring up his redoubtable, fearsome aunt in a place like this.

A few minutes later, he glanced up to see the beautiful young woman who'd admitted him standing in the doorway.

"Madame Chambon has sent someone in search of the thief who will be found," she assured him. She moved languidly towards a bell pull. "Would you like some tea while you wait?"

He shook his head, despite the thought flitting into his mind that it would be a novelty to take tea with a beautiful woman like this one. In his busy life, he rarely had time to do more than squire his sister to the events where she wished for a male escort.

"Will your sister be anxious that you're gone so long?"

He jerked his head up, surprised at such a reasonable question. In her fashionable, figure-hugging princess-line polonaise, she could have been anyone his sister associated with. Her accents, too, were polished. Yet, she was no one his sister could ever know. This woman had traded that right by choosing vice and its ill-gotten gains over respectability.

"I'm afraid she will." He sighed. "I'd just stepped out of the carriage to investigate a hold-up in the traffic, when the thief dashed past and opportunistically made off with the bonnet which my sister had just removed. Of course, I took off after her."

"A man of ungovernable passions, by the sound of things."

Through narrowed eyes, he took in her gentle humour.

She was smiling at him. "I sense that you've never been in a house like this, and you're uncomfortable. Yet your actions suggest you are prone to acting on impulse, nevertheless." She raised an elegant hand when he opened his mouth to protest. "I'm not about to make any offers, have no fear of that, Mr…?" She looked at him inquiringly.

"McTavish."

"And I am Celeste. And here is Madame Chambon with, it would appear, the person who is responsible for abducting your sister's bonnet and spoiling your otherwise pleasant afternoon." With an incline of her elegantly coiffured dark head, she withdrew from the room.

And Hamish found himself face to face with the large-bosomed, fearsome red-headed Madame of the establishment, whose grip upon the elbow of a bedraggled creature reassured him she would not be escaping justice. Lucy's pink-ribboned bonnet dangled from her hand.

"Mr McTavish, I am sorry for the ills you and your sister have suffered this afternoon." Madame Chambon huffed out a breath and gave the personage a shake. "I found her hiding in the cupboard beneath the stairs. This is yours, I take it," she added, relieving the urchin of the bonnet and handing it to Hamish. "Rest assured, she will be punished. Unless you would like to hand her over to the police personally?"

With Lucy's bonnet safely in his possession, and the embarrassment of his surroundings weighing upon him, not to mention the amount of time he'd been absent, Hamish shook his head.

He stared at the girl. Her face had a greyish hue to it, which he recognised from the malnourished poor he'd had occasion to administer to when they'd come to him asking for dispensation or favours. He was generally sympathetic to those who had so little, but he nevertheless had stern words for the girl.

"Hard work will be rewarded, but theft cannot be condoned," he said, frowning. "I'm sorry for your poverty, but it does not give you license to take what does not belong to you."

The young woman gave a slight toss of her head as she said proudly, "The bonnet was about to drop to the ground, sir. I merely snatched it up for safekeeping before escaping the wheels of a cooper's wagon."

The effect of her performance was incongruous. She was like a shopgirl—no, a gin-sodden slattern for no shopgirl would present herself with the dirt ingrained in her skin and her hair in greasy strands—trying to imitate a duchess.

Hamish was still trying to reconcile the modulated sylla-bles that spilled from her mouth when Madame Chambon stepped forward. "I trust Celeste offered you refreshment, Mr McTavish?"

"She did, thank you." He was impatient, anxious to leave.

Madame cleared her throat. "You did not wish to..." she hesitated, her smile cloying, "spend a little time in her company?"

Horrified, Hamish shook his head then immediately added, for fear of causing offence, "Celeste was charming, but I...no."

"Perhaps you are not so fond of brunettes." A thoughtful frown creased the woman's forehead. She was still clutching the arm of the thief, and now she pushed the creature in front of him. "Celeste's composure can be intimidating, I agree. Perhaps you prefer to...dominate."

Hamish tried to hide his horror while his nostrils quivered with disgust. "No, I would never..." He checked himself. "I must go."

"So, you do not care what becomes of the baggage?

Half-turning, Hamish sent a distracted look at the young woman. Her earlier dignity had deserted her, and now her frightened eyes looked much too large for her pinched face, and her mouth trembled.

"I'm happy to spare her prosecution, if that's what you mean?"

"Please, sir!" The young woman put out her hand suddenly and Hamish stepped back. "Please...help me." She dropped her hand, and Hamish looked at her, in shock and surprise, before Madame laughed and said, "These thieving rings grow more brazen by the day. Listen to how she's refined her accents for her pretty pleas." She sighed. "I think they are lost on a kind sir who has exhausted his charity for one day, girl. Good day to you, Mr McTavish. It's always a pleasure to assist handsome young men." Madame began walking him up the passage, still grasping the young woman by the arm. "You know where to find us."

HAMISH STEPPED onto the street from a side entrance feeling lightheaded and disoriented by the bright sunlight.

So that was what Madame Chambon's establishment looked like from the inside.

He'd heard tales of its infamy, and had he known where he was headed as he entered, he probably would have chosen to let the chit have Lucy's bonnet rather than risk being seen where he definitely would never enter of his free will. The demimondaine was a vice-filled pit for which he had only contempt.

He was retracing his footsteps along the pavement, Lucy's bonnet dangling by its ribbon, when a tall, rangy gentleman with a sharp nose and eyes, and too-fashionably coiffed and oiled hair, and side-whiskers, approached him and asked, with a nod of his head indicating the bonnet, "You found her then? The woman who stole the bonnet?" He glanced with shifty eyes over Hamish's shoulder at Madame Chambon's famous establishment and flexed his bony fingers. "She's in there?"

Hamish hesitated. Something about the man was disconcerting, yet it appeared that the thief had not confined her crimes to Lucy's hat and that this gentleman had obviously been swindled too. So, he nodded and replied, "She is," before continuing towards the main thoroughfare, where he could see the open carriage in the distance parked by the side of the road, and Lucy anxiously scanning the street.

Her face broke into a smile when he held up the bonnet, and she called out gaily as he drew closer, "Since you were gone, I've decided it's my favourite bonnet. Thank you for rescuing it for me, Hamish. I hope the little thief who took it rots in gaol."

Hamish remembered the look on the face of the gentleman he'd passed near Madame Chambon's and felt a frisson of foreboding. "I think she's about to get her reckoning," he said as he climbed in beside Lucy, casting her an admiring look as she tied the bow beneath her chin. "And you look the picture of spring beneath all those blooms. Don't be too harsh on the poor creature who snatched it. No doubt she'd never seen anything half as grand, and it was poverty and desperation, rather than greed, that motivated her."

"Now you sound just like those prosing old reformers

you do love to feature in Papa's improving periodical," Lucy said with a sigh. "The dangerous ones who'd have her serving me tea as some sort of dangerous social experiment instead of where she should be—breaking stones or whatever it is prisoners do to pay for their crimes."

Hamish looked at her with amusement as he picked up the reins.

"Men break stones; women work in the laundry. My, Lucy, you don't believe in leniency for wrongdoing, do you? You're more like Papa than you'd care to admit."

Lucy flashed him a warning look. "Unlike Papa, I am of a forgiving temperament when a wrongdoer has proper justification for their crimes. But that creature who stole my bonnet was from the gutter and clearly meant to gain some ill-gotten coins for her crime by selling it afterwards. If she'd wanted my bonnet because she admired it and harboured romantic dreams of wearing it in public, I might have felt differently. But did you see her, Hamish? She was perfectly hideous. Filthy and skin and bone. Far too sunk in poverty and, no doubt, vice and dissipation, to have any hope of being redeemed. Housing her in a prison, I suspect, would be doing her a kindness."

CHAPTER 4

When Lily finally found her tongue, after the gentleman had left bearing the stolen bonnet, she glanced up into the implacable, uncompromising face of the fiery-headed woman still gripping her arm and asked, sullenly, "Why didn't you just let him hand me over to the police as he wanted?"

The woman hustled her along the corridor and pushed her into what appeared to be her office, closing the door behind them. "Did you really think he was going to hand you over, my girl? Maybe he really was the moral arbiter he claimed. Then again, maybe he wasn't." Dropping her hand, she contemplated Lily from top to toe. Her nostrils quivered. "What's your story? You look like a guttersnipe and speak like a duchess."

Her words were cut short by the reappearance of the young woman who'd admitted Lily.

"Yes, Celeste?"

"Madame, there's another gentleman here." She looked askance at Lily, who felt the great gulf between them like she never had before; not even when she had been the baronet's wife, feted for her beauty, and a rival had stepped into her orbit. For this was a working girl. A woman who traded her body for money. Lily had never been so close to a prostitute, having only come to London once many years before.

"He says he's looking for the girl who stole the bonnet."

Lily froze. Mr Montpelier had found her?

"Stay!" Madame Chambon was too quick as Lily tried to evade her painful, grasping fingers. The older woman pressed her face close. "You're very popular, aren't you, young lady? What have you been up to now, then? Not just bonnet-snatching, it would appear. I won't have a runaway risking the fine reputation for law abiding that I've built up. Let's hear what he has to say."

Effectively imprisoned, Lily glanced down at her boots to avoid having to dwell on the satisfaction and contempt she saw in Mr Montpelier's expression as he stood upon the threshold. But as she looked up and saw her abductor, top hat in his hands, regarding Lily like she supposed a tiger would regard a pheasant, or whatever it was tigers preyed upon, she knew she was vanquished.

"Apologies to trouble you, Madame Chambon, but this young personage and I have unfinished business." He bowed. "Allow me to relieve you of her charge. To be sure, I'm very grateful to you for detaining her."

But Madame was not about to relinquish Lily so readily. Lily's refined accents had obviously whipped up her curiosity, and Lily knew Madame was the kind of woman who'd exploit any advantage. Clearly, she saw one in Lily and this gentleman's desire to have her.

"What, did she steal from you too, sir?" Madame asked. "Shall I summon a constable?"

"She belongs to me, Madame. She is not a thief. No need to call in the law."

Although Mr Montpelier said it with an air of casual

disregard, Lily sensed what Madame too, must have sensed—that he was trying too hard to appear unconcerned at the mention of the law. And since he'd evinced a plan not half an hour since which implicated Lily in something so unthinkable, she didn't wonder at it.

"I won't go with him!" she said suddenly, readying herself for flight. "I'll do whatever you want. Just let me stay here."

Mr Montpelier looked down his bony nose at her with dislike. Madame looked out of her folds of smug complacence with interest.

"My, my, but the little baggage does know how to ape her betters to an impressive degree." The woman who held her patted her head. "And just who might you be impersonating so prettily. Lady Astor? Lady Vanderbilt?" She pinched Lily's arm, causing her to cry out in pain before she went on, "Pity you look so like a guttersnipe or a waif from Seven Dials, otherwise the gentlemen might indeed be flocking to try out the wares of such a fine society dame if she had but her voice to recommend you." The woman tugged on Lily's arm as she looked at Mr Montpelier. "You'll have to feed her up if you're to reap the rewards of her refinement." She spoke the words with careless disdain, but Lily didn't miss the thoughtful look that crossed Mr Montpelier's face.

"She's not worth much to me, skin and bone," he agreed. He ran a hand through his oily locks. "Truth to tell, I hadn't factored in just how unattractive a woman is who lacks nourishment. This young woman owes me a debt, you know, but I don't wish for the trouble of keeping her incarcerated for the time it takes to…groom her sufficiently for her to repay it." His eyes darted about the room, resting a moment on the portrait of the queen, sliding over the various doors and curtains to secret rooms and closets. "Perhaps, Madame, you and I could discuss a little business that might be to our mutual benefit?"

Madame clapped her hands. "Celeste?"

The tall, beautiful brunette, who was obviously awaiting orders on the other side of the curtain, reappeared.

"Take this young person somewhere secure while I make a few arrangements." Madame smiled at Mr Montpelier, who, Lily observed, smiled back for the first time. The effect was not comforting. The relaxation of his facial features merely emphasised the hardness of his eyes.

"Come to my office, Mr Montpelier. Celeste, entertain our unexpected young guest while I'm gone. I'm sure we both want to know a little more about her."

So, she was to be a prisoner after all.

Lily closed her eyes as she leaned against the wall of the small withdrawing room to which she'd been led.

The young woman who had led her there—Celeste— seemed to regard the duty as rather tiresome, for she sighed in irritation as she wandered to the window and looked out over the small garden.

"You've certainly caused a great deal of trouble today," she said. Though Celeste was undeniably a beauty, there was a hard, speculative look in her eye as she turned to study Lily for a long moment before her mouth curved and she burst out in mimicry, "Please ma'am, I'll do whatever you want!" She sighed, adding in jaded tones, "Where did you perfect such a perfectly plaintive little speech? Well...It won't work on Madame. She sees through everyone who comes to work here and—"

"I am not coming to work here!"

Celeste widened her eyes. "Goodness, you really have perfected the talk. I thought you had only a couple of lines. Go on, tell me where you're from."

Lily stared. What could she say? I'm Lady Bradden? A glance at her emaciated form and her shabby clothing was enough to remind her that the truth was both beyond belief and dangerous. And even if she were convincing enough as to her real identity, the moment someone from her husband's circles got wind of the possibility she'd absconded from her *maison* of the insane in Brussels, then her freedom would be at an end.

"I'm not from the gutter even if I look it," she muttered.

"Good lord, you're very good," Celeste said admiringly. "I, too, have had a spectacular fall in circumstance, but I grew up speaking like this. You must surely have learned from imitation? Your employer, perhaps? Or were you on the stage?"

Lily was saved from answering by the voices of Madame and Mr Montpelier, though he was not by her side when Madame opened the door.

Clapping her hands, she beckoned to Lily. "It has been arranged. Come, my new protégé. Mr Montpelier has provided me with a small stipend to go towards improving your appearance and prospects. He shall return in a month to collect you."

Lily jerked her head up in shock, Celeste's gloating look wiped from her face as Madame turned to her.

"I've had enough of you queening it over the rest of the girls! Celeste, I've decided you will share a bed chamber with our new guest so as to keep her...safe and sound with us." Her warning look quelled Celeste's fulminating response, before she added, "It's only for a month so no complaints. Now! Mr Renquist is here for you and I know how eager your are to entertain him. So go!"

Once Celeste had obeyed with ill grace, Madame regarded Lily thoughtfully. Sunlight streamed through the windows highlighting the caked powder in the wrinkles between her nose and mouth as she smiled.

"My, my, I think it has been a providential day." She grasped Lily by the chin, frowning as she studied her face. "I don't know what your story is, my girl, but I can see a beauty hidden beneath your veneer of poverty."

Releasing her, she stepped back, nodding in satisfaction.

The sounds of a tussle in the street outside floated through the window, contrasting with the silence of Madame's establishment at this time of day.

But the scrappers moved away and the unaccustomed heavy, portentous atmosphere that now enveloped Lily was strange and disorienting after so long in a noisy asylum.

Though which was better, she didn't know, when her new warder said, softly, regarding her as if she were an insect on a pin, "If I were a betting woman, I'd say that Madame Chambon's House of Assignation has just secured the brightest star in its firmament."

CHAPTER 5

Hamish removed his bowler and was shrugging out of his dark woollen coat when he glimpsed the photographs that littered his desk.

One in particular struck a note, and he froze, wondering if his mind was playing tricks.

Then, slowly, he finished removing his outerwear and settled himself in his chair.

The previous edition of the periodical of which he was editor, *The Family's Guide to Manners & Morals*, had included three photographs taken by a talented street urchin turned photographer named Archie Benedict. Several society matrons had edged out the whiskered men of the church that had hitherto been the usual pictorial fare, of what had begun as a monthly news sheet established by Hamish's father before it had become one of the country's greatest treatises on exemplary behaviour. For all classes of society.

The response from the magazine's readership at Hamish's attempt to lighten the tone in the last issue had been mixed.

Now Hamish drew the first photograph that lay on his desk closer. It featured a dark-haired beauty in a fashionable polonaise, draped over the arm of a high-profile minister in Disraeli's government.

Hamish swallowed, blinked, and then brought the photograph up to the light.

It was the woman he'd met briefly at Madame Chambon's.

Celeste.

He did not know her by any other name, but the curve of her swan-like neck, the swell of her bosom, the brightness of her eyes, and the glossy curls of her hair set her apart from other beauties.

Or was it the challenging twist to her lush mouth? Few society women looked at anyone like that. And no woman pictured in *Manners & Morals* had ever looked like that.

Hamish felt an uncomfortable stirring of his loins as he studied the pair.

Lord Carruthers was a married man; his wife was the daughter of the Earl of Clunes. There was not a chance in Hades that Hamish could publish the photograph, and he wondered if Benedict knew the potential for cashing in on a large blackmail payment if he showed this to Lord Carruthers, who, clearly, had not known he was being photographed.

He put it to one side. Hamish was not in the blackmail business, but as he was the photograph's custodian for the moment, he had a moral imperative to ensure it never saw the light of day.

The next couple of photographs were posed social gatherings. The Derby, tea at the Dorchester. Fashionable men and women. Benedict would shop these around until he found a buyer. Probably some ladies' journal.

The next photograph once again featured Celeste, but this time in company with a delicately featured golden-haired woman. One so dark, the other so fair. The composition set the pair off to perfection. Both sat on a love seat staring into the distance, as if they had no idea their likenesses were being so carefully committed to posterity. In fact, Hamish suspected they did not know, for there was no trace of self-consciousness or suggestion of careful posing. They were in a room where the background was a blur of movement, suggestive of couples dancing. He brought the photograph closer towards the light and stared at it for much longer than a busy man with no interest in these kinds of women ought to, he knew.

He'd thought Celeste beautiful, but her brazen, lush beauty seemed to pale in comparison with the fragile perfection of her companion. He felt his mouth go dry, the blood fizz near the surface of his skin, and was surprised at such a visceral reaction. He was often in the company of beautiful women who had no effect on him.

And he was not a man who forgot his scruples the moment temptation came knocking.

Finally, there was one photograph left. It was less well developed than the others, and not of sufficient quality to make it into a publication so that he might have discarded it if the woman had not again caught his eye.

This time, the awareness that roared through him was magnified.

It wasn't just that it was beautiful, immoral Celeste.

It was that she was draped across a white-haired man Hamish knew to be a Russian diplomat with suspected criminal connections. A man who certainly should not be seen in the company of a woman who consorted with government ministers. Namely, Lord Carruthers.

Warily, he withdrew the first hidden picture of Celeste,

and lined it up next to the second. Frowning over both of them, his brain whirled with the ramifications.

A British Cabinet Minister and a suspected Russian spy. Each consorting with the same woman. A prostitute. Possibly both sleeping with her, given her line of work.

He wasn't aware of the faint rap upon the door, or the protest of hinges and the fact he was no longer alone until the cheery, "She's a beauty, ain't she?" made him jump.

Dumping a leather bag of photographic equipment at his feet, the man who had taken these pictures, Archie Benedict, glanced from Hamish's face to that of the dark-haired young woman in the photograph.

"Where did you take these?" Hamish asked.

"At Madame Plumb's Dancin' Rooms." Then, deducing that Hamish had no idea who Madame Plumb was, Archie went on in his thick cockney accent, "'Tis the salon where the Fair Cyprians go ter dance an' cast their nets. The place ter find beautiful women."

"Did you take them on the same night?"

Archie shook his head. "Takes a fair bit o' time an' work ter get a good photograph when the subject don't know 'bout it."

"Only a true artist could achieve something like this." Hamish picked up the photographic plate of the two beauties, dark and blonde, while Archie puffed up his chest making an impressive show of his barely five feet tall stature as he responded proudly, "The past belonged ter the painter. The future belongs ter the man who can use a camera like an artist." Grinning his sly, broken-toothed smile, he indicated the cumbersome equipment at his feet. "Gettin' easier an' quicker all the time ter set this gear up, though. An' ain't the brunette beyond description?"

"I'm rather partial to the blonde," Hamish said without thinking as he perused the photograph once again. He glanced at Archie, who muttered, "I reckon I oughtn't tell that ter yer ol' man. Glad yer are takin' the magazine in anuvver direction so I can sell yer more o' me wares."

Hamish considered his response. He was tinkering with the pictorial content only. The readership was loyal, and his father would not sanction changes. But Archie was valuable to him, and he couldn't afford not to see what he had to sell in the future if the Cockney thought Hamish remained interested only in whiskered churchmen.

He especially wanted to keep an eye on Celeste in case future actions on her part should have political ramifications, considering a fair proportion of his magazine's upstanding readership included government ministers and their families.

"So, yer goin' ter take all o' 'em?" Archie asked, making a sweeping motion over the photographs.

Hamish pulled out his fob watch and consulted the time, saying distractedly, "What do you think, Archie? I have room for three, but I want to take these, also." He drew across the three pictures that contained Celeste, in addition to the dreary-looking personages he meant to publish.

"Wot do yer want wiv 'em if yer don't mean ter publish 'em?"

"I may include them in a later edition."

"Reckon yer jest sayin' that."

Archie wasn't stupid. Of course, *Manners & Morals* would not publish a photograph of women like these. "They don't come cheap."

"Doesn't matter. I still want to buy them."

Archie sent him an uncertain look. "Yer said yer liked the blonde. 'Tis the brunette who's in all three."

"I like both." Hamish wondered what he could say that would not arouse suspicion of his motives. He did not want the picture of Celeste to make it into any rival publication.

Or to find its way to Lord Carruthers. Perhaps if Archie thought the interest was personal, he would think no more of it. So, he asked, "Do you know where I might make her acquaintance?" in the hope of putting him off the scent.

Archie stuck his thumbs in his suspenders and rocked on the balls of his broken boots and grinned. "Nevva 'fought I'd 'ear yer ask me a question like that, guv? But I reckon I's jest the man ter show yer ter places the readers o' *Manners & Morals* would curl up their little toes an' die jest ter know they existed."

"Good man."

Archie was from the gutter, and proud of it. With a loose tongue and ready to swim wherever the tide would take him, Archie was like a water rat, a survivor; the kind of man who might one day prove valuable, for he knew how to infiltrate the palaces of the rich via their underground servant's corridors, and learn the business of those upstairs, just as well as he knew the rookeries of the poor.

"In fact, I could take yer ter meet this young lady ternight, if yer desire."

"The brunette or the blonde?"

"Both. But women like this don't come cheap. Like me photographs." He laughed in response to the twitch of Hamish's nostrils. "I weren't sure if yer took me meanin', guv. Reckon maybe yer not so interested, now. But I'll take yer ter Madame Chambon's. There's a girl there I quite fancy, meself." When he saw the expression Hamish failed to hide in time, he let out a guffaw! "Lor', the pleasure o' one o' 'em girls would cost me a year's wages. An' I don't really fink yer in the market, either," he added shrewdly, glancing between Hamish and the women in the photograph. "No, the girl I's interested in works as a servant there. Course, yer interest is 'bout warnin' yer readers o' the moral dangers o' bein' taken in by one o' Madame's girls. Easy ter get taken fer a ride if yer don't know the dangers." Archie tapped the side of his nose. "That's the story, ain't it, guvnor?"

HAMISH WAS careful to arrive by the discreet side entrance. Some bolder personages, or those entering or leaving in the dark, were not so concerned about being observed, but as editor of a magazine that upheld morality, Hamish was taking an enormous risk.

But integrity and honesty required him to investigate whether this woman, Celeste, might be compromising the safety of the country through her intimacy with two men with opposing agendas.

It was midafternoon as he stood in the dim entrance, blinking to accustom his eyes to the gloom. There was little sign of activity. A faint perfume permeated the air. Pleasant and sophisticated; not the rank, cloying odour he would have expected, though he remembered, of course, that he'd been surprised by the sophistication of his surroundings during his last brief visit.

When he asked to see Celeste, he was embarrassed that his request was misconstrued, though the fault lay with him, he knew.

"I wish to speak to her on a matter of business only," he tried to clarify. But the young woman he addressed merely said patiently, "Celeste doesn't do business at this time on a Thursday. I'm afraid you'll have to come back tomorrow, sir. However, Karolina is available. I'll go and see if—"

"No!" he responded sharply, realising that his voice sounded too loud. "I'm here to see Celeste on a matter quite different."

He was heartily wishing he'd not come at all when another voice intruded, and he glanced up to see a golden-haired beauty. She'd paused halfway down the stairs, and as she looked into his eyes, he felt the shock of recognition like a branding. She smiled. "Perhaps I could pass on a message, sir."

Hamish was tongue-tied. It was rare that he truly could not find the right response. She was even more beautiful and poised than she'd appeared in the photograph that had crossed his desk earlier that day.

The sunlight behind her burnished her golden ringlets and made her milky skin glow like sun-kissed rose petals. Her teeth were white and pretty, and she carried herself like a duchess, not a woman from the gutter, or a fallen angel, or anything else that was rotten on the inside and eaten up with vice and sin, which he knew would have to be the case if she worked here.

She put her head on one side to regard him with faint amusement. "What is it, sir? You look as if you've seen a ghost. Or have we met in another life? There are plenty of gentlemen who like to say that."

"I beg your pardon, madam," he floundered. "I...I thought I recognised you."

For, although Hamish recognised her from the photograph in his satchel, as she took another step into the light, the faint tug of memory had him floundering even more.

In the flesh, the sense of having seen her before was even stronger than what he'd felt just looking at the photograph.

She tilted her head, her eyes meeting his in challenge, forcing him to study and acknowledge her as she apparently felt she deserved.

Was she mistaking his identity? Did she believe him to be one of her myriad admirers? After all, she must have had many. Certainly, with a face and figure like that.

She gave a short laugh. "I hope your sister was relieved to get her bonnet back. Mind you, that shade of pink does little for my complexion, so like as not, I'd have returned it."

Her words froze him to the spot. He blinked rapidly as his brain struggled to assimilate the bag of bones and lustreless hair and eyes of the guttersnipe who'd snatched Lucy's bonnet with the woman before him. But Hamish was a man of imagination who spent a good deal of time poring over photographs and studying the features of their subjects for a popular segment his father had introduced on page 7 of the magazine called *Saint or Sinner?*

Hamish deplored the segment but the readers delighted in writing in to suggest why the physiognomy of a convicted felon should have proclaimed him—without need of magistrate or jury—instantly guilty.

This woman would have had his readers in raptures over her saintlike features—had she been proclaimed for her good works. Her skin was unblemished, her hair was thick and glossy and arranged in the intricate twists that were fashionable. There was an air of saintlike innocence about her that was so at odds with what he knew her to be. A thief, at the very least.

By the same token, Hamish knew that if her photograph had been printed proclaiming her to be a husband-murderer, those same readers would have written in decrying the deceptiveness of the devil in fashioning their creature as a heavenly manifestation of what was, in truth, a fiend who should burn in Hell.

"Good lord!" he exclaimed! This time, he really struggled to get out the words. "You!"

"Yes." She leaned a little over the bannister, smiling artlessly at him as she said, "Though I am not in the habit of being greeted in such a cavalier fashion."

He shook his head. It didn't make sense. How could the beautiful, cultured woman before him be the thieving urchin he'd pursued a little over a month ago? He blinked again. The girl was…astonishing.

"I see you are lost for words, Mr McTavish. Now, you are here on a matter of business, I couldn't help overhearing. Pray, what business is that? If you'd like to follow me into the drawing room where we will be undisturbed, perhaps I can help you."

CHAPTER 6

Lily led him into the reception room, which she was relieved to note, was empty of the occasional mooncalves who sometimes waited for hours to see the ladylove to whom they'd decided they'd lost their hearts.

And to whom they'd soon lose a small fortune, for the women at Madame Chambon could be afforded only by those with long purse strings.

These women lived good lives, often much better than the lives they'd lived before they'd 'fallen'. But Lily didn't intend to emulate them. She lived for the moment she could leave Madame Chambon's.

In four weeks, she'd learned much about a world from which she'd been protected, both as a lady of gentility and then as an asylum inmate.

The disgust and horror of living in a den of immorality had abated, but she had made no real friends. Karolina was sweet and naïve, but the others had only an eye to the main chance. Celeste included.

The only benefit to being here was that Lily could grow

strong and beautiful again. A woman's power depended upon being strong and beautiful.

But any power Lily might have gained through regaining her health and looks would come to nothing if her circumstances were revealed.

While she would never return to the privileged position of baronet's wife, her dreams of quiet, modest respectability would be destroyed if it became known she'd spent any time beneath Madame Chambon's roof.

Her affair with Teddy fell into a different category, of course. Many long-married women of her social station had discreet liaisons to which the rest of society turned a blind eye. Nor had her affair with Teddy been the primary reason for Robert banishing her to the *maison* in Brussels. Lily had only succumbed to Teddy's charms in response to Robert's liaison with Mrs Scott and years of complete indifference— or rather, contempt—from her husband.

No, Lily had been banished to the *maison* for quite another reason, and the fear of a return of her malady terrified her, though not once in two years had she been afflicted by the mental disorder that had provided Robert with the excuse he needed to be rid of her.

Right now, time was not on Lily's side, she knew, having learned from an overheard conversation passed on to her by Karolina that Mr Montpelier would return in four days.

In order to plan her escape, Lily had to utilise whatever opportunity she could. And whomever she could.

"Please, take a seat, sir. Grace will bring us refreshment in a moment." She had to do all she could to charm this man, for who else could she petition for help? Not one of the regulars who came to Madame Chambon for something entirely different. Something that Lily was not prepared to barter.

Silently he obeyed her, the confusion on his face almost

amusing, except that Lily didn't have time to waste, pandering to amusement.

The previous night, Madame had offered her a position as one of her girls. This, Madame had insisted, promised her comfort, security, and was her best opportunity for making a profitable alliance and shoring up her future. Some of Madame's former girls had snared princes and nabobs. One had married into the aristocracy.

Madame had intimated that with Lily's face and figure, nothing was too great a flight of fancy.

However, working as a prostitute for Madame Chambon was something Lily would never do, nor would she become Mr Montpelier's prisoner once again.

So, pretending a composure that was far from the desperation that clawed at her insides, Lily smiled as the gentleman settled himself in a plush velvet settee while she asked pleasantly, "What brings you here, sir?" as she seated herself demurely in an armchair opposite him before a crackling fire.

Alert for signs that one of the other girls—or Madame— might overhear their conversation, she leaned in a little closer. At least Celeste was asleep. Celeste had been entertaining Lord Carruthers and was resting before she would make her appearance in another hour or so.

But if Mr McTavish had an interest that Lily could satisfy —other than through physical means, of course—he might be in a position to help her.

Unless she heard from Teddy in the next four days.

Her other avenues of hope had turned into dead-ends. There would be no succour from her aunt. No forgiveness from her husband, only more incarceration.

But Teddy had loved her. He'd rescued her from Robert once.

Surely he'd rescue her again? Once her letter reached him?

"I'm sorry we met under such inauspicious circumstances, Mr McTavish," she added, smiling. She'd not missed the flare of admiration in his eye. The fact he was an attractive man made it easy to adopt the slight flirtatiousness she felt would best make its mark.

He shook his head, clearly bewildered. "Can it really be you? I don't understand." Then, after a pause, "Who *are* you?"

She wanted to ask him the same question. Who was he? What was his position in society? Could he help her? *Would* he help her? Instead, she simply shrugged and said lightly. "You wouldn't believe me. Let's just say I'm a widow who fell on hard times, and was at my lowest ebb when you inadvertently became the means by which I managed to…survive. I might have been fleeing from you four weeks ago, but in fact you proved my salvation. I owe you a debt of thanks, Mr McTavish."

"Good god! Working at Madame Chambon's is not surviving, madam. Surely I am not the only reason you are here?"

There was an intensity to his manner that was intriguing. This man was respectably middle class; she knew that. He did not mix in her circles—well, the privileged circles she'd formerly inhabited—so he did not pose so great a threat as some of the gentlemen who frequented Madame Chambon's.

Then how might he have recognised her? A tremor of doubt ran through her. She'd seen a man taking photographs that night at Madame Plumb's. Madame Chambon had insisted Celeste take Lily along to the popular lightskirts' haunt; however, neither had posed for any photographs. And surely one of those cameras had to be trained upon a subject for some minutes. She'd have noticed—wouldn't she?

Still, Lily reassured herself, she had not inhabited a

social arena beyond her small provincial sphere in Norfolk, and had only been to London once as a newly-married baronet's wife six years before. She did not fear recognition.

"Make no mistake, I have not worked here in any capacity, Mr McTavish," she was quick to point out. "After you chased me into the first house I came upon, Madame kindly agreed to look after me for four weeks during which time I have made every effort to be reunited with my family. Alas, to no avail." She dropped her eyes, saying, "But enough of me. What business do you have with Celeste that I may be able to help you with?"

He clasped his hands together between his knees, studying her a moment, and Lily recognised a keenness of intellect and a suppressed energy, like a coiled spring, that was faintly, disturbingly exciting.

"Celeste has certain connections that are of interest to me. I wanted to ask her about them."

Lily laughed. "Celeste does not divulge that kind of information to anyone but..." She dropped her voice. "We share a bedchamber, you know. I am familiar with Celeste's habits and connections. I am happy to answer your questions if they do no harm."

Yes, Lily was happy to do anything to win Mr McTavish's trust. If he could only help her leave this place before the next four days, and offer her some form of future employment that didn't require her to sacrifice her scruples, it would be a start.

And the interested way he was looking at her gave her hope.

"What do you know of Lord Carruthers? Is he a regular consort of Celeste's?"

Lily met his level look. "I know a great deal about Lord Carruthers, though I've never entertained him as Celeste has, as I made clear earlier." She hesitated a long while before adding, "My late husband knew him, you know."

He leaned back. "Really, madam?"

Lily shrugged. She could tell him every detail about her life—all true—and he'd not believe her. "Lord Carruthers is Celeste's regular Wednesday night guest." She smiled. "Carrots, the girls call him. Not Celeste." She smiled. "Celeste lacks humour at times." Lily made to rise. He was interested in what she had to tell him, but it had to be worth her while. "Madame will soon be in to remind me of the value of a lady's time. As I said, she wants me to work for her, though I'd rather starve in the gutter."

"Please, just one more moment of your time." Mr McTavish dug in his jacket pocket and peeled off a note from the wad he retrieved, before he resumed his questioning once she'd sat down again with a calculated show of reluctance. "How long has she been seeing Lord Carruthers, how long does she entertain him, and who else does she entertain?" he asked, reaching forward with the money.

"You don't look the jealous kind, Mr McTavish. But then, you did go to great lengths to please your sister so you are a man of uncommon passions, it would appear." Lily cast a surreptitious look at the doorway as she closed her hand over the notes.

When he said nothing, she answered, "Every Wednesday for as long as I've been here."

"And the Russian?"

"The snowman? I believe that's the man you are referring to. You *are* well informed. Mr Novichov has been coming for the past three months, I believe." She reflected a moment, adding, "Celeste never speaks of politics."

"Perhaps because she's been cautioned not to. Why the Snowman?"

Lily looked down at the pound notes in her hand. Once, it

would have been a trifle she'd have used to tip a servant following a visit to a stately home. Now it was a valuable addition to what she must set aside to fund her escape.

Though to where, she had no idea, for who would help her when she had nothing? Not even a past she could lay claim to, without revealing the truth which would put her in mortal danger.

"His bulk and his head of snowy-white hair, for all he's handsome enough, I suppose, in his way." She shuddered. "I wouldn't like to deal with him, but then, I wouldn't like to deal with anyone in this house." Surreptitiously she bent down to slip the notes into her right boot. "But let me make plain, sir; I am not a common spy," she said. "I don't particularly care for Celeste, but I have no reason to cause her harm." She pondered the situation before saying frankly, "I have no affinity with any of these women, yet we must be able to trust each other if we're to…survive."

Mr McTavish sent her another curious look. "I asked you this before, but you told me a story I didn't quite believe. A beautiful widow with supposed connections doesn't inhabit a house like this, even if her husband—or late husband—you were not quite consistent there—threw her into the gutter. And you were in a…let me say it quite frankly, terrible state when you first came to this house. Now, you could be… anyone." He scratched his jaw. "I'll ask it again. Who, exactly, are you, Mrs…?"

Lily sighed. "I haven't properly decided." On the side table lay a volume by Anthony Trollope. She squinted at the title: *The Eustace Diamonds*. "Perhaps I shall be Mrs Eustace," she told him. "Yes, that will do for want of anything better."

"When you stole my sister's bonnet, you'd fled right out of the rookeries. I saw it myself."

"The rookeries? Why, I wouldn't even know where they were. I'm from the country and have barely been to London.

But I will tell you that the day I snatched your sister's bonnet, I was fleeing from a man who would have me be someone I had no wish to be." She weighed up how much to confide in him. But no, she couldn't tell him the real truth of her past in one great rush that he'd take with no more than a grain of salt. If that.

This needed to be a relationship she could nurture. He was a gentleman with money and connections, clearly. Could she persuade him to return tomorrow?

"A gentleman was after you." Mr McTavish sent her another of his long, considered looks. "Tall and dark-haired."

Lily nodded. "Yes. He was going to take me away, but instead he made an arrangement with Madame. He intends to return for me."

He appeared to weigh this up for a moment. Then, to her disappointment, he merely said, rising, "I'll come back in a few days, and perhaps you'll have some more information for me."

"Come back tomorrow." Lily struggled to hide her anxiety. She'd made some headway with this man, but she couldn't afford for him to delay beyond tomorrow. She dropped her voice as she moved closer to him. "Midday. I'll have more to tell you, though…it would help to know why you want this information so I can better question Celeste."

She followed him to the door where he arranged his hat and cane, ready for departure. Already his demeanour was distant. "With no disrespect, I would prefer to speak to Celeste."

Lily felt her desperation rise, but she could do nothing but hide her feelings as she waited while he reached into his pocket, perhaps to withdraw a handkerchief though his card case fell to the floor and spilled open in the process.

Lily was quick to reach down first. He'd not wanted to introduce himself beyond his name, but an understanding of how he might help her would be to her benefit if his card named his business.

"McTavish and Sons publishers?" Lily jerked her head up from reading his calling card. "You are the publisher of *Manners & Morals*?"

"The editor, madam."

She pressed her lips together. "Your magazine is widely read, sir."

"Indispensable literature for the servants' halls, the parlours of the middle classes, and the salons of the aristocracy, I have been reliably informed." His tone was dry.

"Are you Mr McTavish? Or the son?"

"My father began it as a newspaper that printed religious texts. Fifteen years ago, he expanded it into the magazine it is today."

"To feed the appetite for self-improvement and chaste entertainment for all levels of society. A weighty moral burden." She smiled at his clear surprise at her pronouncement, her thoughts running over why he should be interested in Celeste and Lord Carruthers. "You have a nose for scandal, then," she said. "And a mandate for stamping it out, given the position you hold?"

He sent her a level look. "Vice and immorality are the hallmarks of weakness, and it is up to every individual to harness such dangerous impulses. I publish a mix of improving instruction, and entertainment." He checked himself. "I am not a prude, madam. But what I provide is wholesome and morally uplifting."

"And Celeste's activities could be dangerous to public morality?" she asked.

"That, and more," he said. He drew in a breath and appeared to consider his words. "I need not reiterate that my seeking information is in the public interest. If it should be revealed that I've even come to this house, I promise you that

I can cause a great deal more trouble than such a revelation is worth."

Lily raised an eyebrow. "I hope that was not a threat, Mr McTavish. Besides, what you have said suggests that you'd not mind, one way or another, what would put Madame Chambon and her girls out of business. But pray tell, what do you propose the women who work here should do in order to strive for self-improvement? Other than read your magazine, of course. What other possibilities are there that might entice them to leave their lives of vice and sin?"

"They should find respectable employment, of course." His tone was full of scorn. "But of course, respectable employment does not pay as well as this."

"What is considered fair pay for woman's work does not keep a roof over her head or food on the table," Lily said. "I have learned this only now, for, like you, I grew up in comfortable ignorance of the fact that a milliner working from dawn til dusk earns a pittance insufficient to pay for the barest necessities of life. As for *respectable* employment, without a glowing reference from some upstanding citizen, these girls can't even choose to step back into the kind of life you propose—moral rectitude." She raked her gaze over the fine cut of his coat and his well-made shoes. "It is all very well to proselytise when you have a comfortable buffer against starvation. But I suggest this is not a place where you will find friends spouting your moralising beliefs."

"There is no excuse for sin other than a deficiency of one's own moral character," he said grimly.

"And you have never sinned?"

His nostrils flared. His eyes grew darker. "I was born a sinner, like everyone. But I have never exhibited a weakness of the flesh that brings men here."

"Men like Lord Carruthers, an upstanding man with a wife and family." Lily hesitated, desperate to exploit the moment. "And women like Celeste who do his bidding." The knowledge she was trying to dredge up, when for two years she'd been absent from any discussion of world matters, was slowly coming back. She swallowed, dry mouthed, the street vendors outside intruding on the quiet intensity of their discussion. Slowly, she tried to tease it out, aloud. "Lord Carruthers holds an important position, and you are looking to shame him in your newspapers and magazines? Reveal, perhaps, the fact that Lord Carruthers has a mistress?" She shook her head, discounting this. "No, printing such sensationalist material would not be well received by your readers. The secrets of what a man does in the privacy of his bedroom are sacrosanct. You can't print that. But..." She jerked up her chin. "The fact that a man holding such an important position has a mistress who is simultaneously sleeping with...with the enemy, could."

His voice was tight as he responded, "I am not a grubby sensationalist. I uphold stringent standards, which is why I am gravely concerned by the implications of what you have just outlined." He breathed heavily. "I came here purely so I could prevent *any* publication possibly putting about anything that might jeopardise our government and our safety and standing in the world."

"The clarion call for noble, middle-class values. Your motives are virtuous indeed, Mr McTavish."

"You mock me, madam. You mock virtue."

"It was a miscalculation to come to such a house if you came in the guise of the upholder of virtue, Mr McTavish." Lily forced herself to keep her calm. She had miscalculated when, in the beginning, she'd been trying to build the rapport between them. Experience had taught her that showing admiration generally loosened a man's tongue. And when a man let down his guard, a woman could learn much valuable information.

Lily needed all the valuable information she could get. She needed him to be her ally but his puritanical outlook suggested he might be more impervious to flattery than most men.

To her disappointment, Madame's voice floated down the passage as she made her way towards them. "You're not leaving already, sir? Surely we can entice you to stay? If our lovely Lily is unavailable, I'm sure one of the other girls—"

"No. Thank you." Tight-lipped, Mr McTavish stared at Lily a long second before inclining his head at the two women. "I merely came to pay my respects. Nothing more."

Nothing more, Lily thought wryly. There'd been plenty more, and Lily could have helped him—and have been rewarded for it.

But now Mr McTavish was gone, thinking even less of her—and certainly not in the mood for playing the heroic saviour.

A reflection that cast Lily into even greater despair when Madame announced that Mr Montpelier would in fact be arriving within the hour to take Lily to her new accommodation, so she'd best prepare herself.

CHAPTER 7

"So yer met the blonde beauty, eh, guvnor? 'Ope yer 'ad a nice evenin'. Me Gracie says she's a real picky one." Archie, who had arrived at Madame Chambon's the previous night with Hamish, had not been seen since, though he obviously knew where to waylay Hamish.

Hamish stopped and turned as he was about to mount the stairs to his club. Somewhere refreshment could be had in peace and quiet, which was what Hamish needed following his unexpectedly charged and turbulent exchange with the 'beauty' to whom Archie referred.

"No." Hamish hoped his clipped tones were sufficiently quelling. He wanted a drink. Just the one, of course, while he read *The Times*. And then he'd return home so he could be in bed by eleven, ready for a long day in the office the following day as *The Family's Guide to Manners & Morals* would be going to press late in the evening.

"Are yer printin' 'er photograph? No shame in changin' yer mind. 'Sides, yer jest printin' wot's in the public interest, an' a picture o' Lor' Carruthers is 'allus in the public interest."

Hamish tapped his fingers upon the top of his cane, impatient as he stepped back from the gate that led to the four-square building to let another gentleman pass. "I cannot print such a photograph in my magazine. No editor would."

"I 'fought yer wanted ter expose the rottin' moral undabelly o' a sanctimonious —"

"Come, Archie, I do not have a death wish. My magazine would be closed down five minutes after such a photograph was published. The public would be baying for my blood; rocks would be thrown through the windows. What a government minister does behind closed doors is his affair, and there is not the appetite to turn that on its head. Surely even you understand that?"

Archie stuck his chin out. "I 'fought yer was changin' direction. I 'eard yer ain't on such good terms wiv yer ol' man an' that yer relished the opportunity fer usin' the magazine fer the public good. Not jest prosin' good works, but exposin' double standards an' the like."

Hamish stilled. There was no point in trying to argue Archie down from his moral high ground, but it was concerning that the private matters of the McTavish family appeared to be in the public domain. "Where did you hear that?"

Archie looked evasive. "I jest 'appened ter be standin' near a door that weren't quite as closed as mayhap yer 'fought it was when yer went ter it, heart ter heart, wiv a trusted friend o' yers."

"You were eavesdropping? Is that why you sold me that photograph? Because you really thought I would publish it?" Hamish was angry. He'd been angry when he'd left Madame Chambon's, but he was mostly angry at himself, and ashamed, for being careless. And for caring. Yes, caring too much about what others thought of him.

Archie, to some extent, for believing he had the stomach to follow through on his beliefs. But namely Mrs Eustace, if that's what she now chose to call herself. She thought him a buttoned-up moral prig, and so did Archie, yet neither knew how deeply he wished he could forge his own path. He was feeling his way, and he would not be rushed. Could not be. Too much was at stake, not least the daily possibility that his father would snatch the editorship from his hands.

But that did not mean he was impervious to opinion.

Or doing what he believed was right.

"Sure, an' don't print me photograph. Yer paid me well 'nuff fer it, an' that's all as counts in me book." Archie looked mulish. "But wot say yer ter more o' that? Not ter publish, necessarily—though it may come ter that if 'tis deemed in the public interest…at some stage. Wot say I keep me eyes an' ears open ter any whispers that," he dropped his voice, "our country's safety is bein' put at risk 'frough the peccadilloes o' 'em wot's bein' paid ter keep us safe an' wot pretends ter be so full o' virtue."

Hamish realised Archie had deduced what he had. He'd not for a moment thought the photographer knew anything about either Lord Carruthers or the Russian.

When Archie looked about to give up the conversation and move off at Hamish's silence, Hamish said suddenly, "Your friend who works as a servant at Madame Chambon's…" he hesitated, "she's a girl who keeps her ear to the ground and likes to tell you things?"

"More like 'ter the wall'," Archie said with a snigger. "Yeah, Gracie likes me well enough so I can pry 'er fer wot yer'd like ter know…if yer make it worth me while."

"Furthermore, you like to frequent places of interest in the hopes of a photograph that'll earn you more than a pot of porter, aren't I right, Archie?"

"Dead right, guvnor."

"Well, the truth is, I am interested in this woman, Celeste."

Archie looked eager. "A bit o' a retainer wouldn't go astray."

"No, I'll stop short of offering that. But..." Hamish hesitated, "The other woman. The blonde—"

"An' yer partial ter blondes, ain't that right, guvnor?"

Hamish refrained from comment. "She tells me she doesn't intend staying at Madame Chambon's, which may or may not be the case. But if your friend can update you on the exploits of this woman, a so-called widow called Mrs Eustace, with blonde curls and a face like an angel, then I'd appreciate learning the details."

"Got a bit o' a reputation, 'as she? Likely ter get 'erself a 'igh stepper, eh?"

"No, not yet. And I may perhaps be doing her an injustice. She claims to be respectable but to have fallen on hard times."

"Don't they all?" Archie blew out a gust of sceptical air.

"Anyway," Hamish hesitated as he paced towards the window and stared out onto the bustling street below. "I just have a feeling that we may be hearing of this Mrs Eustace in the not-too-distant future."

Now ensconced in her new quarters, Lily sat on the narrow iron bed and ran her hands over the cheap cotton counterpane as she listened to a heated discussion through the thin walls.

Her lodgings were a comedown from Madame Chambon's, but the boarding house, while populated with the working class, was respectable. And it was the last place

Robert would think to look for her, if he even knew she was missing.

"So, what am I required to do to keep a roof over my head?" she now asked, looking up to see Mr Montpelier's black-eyed gaze fixed upon her. He was seated on a chair in the window embrasure. A man in a respectable woman's bedroom should have been unthinkable.

But she was no longer respectable. And she shuddered to think what this might cost her.

"Yes, this entire charming little bower is yours."

"At what price?" The only thought that gave her any peace was his initial inference that he would not be her pimp. And if using her for her body was his intention, he surely could have made a handsome bargain with Madame Chambon.

"So, you have brought me here to this rented room," she prompted, "and given me clothes that were, perhaps, fashionable two seasons ago." She studied the polonaise with its tight skirt, natural form bustle, frowning at the style of its trimmings. It had been *de riguer* when she'd been taken to the *maison*. Two seasons on, it would show that its wearer had not the funds to keep up with fashion or had bought it secondhand. She sighed. "What is it that you wish of me, Mr Montpelier? You snatched me from the *maison* for a reason, and for the last four weeks, I've plotted my escape as I regained my health."

"And your looks, Mrs..." Frowning, he said, "I had not thought of a name, madam. That is something that will need to be remedied. Something not too unusual, but not too common, either."

"I read *Lady Eustace's Diamonds* at Madame Chambon's," Lily said sullenly. "Eustace has a nice ring to it."

"What was your name before you married?"

"Taverner."

"Taverner, ah yes, how could I have forgotten? No, we

don't want any connection with your past, do we. In that case, Eustace will serve well enough. Lily Eustace." He paused, obviously thinking. "A wardrobe of clothing two years old is just the thing. Not too expensive but just what the woman you need to be would have worn."

"You speak in riddles, Mr Montpelier. That is, when you speak at all." A new kind of desperation was struggling to find an outlet. She gazed out of the grimy glass panes but could see nothing other than buildings, cheaply built and nondescript. "What is it that you want of me? And why me? There are plenty of vulnerable women with no family to protect them who would have been far less a risk to you, even grateful, perhaps. But you are keeping me against my will." She put her hand to her breast and strove for calm. "I ask you again. Do you think I should be happy to exchange one prison for another? That I will be *grateful*?" Agitated, she rose and began to pace before turning, tilting her chin mutinously as she went on, "You think you can bend me to your will, but you are wrong, Mr Montpelier. I will not be used like some...some servant or slave or..." As she said the words, the terror of what he really did have in mind for her grew. "You cannot force me to act against my will just as Madame Chambon could not force me to become one of her girls. I would never demean myself like that. I have morals and integrity. I'm not like one of...those women." Her breathing grew more laboured, and she wrung her hands.

"Are you any better than those women?" He raised an eyebrow. "You cuckolded your husband."

Lily's hand went to her throat. "I fell in love—" But even as she said the words, she knew they weren't true, though at the time Teddy offered her salvation from a loveless eternity with Robert. And besides, how did he know this? Mr Montpelier was not of her class, nor from her locality. Though he tried to speak like a gentleman, he was more likely from the slums of London.

She thought of the letter she'd sent to Teddy. Had he received it? *When* would he receive it? Was he looking for her? Would he go to Madame Chambon's when he received her entreaty?

"You might do well to remember, madam, that I have not so much to lose as you do if you do choose to bow out of your…contract, shall we call it. I was already in Belgium when your sad story was communicated to me. When you learn what you are to do I think you will see the benefits to yourself."

Lily spun on her heel. She felt like crying but would not. "You've told me nothing! Not even what I'm to do! How can I stay here when for all I know, my life might be in danger!"

"I'd imagine your life would be in far greater danger on the streets." He looked out through the window, where the noise of the rumbling carts and carriages and the shriek of a fishwife competing with a newspaper vendor seemed to fill the room. "Or back in Brussels. Are those not your choices? Unless you'd like me to return you to your husband."

"To Robert? Dear God, not that," she muttered, sinking down onto the chair nearest her. "Not now that I have *some* freedom, I suppose."

"And you have no friends or family who will take you in otherwise you'd have left Madame Chambon's at the first opportunity." He clicked his tongue. "I was not pleased when you bolted from the carriage, but events worked out surprisingly well. I admit, it had been something of a shock to discover the poor physical condition of the apparently exquisite Lady Bradden. In fact, I nearly left you where you were. But the possibilities of what you *could* achieve should you regain your former glory were too intoxicating." He gave a short laugh, treating her to a view of yellowing teeth and mottled gums. "The fact that you chose the most notorious brothel in London to seek refuge would have been comical if it hadn't proven such a boon. Madame was happy to feed and clothe you for a nominal fee. She could see what I could not —that you had potential. No doubt she has vast experience of what feeding and decent clothes can do for a girl. And when a girl has no protectors, but the potential to be a beauty, a bit of food and a shelter is worth a punt. Incidentally, she's more than willing to take you back."

"You mean, if I don't perform to your standard."

"Oh no, you are too perfect to fail at what I have in mind. Have no fear on that score."

She gripped the curtain that hung limply from its railing. A sad, faded floral. "I have fears on many scores, Mr Montpelier, but since you refuse to enlighten me, I have no choice but to kick my heels and await illumination...or rescue."

He rose and, at the door, stopped and turned. "I wouldn't hold your breath, Mrs Eustace." His sharp, bright eyes raked her newly replenished form but there was no admiration there. "You might be beautiful, but there is little else to recommend you to any would-be protector, it would seem. I have made enquiries."

Lily sucked in a breath.

No one would claim her. After her mother had died her father had declared her a child so unlovable he'd sent her away for the next seven years.

Then he'd bartered her to a husband for whom she held no interest.

A husband who would no doubt be delighted to learn that the disappearance—and presumed, death—of his barren wife might be replaced by one who would give him heirs.

Lily glanced up, unaware Mr Montpelier was still there until he spoke.

"I'm satisfied now that you will not be recognised by any

concerned party from your past." He drummed his fingers on the door frame, as the most satisfied smile Lily had seen played about his lips. "Even though you have regained you former looks." He studied her with dispassionate interest. "Have you been locked away so long that you are perhaps unaware of the new craze sweeping the land?"

He waited, keeping her in suspense, for she knew nothing of how society had shifted during the two years. It was partly why venturing outdoors was so terrifying. She felt like a vessel, not sturdy enough to cope with the uncertain tides of the ocean.

"Spiritualism, Mrs Eustace. You've at least heard the term."

Lily nodded. She knew some people believed one's character could be foretold by the bumps on their head. Phrenology. Robert had used the dubious practise to bolster his claims regarding his wife's precarious mental state. Near the end, he'd threatened to call in a spiritualist to banish the demons from her.

Lily closed her eyes. He hadn't needed to follow through.

As it transpired, Lily had needed no help to provide all the evidence he'd needed.

"Spiritualism, my dear Mrs Eustace, is the world in which you are about to be plunged," Mr Montpelier went on. "Your new duty, is to delve deep into the past for someone for whom, you will be delighted to hear, you hold a very particular interest."

And upon these enigmatic words, he turned on his heel and left.

CHAPTER 8

Another issue of *Manners & Morals* was almost upon him and, as the deadline approached, Hamish felt increasingly desperate, as he always did.

If he published what he wanted to publish, he'd not retain the editorship reluctantly ceded to him by his father.

But if he could push the boundaries just a little more with each issue, he might also train both his father, and the readers, to take an expanded view—his view—of the world.

Gloom was all about him, both outside, and in the small office where he sat, studying Archie's latest photographic offering. A parliamentary debate. A dry discussion that would be of interest to some readers.

In addition, Archie had photographed an archery competition. It featured both men and women drawing their crossbows, and certainly was of greater interest, visually, than anything else Hamish had before him. Lady Whittington, a famed society beauty, looked majestic in her gown of black-and-white stripes.

With a fingertip at the bottom of each image, Hamish

moved the former to the left, and the latter to the pile of possibilities on his desk just beneath the inkpot.

The left would definitely be included in the next issue of *Manners & Morals*. It would inspire some robust debate in the Letters to the Editor section which would please the magazine's founder.

And pleasing his father was, after all, Hamish's chief responsibility if he wished to remain at the helm while old Mr McTavish was on his sickbed.

If he included Lady Whittington's picture, he'd have to jettison his plans for a serialised adventure story that contained a suggestion of romance and replace it with a more prosaic homily for children.

"Thank you, Archie," Hamish said in dismissal. The photographer was standing close by his left shoulder, having just delivered the selection of photographs Hamish had requested. "That will be all."

"I ain't done, guvnor," said the photographer, his final offering already between thumb and fingertip, a secret little smile playing about his lips, Hamish saw when he glanced up. Silently, and with an air of triumph, Archie dropped the photograph onto the desk in front of Hamish.

Hamish drew it before him and frowned. The photograph was not up to the technical standard of the archery competition or the debate. Those subjects had obviously posed, unmoving, for the requisite time.

In this photograph, the subject was clearly not aware she was being photographed, though the fact she and her companions had kept still for a sufficient length of time made the younger woman easy to identify with just a slight blurriness at the edges.

"Ain't she the one yer wanted me ter find?" Archie asked. "The blonde, not the brunette? Or were it both, cos the brunette weren't there? Nevva mind, I knew yer was lookin' fer the blonde 'cos yer couldn't resist 'er enticements fer all yer'd not admit it even ter yerself."

"Lord, Archie, that's not true—"

"Reckon 'tis," said the photographer, his sly grin stretching wider. "That is 'er, ain't it?"

"Mrs Eustace? Yes." Hamish held the photograph up to the light and tried to place her surroundings. She was in a room, seated on an elegant sofa, a tall, broad-shouldered gentleman standing at her right shoulder, a stout, middle-aged woman in black seated beside her, both with their hands upon a card table in front of them.

"What are they doing?" Hamish's frown deepened.

"It were Mrs Bennet's Wednesday 'At 'Ome' an' I were photographin' 'er little crowd in diff'rent vignettes, as she called it. Yer can imagine me excitement when I recognised Mrs Eustace."

"Why did Mrs Bennet request your services?"

"'Parently she's a member o' a spiritualist group wot talks ter the dead. People come ter 'er At 'Omes an' listen ter spirits rappin' on the table, an' the like, tryin' ter talk ter their loved ones. Least, that's wot I were told."

Hamish looked more closely at the gentleman who appeared, on closer examination, to be focusing his gaze down Mrs Eustace's bodice rather than upon the baize-topped table.

He was surprised at the discomfort this occasioned and refused to recognise it as a twinge of envy. "And who is the man?"

"Lor' Elkin'ton wot's big in spiritualist circles." Archie leaned over and took possession of his photograph. He held it up and gazed at it lovingly. "A real beauty, ain't she?" he murmured. "Reckon Lor' Elkin'ton 'fought so too."

Hamish tapped his fingers on the table and stared

through the window. "Is that the impression you got?" he asked with a contrived show of unconcern.

"Well, 'e didn't want ter stop talkin' ter 'er. An' then 'e got mighty excited when he 'eard that she were a medium an' all—"

"What?"

"A medium. I 'fought I tol' yer. Someone wot talks ter the dead 'an conveys their messages ter the livin'—"

"Yes, I know what a medium is. But…he didn't believe her, did he? Good lord!" Hamish rose and began to pace his office, trying to keep his breathing under control. "Does she have this effect on all men? Is she going to pull the wool over his eyes like the charlatan she is?"

He realised he'd gone too far when he glanced up to see Archie's interested look. "'Ad no idea she'd got ter yer like that, guvnor. Yer shoulda said the word ter 'er when yer 'ad the chance. She were only too keen ter get out o' that Madame Chambon's place, me Gracie tells me. Woulda jumped at *any* offa. But then, yer not in the market fer that kind o' piece. Not a Puritan like you."

"I am a Methodist, not a Puritan."

"Same thing." Archie didn't appear to notice that Hamish had taken umbridge. Or perhaps he did, and that's why he went on with a broadening grim, "Terrified o' beauty. Or rather, o' beautiful women like this Mrs Eustace."

"I object—"

"Course yer do, course yer do, guv, but that ain't me concern, 'ere. I want ter sell yer me wares an' yer ain't interested in wot I reckon is me best photograph by a ragged mile, so I's jest gildin' the lily, so ter speak." He flicked a cheeky grin at Hamish over the top of his hands, for now he was holding a fistful of five photographs and going carefully over each one.

"There!" he said again. "Mrs Eustace, encore! Knew yer'd not be able ter resist in the end. 'Ere she is discussin' spiritualism wiv Lor' Elkin'ton wiv their 'eads close together. Mighty 'andsome couple they make, don't they? I's given yer the caption an' everyfink. Yer don't reckon the public would be interested? Then yer've lost yer touch, I reckon." He dropped the five photographs onto the table with a dismissive snort.

Hamish gripped the tabletop and kept his temper in check. "Sometimes you go too far, Archie," he growled.

"I'll go as far as I need ter," the little photographer said cheerily. "Now, wot'll yer pay me fer these? Every one is front page worthy."

Of course, Archie bested Hamish. Archie could sell fish to the Greenlanders, Hamish told him as he'd forked over a handsome sum for the dubious pleasure of owning Mrs Eustace's image, earmarked for his bedside table drawer rather than *Manners & Morals*, together with a horse-racing scene and a couple of standard society photographs, the type of fare his subscribers were used to seeing after a surfeit of missionaries and ministers.

Now, as the sun dipped beneath the roofs of the buildings across the road, Hamish hunched in his chair and surveyed the articles, drawings, and photographs that littered his desk.

His concentration was intense, as usual, so that he leapt at the sound of a brisk rap on the door which opened peremptorily without waiting for invitation, and a pert, bright-eyed face peered at him.

"Goodness, Lucy, have you not heard of knocking to announce yourself?" he barked.

"I did, but I knew there was no point in waiting for an invitation," his sister said, undeterred by the set down. "Here, I've brought you something from the pie shop so I don't find a corpse when I get back from my visit to Aunt Periwinkle."

She sighed. "Are you sure you don't want to join us on Saturday?"

He shook his head, ignoring the canvas bag on the table from which emanated an appetising aroma. "No point when there'll be so little time. Do send her my regards, naturally."

"Naturally."

He looked up at her sarcastic tone, raising his eyebrows with what he hoped was an admonishing look. "You didn't come here alone, did you, Lucy?" he asked.

"As a matter of fact, I did," she said with a complacent smile. "I'm twenty years old, Hamish. And I have no mother or father to answer to."

"If you don't show sufficient respect to your brother, then I promise I *will* return you to Father."

She blanched at this and immediately Hamish was sorry for the thoughtless remark. "An idle threat. Pay me no mind. Now, tell me why you're here, but not before you tell me why you're unaccompanied. It's dangerous for a woman to walk the streets alone."

"It's not dark, Hamish. And besides, there's every chance I shall be a comfortably married matron before the end of the year and able to do what I like." She reached across and put her hand over his, giving it a gentle squeeze. "That is, if you'll only agree to let Mr Myers call," she added cajolingly.

"Not a chance." Hamish leaned back and closed his eyes briefly, though he gripped Lucy's hand before she could withdraw it in pique. "He's not good enough for you and I won't see you throw yourself away."

"But I love him, Hamish. It's true that his position is lowly but he has prospects, and he loves me and I love him." Her voice grew tighter. "Are you really going to turn into Papa?"

"You know I'm not, otherwise I wouldn't have fought the battle I did to let him relinquish you so you could live with me," Hamish muttered.

"And for that I'm eternally grateful. And you would change your mind about Mr Myers if you only got to know him," she said with fierce determination. "Do you know how easy it would be for him to call without you even knowing of it. There, see how honest I am?"

"You're not honest. You just know that Maggie doesn't let anything you do pass her by, and you'd be found out and I'd be told of it—"

"And what would you do then? Throw me into the street? Gracious, Hamish, just thinking of it makes me shudder. I truly thought Father would when I defied him one too many times. We both know he is capable of such callousness. You're not." She grew thoughtful, withdrawing her hand and murmuring as she rose and wandered about his office, "Imagine what I should do if I *were* cast into the streets simply for displeasing you? I'd be ruined, of course. I'd have no future and end up selling turnips from a fruit and vegetable barrow." She shuddered before saying more force-fully, "For all your concern about people's morals and manners, I think you should be *more* concerned about the cruelty of a society that offers no support to women who are cast out into the world and forced to become what they have no wish to be, simply because they have no choice. Papa would never listen to such talk, but I'm not a child, and I had a friend, Dorrie, at the Ladies Seminary—she was a servant, actually—but she sometimes told me about what life was like for girls like her. How hard it was to earn enough to be considered *respectable*. How hard the men were on their wives and daughters. In a different way, Hamish." She looked stricken. "Papa clipped my ear and used the birch rod often enough, but if it hadn't been for you launching in to save me from an even worse hiding, which was becoming a habit, I'd have been like Dorrie and her sisters, and so many other young girls who worked their fingers to the bone dragging buckets of water up and down stairs and blacking the grates. The only difference being that I'd be wearing fashionable clothes. At least I'm looked after properly...and kindly...by you. I hope you know how much I appreciate that."

Hamish stretched his long legs, uncomfortable by the shift in conversation. "You were not so forgiving of the woman who stole your bonnet," he reminded her. His throat felt dry. Imagine if Lucy knew what Hamish knew about her.

Felt about her.

"She was different. She was a filthy beggar who had been born in the gutter and had no concept of morality so, sadly, would have had no hope of being guided into a better life. She wasn't like Dorrie who worked so hard but who would never commit a crime like *stealing*. I'm talking about women who were once good and virtuous but who, through no fault of their own, suddenly are cast adrift. Why don't you write about their plight in your newspaper, Hamish?"

"Because our father would remove the editorship from my hands, you know that." Hamish was feeling more uncomfortable by the minute. He changed the subject. "I'm sorry you're cross with me, and I have said that if Mr Myers can demonstrate that he can support a wife, then he is welcome to call and state his case." He paused, adding, "And I'm sorry if I didn't fulfil my brotherly obligations earlier, Lucy. You know I would have if I'd had an inkling. I'd have come back from France on the next steamer."

"Gracious! An apology is not what I was expecting," she said, making light of what had been a frightful time in Lucy's life when their father had, indeed, lost his temper to such a degree that his violence had nearly gone unchecked. Hamish's return had been just in time. "And nor is it like you, Hamish, my darling brother whom I have never heard apologise to anyone in his life."

"I would be the first to admit when I was in error." He cleared his throat, wanting to believe it.

Lucy put her head on one side and crinkled her brow. "Then you must never have been in error and I should rejoice at my good fortune in having grown up with a paragon."

Hamish laughed. "I don't know if I should send you home with a clip over your ear or thank you for relieving the tension. Lord knows, it's needed around here as we prepare to go to print." He reached for the food she'd brought. "Thank you for taking such good care of me," he mumbled, his stomach growling as he realised he hadn't eaten since early morning. "I don't know what I'll do with myself when Mr Myers proves himself worthy and you leave me."

"Lord knows, you can't look after yourself. You'll have to find yourself a wife, of course," Lucy said.

"I haven't time for that." Hamish took a bite.

"Time? Or inclination?"

"Both."

She studied him a moment as he ate, before one of the photographs caught her eye and she reached across and held it up to the light. "Now that's a beautiful woman, indeed. And she is with, if I'm not mistaken, Lord Elkington. She's not his wife, is she?"

"Heavens, no!" Hamish expostulated and was immediately embarrassed for she looked at him with obvious surprise and the expectation of elucidation. Awkwardly he said, "She's not the kind of woman you should associate with, that's all I can say, Lucy."

"You can be such a Puritan sometimes, Hamish," she grumbled, looking more closely at the picture. "How would you even know that? She looks perfectly respectable to me."

"Looks can be deceptive," he said. "And I am not a Puritan. Someone else called me that today and I took exception."

"Well, you are buttoned-up and judgemental which is tantamount to the same thing." Lucy flashed him a smile. "You need to fall in love with a girl who will make you forget that you're just a sinning mortal here on this earth for only a short time."

"I believe that is the philosophy behind what these people are so very interested in refuting," Hamish said, indicating Lord Elkington. "His lordship regularly communes with his dead wife at Mrs Bennet's seances."

"And this woman?"

"Mrs Eustace?"

"Oh, you're familiar with her?"

The artless question made his body stir. "I know nothing about her. You know I don't believe in this quackery."

"You don't believe in spiritualism, dear brother?" she asked in mock horror. "When the spirits are all around us?"

"You know me, sister. I only believe what I can see."

"Except for our Heavenly Father."

He grunted. "You should be heading back, Lucy. Thank you for the pie. It's much appreciated as I shan't be home for hours. Get Mrs Dawkins to walk you home. It's nearly time for her to leave, anyway. I'm sorry but you'll be dining alone, tonight."

"It's hardly a surprise." Lucy paused at the door. "But do think about what I said."

He frowned, blank. "What *did* you say?"

"About finding a wife."

"Oh, I doubt that will happen very soon. I'm far too busy for that."

"Or are you perhaps afraid of courting rejection? Maybe after what happened in France which you refuse to tell me about?"

He took a second to gather his wits before dismissing this. "Nothing to do with that! I just haven't thought too much about marrying, to be perfectly honest." He glanced at the piles of papers and photographs upon the table and felt a sudden surge of desperation. "Not when there is so much work to do."

"And too much work makes Johnny a dull boy. Which is why I doubt you'll find a wife, either, Hamish, and that is a concern to me." She retraced her footsteps to put her hand on his shoulder to give it one last sisterly squeeze. "For you are a kind and endearing chap when one gets to know and understand you but, alas, I think I will be the only woman who ever will."

CHAPTER 9

Lily cast a final eye over Mrs Moore's drawing room while she bottled up her feelings about what lay before her. Unlike Mr Bennet's well-appointed drawing room, Mrs Moore's salon was draped with black velvet hangings, the lamps turned down, giving it a sombre, eerie feeling.

Lily had been left alone for just a minute, which was long enough to feel almost overcome by fear and dread, for Mrs Moore and Mr Montpelier had been like spectres of doom as they'd instructed her on the role she must play.

Of course, she'd heard the terms the two of them now bandied about. Theosophism, spiritualism, supernatural phenomenon.

But, rusticating in the country as she had all her life, these were terms that had been used with scorn by the horse and hunting crowd, who were Robert's cronies.

Lily didn't like what she must do, though she supposed it was better than many alternatives. A bit of pretence to cheer a few of Mrs Moore's bereaved clients was hardly going to do harm, she reasoned.

"They're here. The first carriage has just stopped by the front steps!" Mrs Moore dashed into the room, clutching her string of black beads, her feathered headdress waving. Her painted face looked comical in its alarm, and Lily wondered how likely these guests were to take her seriously. Especially as they'd been described as respectable, 'normal' members of society. "Get out, Lily! Go into the next room and down the stairs. Go, go! Then wait until you hear the sign that your presence is required. You know what to do!"

Mr Montpelier, who had followed in Moore's wake in his usual unhurried fashion, raised an eyebrow. "You look just the part, my girl. Nicely done." This last, however, was directed at Mrs Moore, Lily noticed as she quit the room, hearing the medium reply, "Such a strong resemblance, Mr Montpelier. The girl could be her living embodiment. Indeed, it is truly remarkable."

Clutching her train over her arm, Lily slipped into the next room and then down a shallow flight of steps and along a short corridor until she was beneath the parlour.

Her gown was, as she'd remarked, two seasons old, so she'd been surprised at how much deliberation had gone into its choosing. That is until she'd seen the photograph which Mr Montpelier and Mrs Moore had been poring over earlier that afternoon.

Enlightenment had suddenly descended, for the girl, who was about eighteen, she supposed, could have been her sister.

If she'd had one.

There was not enough time to dwell on the ramifications of her resemblance to a girl in a photograph, though, as she nervously waited below the trapdoor that would open, the sign at which she would step dramatically into the room. She wasn't quite sure what would happen then. Or what her reception would be.

But these were her instructions. And if she wanted food and shelter, she had no choice but to obey.

As for hope in the longer term? Lily really didn't think she had the courage she needed to think that far right now.

"Oh…oh…ohhhhh!"

She heard Mrs Moore's grating cry, growing louder and echoing about the room to the accompaniment of tinkling percussion. Steadying herself, Lily picked her way carefully up the steps, pushing open the trapdoor, closing it carefully and quickly behind her, before emerging amidst a cloud of smoke and clanging into the middle of the drawing room. As her eyes became accustomed to the gloom, she saw that a gauze curtain separated her from several rows of chairs, upon which were seated five people.

The most prominent of these was a whiskered gentleman with a head of thick, snowy-white hair, wearing a dark suit and waistcoat, his gold fob watch twinkling in the lights that lent the room the air of a mystical fairyland.

"At last! At last she has come to us…We have summoned the spirit. Cassandra's spirit! She is here at last," Mrs Moore intoned.

Lily stood very still, observing the shock and alarm her sudden presence seemed to generate. She kept her look blank and staring, eyes trained into the distance, as she'd been instructed; silent until the sign to speak.

Haltingly, she repeated what she'd been told, as she stretched out her arms, "Papa…Papa, it is so good to see you again." It was strange to utter such things, having never spoken like this to her own father whom she'd not seen since her marriage. "Papa, I have missed you so very much." Then, in a forlorn voice, as instructed, "I'm sorry I went away."

Before she'd even finished speaking, another burst of smoke and mist enveloped the room, obscuring her from sight as cymbals clanged and bells tinkled. Suddenly the two ladies on either side of the man whom Lily had heard referred to as Lord Lambton began to wail, and then to cry out as they stretched forward their arms, "Cassandra! Cassandra! Stay and talk to us!"

"I must go! I must go now. But...but I will return!" Lily swayed where she stood for a few seconds until the mist became all-encompassing. It stung her throat and eyes, and she struggled not to cough.

Just as she was about to step back down the steps and pull the trapdoor over her head, Lord Lambton got to his feet and also threw out his arms.

"Don't leave me again, Cassandra!" he begged in a broken voice. "Don't go! What will it take to make you stay?"

Lily saw Mr Montpelier crossing the room to restrain the elderly and clearly much-affected gentleman, and nervously Lily retreated, thankful for the obscurity afforded her by the swirling mist.

The performance had been short, carefully choreographed, and, she guessed, effective.

With difficulty, she closed the trapdoor above her as she descended, but then it was too dark to see as she crouched on the steps. The silence that replaced the mystical chanting and odd music was daunting, but now she was terrified that she would trip over her train and tumble the last few steps, possibly breaking her neck.

The reflection that her death would cause no great lament in the hearts of anyone else, and that in fact it was likely to go completely unnoticed except to the pair who had found a use for her, and whose pockets she'd no doubt gilded nicely, was painful, as she crawled down into the depths of the room.

A few moments later, the trapdoor above her opened again, and a dim light penetrated. Mr Montpelier eased his way down, like a spider, until he straightened before her, brandishing a lantern as he declared, "Magnificent! They were entranced! They loved you, Mrs Eustace! Well done!"

Lily blinked in the light. "Are they going? Can I go upstairs yet? It's very cold down here."

"Nearly, nearly. Mrs Moore excelled in building up to the great reveal." His eyes glittered with satisfaction. "They were full of doubt when she sat them down. Said they were non-believers, but it was Mrs Bennet who persuaded them."

Lily had never seen Mr Montpelier in such an expansive mood. While she leaned against the steps and shivered, he afforded her a running commentary on the method by which respectable Mrs Bennet had engaged Lord Lambton's sisters in conversation, persuading them that she knew someone who could summon their dead niece's spirit, but encountering enormous scepticism along the way.

"They were the ladies?" she interrupted.

"That's correct. Lord Lambton's sister and his aunt. There were many tears as they spoke of their loss and their hope that they would be treated to a final glimpse of the child they loved so well."

"I'm hardly a child," Lily muttered.

"Cassandra was not yet eighteen when she died." His smile was unusually expansive. It didn't sit well on his gaunt, hard face. "And you look barely older than that with some mist and gauze to muddy the waters. Oh, but you were better than we could have expected." Mr Montpelier shook his head as he raised the lamp to peer at her. "You'd not believe how fortune favoured me. I barely attended when I saw a photograph of Lord Lambton's poor, dead daughter in the death notices. But less than a week later, I was in Brussels, using an old newspaper to polish a pair of boots and…there you were!" His long, thin teeth gleamed in the light. "A picture of the maison's most notorious inmate. It's most beautiful inmate and I was suddenly struck by your remarkable resemblance to Lambton's poor, dead child." He rolled his eyes. "I must say, when I discovered you so reduced, I really did think to abandon you to Madame Chambon. But my early hopes have paid off, and you, too, are the better for it, my dear Madame Bradden. You are free from your incarceration and free from your husband. Tonight, you have been put through your paces, and you were a triumph."

Lily drew back as he went to grip it, and he narrowed his gaze. "Have no fear that my interest in you goes beyond what you can do for Mrs Moore and myself." She clearly had offended him, for he pinched the tip of his long bony nose and raised his eyes heavenwards. "If next time goes as well, you will be rewarded. I am a fair man, and it has not escaped me that you have nowhere else to go. Except Madame Chambon's."

Lily was about to make some perhaps unwise rejoinder, but asked instead, "Lord Lambton was much moved? I retreated when I saw him rise from his chair. I was afraid—"

"You were in no danger. He would not have gone beyond the curtain."

"I wasn't afraid for myself. I felt sorry for him." Lily lowered her voice. "Surely he only wanted to believe I was his daughter?"

"My dear, you underestimate how compelling Mrs Moore can be. She has quite the reputation. And you, Lady Eustace, were entirely believable. Don't let your conscience smite you." Mr Montpelier laughed softly. "We are selling him happiness."

Lily opened her mouth to speak, but long habit stilled the words on her tongue.

There was no point asking him at what cost.

CHAPTER 10

"I won't take no for an answer, Hamish. It's far too nice a day for you to spend all of it closeted inside your office."

Hamish considered Lucy's mulish expression, and the clear blue sky behind her, and weighed up the work he should be doing, and the amount of time he was likely to waste arguing with her.

"You always get your way in the end," he muttered as he rose and offered her his arm. Together, they descended the stairs to the pavement and headed for Regent's Park, a short distance away.

"If I didn't, you'd be even more deadly dull than you already are," she said brightly. Lucy was like a child with a new toy each time she bent him to her will. "Now, as I was saying only yesterday, you just need a pretty, long-suffering, but necessarily cheerful wife to be a foil to your perpetual gloom."

"Lord, Lucy, you make me out to be some nocturnal creature who scuttles about in a basement, shunning joy and fresh air when nothing could be further from the truth,"

Hamish countered as they traversed the gravel path. "I walk to work every morning, breathing deep the pea-soup fogs of this time of year, and I smilingly compliment all the nannies on their bright and energetic charges. If I don't smile, it's not because I'm unhappy but rather—Oh, I beg your pardon!"

He stepped back quickly so as not to impede the path of a woman in a fashionable gown, a thick veil concealing her face.

"Why, Mr McTavish!" the pedestrian said, raising the veil and revealing herself to be the beautiful blonde whose image haunted him and who seemed determined to bring him to account in the flesh.

"Mrs Eustace," he acknowledged with a bow.

In her heavily adorned gown of red-and-white stripes with black fringing set off by a pert black velvet hat with a curling plume, she looked extraordinarily fetching, and Hamish had to work hard to show how unmoved he really was.

Hamish introduced her to his sister with misgiving, heightened when Lucy put her hand to her lips, saying, "I knew you looked familiar!" She shook her head disbelievingly. "Why, I saw your photograph on Hamish's desk only yesterday. I thought you so beautiful."

Instead of moving on in embarrassment at the first opportunity, as Hamish had hoped, Mrs Eustace inclined her head and said with a twinkle in her eye, "You are kind. Might I, in turn, compliment you on your bonnet, Miss McTavish? The fruit looks so edible I'd worry some urchin might dash past and snatch it right off your head."

"Heavens, but can you believe it! Some urchin already tried!" Lucy said with a surprised laugh. "Hamish went in pursuit and fetched it back, of course, though I think the creature got off lightly since he didn't drag her before the police constable. Not too long ago she'd have been sent to the colonies for her crimes."

"Indeed. Well, let us hope the urchin mended her ways, having got off so lightly this time and has taken advantage of being given a second chance." A smile tugged at the woman's lips. "That's if you are a champion of progress, Miss McTavish. I am a regular reader of your brother's improving magazine, and I am still undecided as to his views on reform now that he has taken over the magazine's editorship."

Hamish could not respond. In the sunlight, standing so close, he could smell the violet scent she wore; she was mesmerising. Who was she?

"My late husband was a subscriber to *Manners & Morals*, and it was clear that retribution, not reform, was believed by the editor at the time to be the key to keeping the lower classes in check and thus revolution from our shores." She spoke with the modulated voice of someone who really did hail from the upper classes and not the gutter, yet Hamish could not be taken in. She was an actress; he had to believe it. A guttersnipe who'd learned to ape her betters, to speak like them. She was parroting someone else's words. Why else would she be friendless? What else could he believe?

"Goodness," murmured Lucy. "My father founded the magazine, you know, and oversaw every editorial decision until he became unwell and my brother came back from France to take over."

"Is that so, Miss McTavish?" Mrs Eustace smiled at Lucy and said in a tone that was clearly meant to convey more to Hamish than to his sister, "Your brother is doing a fine job of keeping his father's loyal subscribers happy, yet there are occasions when he shows flashes of surprising tolerance towards those who transgress. For several years, I had no occasion to read the monthly edition of *Manners & Morals* to which my late husband was addicted, but very recently I resumed a very great interest in it. Such an improving magazine with so many tips on how I might better myself, which I take quite to heart." Her eyes flashed a smile that did not reach her lips as she transferred her look to Hamish.

"I am delighted that you find it such a useful resource, Mrs Eustace," Hamish said drily.

"And you, Miss McTavish? It must be challenging, at times, to have to live up to the ideals of two such upstanding men. Your father and your brother."

She said this with feigned cheer, but the blush that suffused Lucy's face was instant as the girl stammered, "I... couldn't. It's why I live with my brother now."

"Oh, my poor child, I had no intention of distressing you. I am so sorry." She put her hand on Lucy's shoulder and leaned into her, her expression genuinely remorseful.

And so utterly bewitching, Hamish had to turn his head away.

"But I am sure it is the perfect arrangement," declared Mrs Eustace. "And you are surely the perfect sister who has no fear of failing to live up to anyone's ideals, least of all your brother's. For who has not sinned, whether in deed or thought, Miss McTavish?"

Lucy made a quick recovery as she put her hand over Mrs Eustace's, looking at the woman as if she were staring at a goddess. "Goodness, I don't think I've pondered the matter as deeply as you have, when I suppose I really should have. I just know that what is wrong is wrong...and what is right is right."

Mrs Eustace considered this. "I once thought like you, Miss McTavish." She smiled at Hamish, adding, "That is until I realised how open to opinion was the concept of right and wrong. Who is to judge, besides?"

Hamish wanted to end the conversation, but on the other hand, he wanted Lucy gone so he could have Mrs Eustace all to himself. He wanted to take her to task for speaking like that to his innocent young sister.

Though, really, he knew that was just an excuse as he felt his own fascination twine through his body, as thick and intense as the vines that grew up to surround the Sleeping Beauty. Only, in the space of seconds rather than a hundred years.

"The photograph I saw showed you with Mrs Bennet, the famous spiritualist," Lucy went on in tones of breathless excitement. "She's held in such high regard. Everyone talks about her. What is she like?"

"Really Lucy, this spiritualist business is humbug," Hamish interrupted, sounding more irritated than he'd have liked, for now he sounded like the taciturn humbug, he realised.

"Calling forth the afterlife?" Mrs Eustace asked with a serene smile, "I don't believe in it myself, it is true."

"Yet you dabble in it," Hamish challenged, and Lucy sent him a concerned look which caused him to flush hotly for he knew his accusatory tone was uncalled-for.

"I'm interested in it, that is true."

"I'm told you took part last night. How can you say you don't believe in it if you participated?"

"Many people act parts they don't believe in," she countered reasonably. "I'm sure there are plenty of vicars who have lost their faith but still need to feed their families. Or peddlers of beauty products who know nothing can hold back the hands of time."

"So, you do attend these spiritualist meetings?" Lucy was wide-eyed, still staring at Mrs Eustace as if she thought her the most beautiful creature she'd set eyes upon. Which was exactly how Hamish was feeling this very minute; a feeling he intended to fight, all the way. "How thrilling. Do pray tell me more? Who was called forth? Did they oblige?"

"A bereaved father recalled his beloved daughter from the grave." Mrs Eustace looked genuinely sorrowful. "He was overjoyed when she appeared."

Hamish cleared his throat. "Lord Lambton, no less, I heard. I hadn't pegged him for believing in such nonsense."

"Poor Lord Lambton. Of course he would believe anything in the hope of seeing Cassandra again!" Lucy cried, excited. "Was it really him? I went to school with Cassandra. She was a lovely girl."

Hamish studied Mrs Eustace for some sign of discomfort. Or embarrassment. And saw none. "So, you called up her spirit?" he said, not hiding his disparagement. "Made her father believe you were his dead daughter?"

"He was overjoyed when his supposed daughter spoke to him." Mrs Eustace looked a trifle defensive. "You mightn't be a believer, Mr McTavish, but it brought him joy. And you can't argue that's not a good thing."

"But it won't bring his daughter back."

"You weren't there, Mr McTavish."

"Are you inviting me?"

"No, I am not," she said quickly. "Mrs Moore does not permit non-believers."

"Despite her star performer being one?"

"I did it to bring him comfort."

"Forgive me, I thought material gain might have been the motivation."

He knew he deserved the scandalised look Lucy sent him before Mrs Eustace inclined her head, saying softly, "I'm sure I'd never question whether you believed everything you printed in your magazine, Mr McTavish. Good day to you both. It's been a pleasure to meet you, Lucy."

"Hamish, what got into you!" Lucy cried as they watched the woman's shapely form disappear round a bend. "You were so rude to her! And you barely know her!"

She put her hand to her mouth, her eyes widening in sudden insight as she gasped, "You do know her. That's why you have her photograph on your desk, even though you aren't going to publish it because of course *Manners & Morals* wouldn't countenance an article on spiritualism." Then, without waiting for him to respond, she went on in a rush, "It's because you didn't know what to say to her that you became all combative and taciturn. Because you're afraid of goodness and beauty! You think the only woman worthy of being your wife should be some dowdy little do-gooder, yet Mrs Eustace makes your heart beat faster, and you're angry with yourself for there being something you can't control!"

"Enough, Lucy!" Hamish snapped, agitation coursing through his veins as he struggled to say more.

For innocent, winsome Lucy, who had no experience of life, let alone lovers, had just summed up the matter with frightening clarity.

CHAPTER 11

After three Wednesday seances, Lord Lambton lived for further, more prolonged glimpses of the daughter he'd lost.

Some said she'd died of fever in her bed. Drowned, by her own hand, according to others.

Lily only overheard snippets of conversation between Mrs Moore and Mr Montpelier describing the success and growing interest in these spiritual evenings, for she saw little being veiled for the most part. The week before, however, she'd stayed longer as the mist had cleared and pushed back her veil, as she'd been told.

The response had been disarming and disturbing.

Lord Lambton had abruptly stood. Then he'd crumpled back into his seat and wept.

"I say give 'im anuvver couple o' minutes ternight ter gaze upon 'is lost girl 'an 'e's good fer a tenner more," Lily overheard Mrs Moore tell Mr Montpelier in a loud whisper as they sat, heads close together, on a sofa in the rather cramped parlour where these so-called supernatural events took place.

Lily hesitated within the curtained embrasure that was just inside the door that led from the passage to the parlour. She'd been on her way to report for her duties for that evening's performance, but as she was kept completely in the dark as to what the pair intended for the following weeks, she wanted to hear as much as she could.

"Top that wiv anuvver tenner, cousin," said Mr Montpelier with a soft laugh. "Ol' Lambton 'ad an iron constitution when it came ter politics, but 'e's nuffink but a sentimental sop at 'eart, ain't he?"

This was not a conversation Lily was supposed to hear. Occasionally, she'd heard them lapse into common parlance. These were the occasions they dropped their guard, no longer caring about pretence.

Concerned, she eased her way further back within the encompassing folds of the heavy velvet curtains. The room was a monument to the craze for the unexplained, with heavily framed pictures of ghostly scenes, photographs of so-called ghosts surprised on Earth as they floated just above the ground, domes containing skulls and books of spells and chants to summon the dead.

Amidst all this were a jumble of sofa and chairs, with the aspidistras and other fernery pushed aside to make way for the increasing amounts of standing room required as word spread of Mrs Moore's mystical evenings, and more and more people jostled to get a ticket.

"'Ow long can all this last afore the ol' cove gets an inklin', Mrs Moore?"

Lily was taken aback, for while she'd surmised their origins, she had not known they were related.

Peeking past the curtain's gold fringing, she saw Mrs Moore preening, running the forefinger of her mauve-gloved hand the length of the ostrich feather that waved from her sequinned velvet headwear. "I ain't stupid, Mr Montpelier.

Course there's a limit ter 'ow long we can string 'im along. Reckon mayhap anuvver couple 'o Wednesdays, mayhap three afore we'll 'ave ter retire poor little Miss Cassandra, eh?"

It was fortunate Lily had the support of the back wall or her knees might not have held up. Another couple of weeks was all they needed? Then where would she go?

Into the spirit world?

She held her breath. If they planned to be rid of her, she couldn't let them know she'd overheard.

"Nevva gave yer the credit yer deserved, Mr Montpelier when yer went inter service instead o' joinin' the rest o' the family on the stage, an' nor were I more ashamed than ter 'ear yer'd bin given yer marchin' orders fer stealin' yer lor'-ship's cufflinks but 'ow nicely it did play out, eh?"

"I were not cut out fer the stage like yer side o' the family, Mrs Moore; that was made verra clear ter me." Mr Montpelier sounded a trifle aggrieved.

"No, Mr Montpelier, that is true enough. No flair! The boy's got no flair or flamboyance, that's wot me mam allus used ter say. Only way 'e'll earn a crust is if 'e goes inter service an' does wot 'is betters tell 'im ter." Mrs Moore gave a satisfied sigh. "But yer surprised us all, yer did, Mr Montpelier, when yer showed yer 'ad nouse 'an nerve."

"'Twere a grave risk, Mrs Moore—"

"An' yer didn't get away wiv it, neither, Mr Montpelier. Stealin' yer master's cufflinks like yer did. Yer got caught an' the fancy footman were no better'n than the rest o' us. I remember 'ow yer did like ter show o' that fine liv'ry o' yours. 'Fought a bit o' gold braid made yer better'n than the rest o' us, didn't yer?"

"I was promoted ter valet ter me gennulman, I weren't no footman." He sounded offended, but Mrs Moore was already running on, "I still can't fink what got inter yer. Stealin'! Fer yer nevva were a chance taker, that were fer sure. Can't imagine 'ow yer didn't bungle it even more an' end up swingin' from a noose."

"I meant only ter relieve 'is lor'ship o' 'is cufflinks long enough ter buy meself a train ticket from Brussels ter the asylum an' see fer meself if the incredible story I'd 'eard 'bout the poor madwoman who maybe weren't mad were true."

"An' if 'is lor'ship's sojournin' in that Froggie land 'and't taken yer so close ter the asylum, wot them dinner guests 'ad bin talkin' 'bout the night afore, yer wouldn't 'ave 'ad the chance ter see fer yerself, eh?" Mrs Moore hiccupped in pleasure. "But the story 'bout the poor beautiful ol' wife, discarded like a piece o' flotsam, were true enough."

"There's the rub, Mrs Moore. She looked like a bit o' flotsam; a bag o' rags when I saw 'er. I nearly turned tail an' fled back ter me master wiv his cufflinks afore 'e 'ad a chance ter realise any o' us 'ad gone."

"'Cept yer used yer nouse, Mr Montpelier. Yer 'fought o' the girl's potential an' 'ow she 'ad no one an—"

"'Twere a prison guard wot said she were a fine beauty when she were brought ter 'em an' as a bit 'o victuals would set the matter ter rights...an' that she'd not 'ad a bout o' madness since she'd got there, when I asked 'im."

"So, yer kept the cufflinks which was diamonds, not paste, an' got the lady an' now we'se rollin' in muck, eh? An' wot's more," Mrs Moore went on, punctuating her conversation with a cackle, "The Widow Renquist came back this mornin' an'—dead set—but she all but put it in writin' that she wants me ter 'old a séance ter find 'er dead 'usband's killer. Or 'is body, more like. She's comin' back t'morra. Says if we can come ter an agreement that makes it worth ev'ryone's while, she wants ter 'old the 'ole smoke an' mirrors palaver next Thursday."

"Well, well. That'll keep Mrs Eustace useful a while

longer," said Mr Montpelier with a chuckle. "Wot's the widow off'rin'?"

There was a tense silence. And then Mrs Moore said with glee, "Fifty ter fill the place wiv suspects, Mr Monpelier. People wot might o' seen ol' Renquist round Shepherd Market, that raffish part o' Mayfair where them bloodstains was found." There was a long, tense silence finally broken by her wheezing whisper, "An' a thousand if we find the body or get us a murderer."

Mr Montpelier seemed lost for words. Lily certainly was.

"A thousand? Lor', Mrs Moore, I ain't sayin' I don't b'lieve yer but –"

"Mr Montpelier, the widow Renquist is a rich woman who wants ter remarry." Mrs Moore clapped her hands. "She can't do that fer seven years if the body o' 'er 'usband ain't found. 'Tis worth at least a thousand if we can do that."

Lily's brief excitement gave way to the pragmatic realisation that, of course, they couldn't do that. How foolish to have let hope bear her up for even a moment.

Mr Montpelier clearly shared her view for he said, "Now, now, Mrs Moore, don't get ahead o' yerself. If we can secure fifty jest fer a few sessions communin' wiv this so-called mort cove, then we'se doin' well. 'Ow do yer s'pose we 'ave any 'ope o' doin' wot the constabulary can't?"

"Why, Mr Montpelier, 'ave yer no imagination? We will publish the story in the newspapers. 'Twill bring the punters in droves an' somewhere 'mongst them all will be the killer who will lead us ter the body. My dear cousin, I's read 'nuff o' them penny dreadful detective stories ter know 'ow it's done. I b'lieve we can do it!"

"Publish? Who'll publish?"

Lily peeked again through the folds of the curtain that sheltered her, to see the smug smile that nestled amidst the folds of Mrs Moore's heavily powdered face. Mrs Moore looked far more indomitable than Lily felt. "Any newspaper or magazine wot likes ter serve up wot the public likes ter read will be fallin' over themselves ter come 'ere an' photograph Mrs Moore the Magnificent, Spiritualist an' Spirit Communer."

"Wiv all due respect, mayhaps a photograph o' a young an' winsome creature might whet the public appetite more. Photographed wiv yer, me dear cousin," Mr Montpelier added hastily. He made an expansive gesture with his hands, unusual for him, but then it was clear he'd offended the mastermind of this little plan. "Experience an' beauty, Mrs Moore."

Mrs Moore greeted this with a harrumph. "The girl will 'ave ter be veiled. Course, 'er appearance can be apprehended, not but that she don't 'ave a nice shape ter 'er. But the 'int o' 'er youth an' beauty will be sufficient. That boy wot checks on 'er from time ter time says she's a good 'un wot don't go out wivvout bein' veiled though more like it's cos she's terrified 'o bein' recognised an' returned ter that 'usband o' 'ers."

Just the thought of being returned to Robert and her former life was enough to make Lily's mind close down for a second. She took a deep breath to try and push aside the horrors of her former life; silently entreating the heavens that this not be a precursor to the insanity that robbed her of all her faculties. Life with Robert, and life in the *maison*, were both tantamount to death sentences.

Mrs Moore rose. "Now Mr Montpelier, 'tis comin' up ter time an' Mrs Eustace should be 'ere by now. Go an' sees if she's waitin' in the cellar an' I'll nip ter me chamber an' prepare meself. If Lor' Lambton were in tears last week, 'es goin' ter be gnashin' 'is teeth an' blubbin' like a baby afore ternight is 'frough."

CHAPTER 12

In the warm offices of McTavish & Son, a battle of wills was taking place.

"But it's wot the public wants, guvnor," Archie protested, causing Hamish to bang his fist onto the table with more energy than he'd intended.

Hamish—Archie's boss, superior and editorial director—reminded his minion of his status, drew in a breath and said in a measured but warning tone, "If I published what the public wanted, we would be written off as purveyors of filth and immorality."

"I ain't sayin' ter lower the tone, guvnor; I'm jest sayin' as yer are missin' an opportunity when the public—rich an' poor—'ave gone spiritualist mad. Why, this Widow Renquist seekin' out yer Mrs Moore ter discover wot 'appened ter 'er 'usband is the perfect occasion fer me ter lug me equipment across town an' photograph all them wot's in the audience, jest like Mrs Moore respectfully requests."

"The woman is a charlatan. She requested that I offer her free publicity at the expense of our reputation to photograph her Lambton seances. I said no, then, and I'm not about to change my mind."

"But that's different, guv," Archie protested. "Lor' Lambton's loss is private. The Renquist case is not. Two months ago, when it were a live murder investigation splashed 'bout in ev'ry newspaper, yer was verra 'appy ter do the same an' give a proper account o' it."

"That was news, Archie. Don't you see the difference?"

"This is news, wiv all due respect," Archie grumbled. "Now wot could be better than that the rich widow is fed up wiv the constabulary failin' ter even get them a suspect, an' she reckons she'll find answers elsewhere? 'Frough a medium. See, immediately yer got a story." He sniffed. "Sure, an' it's true enough that Lor' Lambton's seances are private, but they's open ter the public. Each week more an' more people crowd inter that 'ouse ter get a glimpse o' the spirit creature wot looks so like the poor dead girl." He sighed. "Yer beautiful Mrs Eustace wot 'as yer all hot and bovvered an' yer won't even give 'er the time o' day let alone publish 'er picture an' make 'er the next beauty o' the decade. Which she could be, yer know."

"She's not my Mrs Eustace." Hamish went to the window. "What makes you think you have any right to speak to me like that?"

"Cos I sees the way yer look at 'er photograph. Yer won't publish, but yer look at it."

Hamish felt his skin heat up at Archie's words and kept his face firmly averted. It was true; he did keep Mrs Eustace's photograph in his desk drawer. Occasionally, he did look at it.

"Mrs Eustace and Mrs Moore are as bad as the snake-oil salesmen who would trick the credulous of their hard-earned money," he said softly. "I will not sink to their level."

"My, but yer nevva 'ad such scruples when yer published a

picture o' the Blood Countess. Didn't that magazine fly o' the stands?"

"Countess Bathory lived three hundred years ago, and it was a woodcut. It's hardly the same."

"An' 'ow many issues did yer last prosing publication sell? Not nearly as many as that one wot featured a bit o' the gruesomeness the public want," Archie persisted. "Yer in the bizness o' feedin' public appetites so as ter make money. Yer not a monk." He gave him an assessing look. "Hmm, maybe that's the problem."

Before Hamish could lambast him for his impertinence, Archie went on, "Don't matter, guvnor; by 'ook or by crook, I'll be at Mrs Moore's Wednesday next ter capture Lor' Lambton's tears an' at the Widow Renquist's séance the night afta that an' I'll sell me pictures ter some'un else. The 'ole country will want ter see a murderer be brought ter justice."

Hamish turned. "How do you possibly imagine Mrs Moore will be anything but discredited through her ridiculous claim that she can discover what the police have not been able to?" he snapped, glaring at the small Cockney, who was already halfway out of the door.

Archie stopped and raised an eyebrow. "I reckon yer've missed the point, guvnor," he said.

No sooner had he gone than one of the clerks tapped on the wood panelling to announce that he had a visitor, and to his astonishment Mrs Eustace was ushered in, with Archie returning in her wake like a bad penny.

Hamish nearly groaned aloud, and was on the point of despatching the photographer with a sweep of his outstretched arm, but was prevented by Mrs Eustace's gasp of admiration as she took in Archie's photographic equipment.

"Goodness," she gushed, "are you the gentleman whose photographs appear in *The Family's Guide to Manners and*

Morals? Why, it is an honour to meet you. You are a true artist." She lifted her veil, and Hamish noticed with misgiving that the effect she had on Archie was as dire as upon himself.

"An' a great many uvver publications, 'sides, not ter mention the fact me portrait photographs are becomin' quite sought afta by the gentry," Archie said importantly.

Mrs Eustace's admiration was replaced by disappointment as she said with a sigh, "Alas, such skill must command a higher remuneration than I am able to pay, but perhaps you may advise me on a related matter. You see," she went on quickly, "I am looking for a photographer to capture a very important—you might even say, critical—event that," she lowered her voice, "involves possibly drawing out a murderer. It's what I came here to talk to Mr McTavish about."

"Mrs Eustace, I really don't believe that is what brought you here since you surely must know that I recently declined Mrs Moore, herself, when she put to me this same request," Hamish interrupted, directing a quelling look at Archie, who appeared dangerously on the verge of crumpling to his knees and offering his services for free as he kissed the hem of the lady's skirts. "And in fact, Mr Archie was just on his way out."

She smiled brightly. "You're right; it was not what brought me here. I was, in fact, going to put an advertisement in the Wanted column."

"You can do that with the clerk downstairs."

"Yes, for a lady's maid and for a photographer," she said, as if he hadn't spoken, smiling instead at Archie. "I have a lady photographer who has offered me her services—"

"Lor' ma'am, but I don't reckon no lady photographer is up ter the skill level o' wot I can offer," said Archie, staring at her as if he were still mesmerised. Then, more eagerly, "An' fer jobs that are in the public interest, I can offer yer me rock-bottom rate."

"Could you? How kind, sir." She turned to Hamish. "And if the event does prove to be of such great interest to the public, perhaps you could reconsider and publish the article in your newspaper, Mr McTavish."

Archie sent Hamish a scathing look. "Reckon 'e might be talked round, ma'am. Our esteemed publisher don't fink that murder is related ter morals so therefore not wivvin the scope o'—"

"That is not what I said, Archie—"

"Anyways, 'e needs ter make money like the rest o' us. An' if 'e don't publish the biggest news o' wot's happenin' in the supernatural world, then some'un else will."

"I publish periodicals to educate, not to titillate," Hamish said. He felt like saying a lot more and in a tone far less measured than the one he'd used; however, it was important that Mrs Eustace understand he was a man who did not easily let go of his passions or his principles.

"Fact an' fiction are summat one an' the same when the world sees it their way," Archie said cheerfully. "Yer may see it as yer job ter educate, but the public won't choose ter be educated by yer if yer don't serve 'em up anyfink ter titillate. A fine balance is what 'tis, eh?" He jabbed an elbow in Mrs Eustace's direction. "Put a beauty like 'er on the front page an' the world will take notice an' then suddenly yer'll be makin' all the money yer need ter throw yer focus where yer wants it ter be—educatin'. But yer got ter get the money ter do that, first."

Mrs Eustace blinked and pressed her pretty lips together. "I think I'd be just as happy not to have my photograph on the front of any newspaper, or anywhere else, thank you. No lady wants to be recognised in such a public way, Mr Benedict." She nodded at Hamish. "But I thought, perhaps, a photograph of the medium, Mrs Moore, and her crystal ball, and perhaps some words to explain the desire of the bereaved widow to bring her husband's murderer to justice, or even to find her husband's body." She hesitated. "And, even more importantly, a photograph of the audience for it may be that the murderer was unable to resist attending?"

"Yer an intelligent woman wiv a mind afta me own," said Archie. "That poor man, a rich industrialist...vanished inter thin air." He clicked his fingers and looked at Hamish. "Bringin' a murderer ter justice must be the greatest duty o' a God-fearin' society. Don't yer reckon, guvnor? A moral duty it'd be to do everyfink possible ter apprehend a heinous perpetrator o' bloodcurdling crimes."

Hamish had a hard time refraining from rolling his eyes. "When nothing was found beyond a few bloodstains, which may not even have been those of Mr Renquist, the police concluded that it was just as likely that he disappeared because he wanted to."

"Or not," Archie said darkly. "Did I ever tell yer that me lady friend wot works at a certain 'igh class establishment, Mr McTavish..." He sent Hamish a meaningful look before raking Mrs Eustace with knowing eyes, "whose name is Gracie, reckons this person o' interest, Mr Renquist, were well known ter Gracie's mistress at this high class establishment ."

"You did not, Archie. No doubt there was nothing to it, either." Hamish wanted to shut down this avenue of discussion very quickly. Of course, Archie knew very well by now that Mrs Eustace was the blonde beauty who had captivated him, and whom he'd photographed at Madame Plumb's, and whom Hamish may have visited on business at Madame Chambon's. Who knew what conclusions he'd drawn as to why she was visiting his office now? Not that it wasn't all rather a shock to Hamish, too.

And he could not be dispassionate about the fact she was standing so close to him, either. The truth was, her very nearness was having a very real and uncomfortable effect on him, which he sincerely hoped was not noticeable to anyone else.

Fortunately, there was none of the tawdry in Mrs Eustace's neat, fashionable appearance that suggested she was a woman of dubious moral character, which could have had serious ramifications for himself and his publication. Not to mention what his father might have done had word come to his ears that his son had been brazenly visited by a barque of frailty in his office in the middle of the day.

Or, any time. Hamish was well aware that Mr Miniver, one of his clerks, regularly gave a thorough accounting to Hamish's father whenever his suspicions were aroused that Hamish might be considering decisions that ran counter to the old man's.

"I think that's all, Mr Benedict," Hamish said firmly, taking a few steps forward as he tried, physically, to edge Archie from his office. Archie was trying to milk this for all it was worth.

As to what Hamish would do with Mrs Eustace, his first thought was that he'd like to offer to walk her home. But he immediately recognised both the danger and the folly of such a desire, and wondered how such a notion could have entered his head.

Archie stood his ground, moving slightly round the table to be closer to Mrs Eustace, to whom he now showed off his shutter box proudly. "Reckon a few photographs wiv this instrument o' magic could go a long way, an' me Gracie said the same fing, though at the time the constabulary weren't askin' 'er or Miss Celeste anyfink an', yer know, Madame Chambon don't like the police, so she said there'd be a ruckus if they blabbled like canaries 'bout wot might a' gone on."

Hamish felt a wave of something quite near to panic as he

glanced at Mrs Eustace. What would she make of this? Archie's reference to Madame Chambon's was too close to the bone. Would she imagine Hamish had spoken slightingly of the women at Madame Chambon's? Of her? That he'd revealed a past she clearly would want kept secret?

He wanted to refute any suggestion but instead said softly, "I think you've said enough, Archie. Please leave so that I may see what else I can do to assist Mrs Eustace. I'm happy to take instruction on what you would like printed in the Wanted column, rather than sending you to Mr Miniver. Please, Mrs Eustace, take a seat."

He sat opposite her, the wide desk taking up too much space.

And not enough. For one moment of madness, he felt like locking the door and reaching for her hand.

A faint furrow creased her forehead, and he said reassuringly, "Archie knows only what he deduced from taking a photograph of you at Madam Plumb's. You should know that…in case it puts you in a difficult position."

She put her hand to her mouth, and her eyes widened in real fear. "There is a photograph of me? In the public domain? Oh, please, no! Celeste simply took me to some dancing rooms. I had no idea it was frequented by," she dropped her eyes, and he was astonished to see deep colour flood her face as she added, "prostitutes."

He might have made some dry rejoinder, but he didn't. The truth was, he simply didn't know what to make of her.

She went on, "I know the photographer took some photographs at Mrs Bennet's séance and that Mr Elkington posed, but I do not recall having been included in anything that might fall into the hands of the public."

Leaning forward, he asked gently, "Why are you here, Mrs Eustace?"

Her gloved hands, he noticed, trembled as she fixed her

beautiful eyes upon his and said with an attempt at retaining her previous bravado, "I was instructed to do what I could to get some public attention for the séance." She swallowed. "After Mrs Moore failed, that is."

He nodded. Good lord, each time he saw this woman, the effect on him was more severe.

"There's a reward, you see." She leaned slightly forwards so that he felt his heart hitch as she said faintly, "It would please me so much if you considered an article for your newspaper, Mr McTavish."

Hamish regarded her steadily. He wished he could say yes, but his father would be vehemently opposed; he was certain of it. The old man's religion took a dim view of those who dabbled in the supernatural.

In the tense silence, he tried to formulate the right response. She was an enigma, a woman of loose morals he had to infer from her tenure at Madame Chambon's. A thief from the gutter, he had to assume after she'd stolen Lucy's hat.

But she was also a fascinating enigma. Clearly, she was so much more than all the things he knew her to be.

Of course, he shouldn't care when there could be absolutely nothing between them. But he hated the fact she thought him a buttoned-up prig beholden to his father. Still, it was a defence against the attraction he felt. Resisting the temptation to reach out and clasp her hand, and touch his lips to the soft, smooth skin on the underside of her impossibly dainty wrist, was hurting his head.

"Sir Lionel to see you, Mr McTavish."

Startled, Hamish glanced up, quickly drawing back his hand as he pushed back his chair. "Thank you, Miniver."

The spell was broken. She stood up, and he rose with her, putting out his hand, nodding as she asked, "You'll think about it, Mr McAlister?"

"I will, but I doubt the editorial board will sanction it?"

"Aren't you the editorial board?"

He smiled, dropping her hand, which he realised he'd retained too long, using brusqueness to cover his embarrassment as he said, simply, "Good day, Mrs Eustace. Mr Miniver, will you please escort my visitor downstairs."

CHAPTER 13

Lily glanced up at the sun and considered her next movements. There was one important visit she had to make before dusk, occasioned by her informative, disconcerting visit to the offices of McTavish & Son.

Informative, of course, because of how much about her the photographer actually knew, as well as his revelation that Celeste had known the murder victim. Mr Renquist's death had occurred just before Lily had been taken in by Madame Chambon, yet Celeste had not mentioned the man's name, nor had any of the other girls.

Perhaps they had been warned against doing so on account of Madame's aversion to the police? Hardly surprising in view of the illegal business she ran.

What had been particularly disconcerting, however, was that Mr McTavish's inability to hide his attraction to Lily had resulted in a quite inconvenient response on her part.

Just thinking about it made her stop in the middle of the pavement as she walked the city streets to take a sustaining draught of air to clear her head.

When Mr McTavish had smiled, she'd been struck by how kind he looked.

Not just handsome.

When he'd stopped playing the insufferable prig, there'd been such compassion in his expression as he'd explained why he couldn't accede to her request, that it was as if a gauze curtain between them had been lifted—Mr McTavish had to answer to his father.

Only, he didn't want to be diminished in the eyes of the photographer by admitting it.

He'd nearly reached out his hand to take hers across the desk. And she'd nearly extended hers when he'd lacked courage.

Her heart hitched. Mr McTavish was composed of more layers and depth than she'd given him credit, but, understandably, he didn't know what to make of her, and he was afraid of showing his feelings when he feared she was the very worst type of woman.

The thought was comforting and emboldening.

She tucked her reticule more firmly under her arm and continued to walk, her mind whirling with possibilities. The sooner she could earn herself a handsome payment for doing what she was currently doing for no more than board and keep, the sooner she could escape from her domestic nightmare and return as the type of woman an upstanding young man like Mr McTavish would honour and revere.

After all, when Mr Montpelier and Mrs Moore had no more use for her, what would she do then? How would she survive?

She needed a protector and Mr McTavish might just answer. Teddy had clearly not received her letter. She had to accept that.

Perhaps he'd left the country.

"Divorce scandal rocks the aristocracy!" The cheerful

shout of a street urchin selling newspapers on the next corner was like being doused with iced water. Of course, it was not the first time Lily had heard about the trials and tribulations of Lord and Lady Dewberry, whose unhappy marriage had been gossip fodder for at least the past two months.

But it was a brutal reminder of the uncertainty of Lily's future.

Bigamist and the beauty! Divorce and Destitution. These were some of the headlines bandied about lately, reminding her that the lower orders had a ghoulish fascination with the domestic affairs of the aristocracy when privileged lives tipped into public disorder.

Not that Lily had been born into the nobility. Her father had been a mere baronet. Landed gentry, not aristocracy. But he'd been rich, and her dowry had been the enticement for Sir Robert, who, while not a gambler or a spendthrift, needed funds.

For his lover, she reflected bitterly.

Not that she'd known he'd had a lover when she'd married him. Her father had told her nothing other than that she'd been admired, and that an advantageous offer would be made if she conducted herself appropriately during Sir Robert's visit.

How Lily had striven to impress both her father—whom she hadn't seen for years—and Sir Robert, who had appeared charmed by her.

She'd felt so proud when her papa had announced over breakfast the day before she was to return home to her aunt that Sir Robert had indeed requested his daughter's hand in marriage.

Lily had done everything she could to please her father. Of course, she'd accepted Robert.

"Can 'e forgive 'er?"

There was another one. Another newspaper seller shouting to the world the private pain of a poor misunderstood wife.

Lily had no doubt that it was the husband's side of the story that garnered public sympathy. He had the money and the power.

Like Robert had after he'd married Lily.

As a young newlywed with no experience of men, Lily had recognised that being the good wife Robert expected meant being agreeable, both at the breakfast table and in bed. Her aunt had told her nothing about what to expect after marriage, though Lily had had it drummed into her that obedience was a woman's greatest virtue. So, it stood to reason that if Lily did nothing else, she must be obedient, even if she hated the painful prodding and pushing that Robert inflicted on her each night while his moist breath panted hotly in her ear.

But it was hard to be accepting and obedient and bite her tongue when Lily knew that Robert kept a mistress: Lady Majors, the squire's wife who came to dinner once a week with her husband, and who had shown Lily such kindness and helped Lily prepare herself for her wedding after her aunt had fallen ill.

It had taken years before the truth was irrefutable—no matter how hard Lily tried, she could never make Robert love her.

Robert partook of his Welsh rarebit at breakfast with as much emotion as he showed when exercising his conjugal rights. Lily was simply another commodity laid on for him. Not for his pleasure, but for his needs, his convenience, and the assumption she'd bear him a son. Or a child, at least.

When, with four years of marriage under her still youthful belt, she'd tearfully declared that Robert could find her kissing the boot boy, and he'd not be jealous, he'd just shrugged his shoulders and agreed, not even looking at her as he'd stolidly crunched through a piece of bacon.

Lily could hear the sound of dead pig all these years later whenever she thought back to that moment. The crunch of doomed hopes that became the squeal of despair for a potential eternity.

Perhaps that was when the madness had come upon her.

Dr Swithins had been called for that afternoon, and, despite the fact he'd been Robert's personal physician for some years, Lily had, for the first time, become aware of him as a man. Several years under forty, he was unmarried, handsome, and athletic.

And the remedy he'd used to treat Lily for her hysteria had transported her into a world of hitherto unknown sensual delights.

Right under Robert's nose, Lily and Teddy had become lovers.

Robert had known, but he'd said nothing. No, Robert would not have cared one jot if Lily had had ten lovers.

She stopped as she reached her destination, careful that her veil was down, and that she went by the side entrance.

"Ma'am, it's right good ter see yer again," declared Gracie as she let Lily into the large red-brick house and led her through to the parlour. Gracie had become a faithful ally to Lily during her tenure at Madame Chambon's. "I'll wake Celeste, if she ain't already up," the young maid assured her when Lily had stated her request. "It's past time she were up, anyways."

A few minutes later, the invitation came for Lily to make her way to the young woman's bedchamber, which it appeared she had to herself these days. Celeste had thoroughly disliked sharing with Lily; she'd made that clear enough.

And her antipathy towards her former roommate had

clearly not abated as she lolled on the bed, combing out her long dark hair, saying when Lily entered the room, "Goodness, what a surprise to see you here. Do you want me to put in a good word for you to Madame Chambon?"

"Lord, no." Lily shivered, sinking down upon the stool at the dressing table. "I'd rather be dead than work here."

Celeste regarded her with dislike as she put a pillow behind her head and leaned back, examining her fingernails, her knees drawn up, the skirts of her pale-blue dressing gown spilling down the side of the bed. Celeste couldn't fail to be beautiful and exotic if she tried. She flicked a disdainful look at Lily and murmured, "All of us here would be dead if we had to live by your morals. Why did you come? To lord it over me? Tell me about some grand society marriage you've contracted?"

It was not a good start. Lily picked up the rabbit's foot brush on the tabletop and leaned into the mirror, idly sweeping a touch of colour onto her cheeks.

Out of the corner of her eye, she noticed the girl's hands were shaking as she began to drag the boar bristle brush through her long, dark locks once again. There was a pallor to her skin and a dullness to her eye, both of which had seemed full of vitality the last time she'd seen her.

Celeste was never one to volunteer information and nor was she a conversationalist. After an awkward silence, Lily said, "I want to ask you about Mr Renquist."

"Lord, that man? I haven't the faintest idea why you'd think I know anything at all about him." Lily did not miss the wariness in her tone.

"He was one of your gentlemen, wasn't he?"

"Before your time. Anyway, he's dead now." Celeste sighed. "There was a murder investigation which came to nothing, so he probably just disappeared to escape his wife."

"I heard that blood was found where he was last seen,

which was why murder was thought possible." Lily put down the rabbit's paw and frowned. "Do you think his disappearance could have anything to do with any of the other gentlemen callers you entertain?"

"Good lord! Are you accusing me of something, Lily Eustace, or whatever your name is these days? Because if you are, you can just leave right now!" Angrily, Celeste lurched forward, pointing at the door.

Lily drew back, startled. "No, no! I don't think anything. I just want to warn you that Mrs Renquist has organised a séance to commune with Mr Renquist's spirit if he is dead, or to possibly lure someone along who might be involved in his disappearance. I thought I'd tell you in case you hadn't heard."

"And you're the queen of the spirits, are you?" Celeste laughed, sounding slightly more relaxed. "I've heard you are drawing the crowds at Mrs Moore's pretending to be Lord Lambton's dead daughter. You think you're better than I am because you're not enticing him into your bed. At least I don't pretend to be someone I'm not."

"I'm making Lord Lambton happy. And I'd like to make Mr Renquist's widow happy." Lily fiddled with the pots of colour on Celeste's dressing table." When someone told me that Mr Renquist was a frequent visitor of yours before he died, of course, I wanted to ask you about it."

"Who told you that?"

"That photographer who took our picture at Madame Plumb's."

Celeste dropped her brush. "What are you saying? There's a photograph of me?" She jerked forward, her interest more aroused by the knowledge that she'd been secretly photographed rather than by the fact that her long list of male consorts was clearly public.

"Yes, a very flattering picture of you, Celeste. Mr Benedict the photographer was trying to sell it to the editor of *Manners & Morals*." Lily tried not to show how much hope she was pinning on this conversation as she toyed with the pots of beauty creams on Celeste's dressing table.

She glanced up to see Celeste's lip curl before she grew excited once more. "*Manners & Morals*? Not quite their fare but, there'd be other publications interested if the photograph is, as you say, a good one." She hugged the pillow as she leaned forward. "What did the photographer say? Did he think I looked beautiful? What is the word? Photogenic?"

"You looked beautiful, Celeste. That's why the photographer was determined to shop it around until he got a buyer." Lily thought quickly. She knew the extent of Celeste's vanity. "And you see, Celeste, I think I could be persuasive enough to get a photograph printed. It would publicise the case and—"

"Who cares about publicising the case?" declared Celeste. "It would publicise me, more to the point. Oh, what I wouldn't do to get my photograph into the newspapers." She raised her eyes to the ceiling; her mind apparently engaged in a tremendous flight of fancy before she swivelled an intense look back at Lily. "How did you propose to persuade whoever it is you need to persuade? I presume you mean some newspaper editor?"

Lily met her look with a shrug. "I'd thought to invite him to where I lived. I think he could be susceptible to a bit of persuasion, and I wouldn't mind doing it, you know, for he is very handsome." A sentiment like this would surely reduce the gaping chasm between them. Celeste saw nothing wrong in selling her body for favours, whereas Lily wouldn't do that to save her life.

But she could let Celeste think it, and hopefully Celeste would not regard her with quite so much disdain and distrust and so would volunteer more information about Mr Renquist.

"Where do you live? A life of ease in some grand mansion?"

Lily laughed. "A noisy bedsit that smells of boiled cabbage where I'm not allowed gentleman callers."

"You really think you can get that photograph published?" Celeste had never been so animated. "I remember I was in fine form that night at Madame Plumb's. There was a gentleman—But no matter. You say this photographer is going to photograph the séance? Can I see the picture? Of me, I mean?"

"The editor of *Manners & Morals* has it—"

"How do you know?"

"I visited him this afternoon. I spoke with both the photographer and the editor."

"You did?" Celeste ran the tip of her tongue over her top lip. "Lily, you must persuade him to publish, or have the photographer find a smart magazine or newspaper to buy it."

Lily nodded. "Yes, I think I can do that. I'll ask again." Celeste was coming round. She'd be more amenable to Lily's next questions, Lily was sure.

"Invite him to *The Velvet Nest* in Mayfair," Celeste went on. "That's where we girls meet gentlemen on certain occasions. Especially if we need a favour."

"Mayfair?" Lily frowned. A coincidence that it was in the area where Mr Renquist had last been seen. Where the bloodstains had been found.

"There's a very cosy bower there. It's in Shepherd Market, so not quite so refined as the rest of Mayfair. But it's fine enough has a grand double bed and all the furnishings. A sweet little house where we girls entertain when we don't entertain here. I'll send Gracie over to prepare it. I'll lend you the key. Just for an afternoon, mind. And then you can persuade whoever needs persuading to photograph me again and to publish."

She collapsed back on her bed with a satisfied sigh, as if she'd said all that needed to be said and was now dismissing Lily.

Lily turned on the footstool. "Do you think Mr Renquist—?"

"Enough about Mr Renquist." Celeste waved her hand languidly. "At the time, I thought him the kindest and most thoughtful of all my lovers. I truly was distraught when he stopped coming and then heard he was dead." She gave a soft laugh and said in the most collaborative tone Lily had heard her use towards her, which is when Lily first suspected her former room mate might not be entirely sober, "You remember how the girls poked fun at me for existing on carrots and oranges? They were referring to Lord Carruthers and Mr Renquist. Fiery red-headed men, both of them. Well, if I had any choice about it, I'd dispose of Lord Carruthers tomorrow, but," she sighed eloquently, "a girl has got to pay the bills. Now, you just see that photograph of me makes it into print in the right places, since you have so much sway with all these important men of business." She'd begun filing her nails now, her attention focused on her beauty regime, though there was an air of suppressed excitement about her.

Uncertainly, Lily rose. She'd spent enough time with Celeste to know the vagaries of the young woman's mood, and that she'd do herself no favours if she persisted with her questioning.

Celeste stopped her when she'd reached the door. She pointed to a heart-shaped jewellery box on her dressing table. "You'll find the key and the address in there," she said. "If you can persuade your editor friend to give me some publicity in his newspaper, I might tell you a little more about Mr Renquist. Something no one else knew about him." There was a wicked gleam in her eye, and her full pink lips were pursed with promise. Or amusement. "I think you might be interested."

Lily opened the door to find Gracie raising her arm about to knock. Her eyes were dark, and her lips pressed together. She didn't look nearly as cheerful as she had when she'd greeted Lily.

"The scary Russian is back," she whispered, before raising her voice to say, obviously for the benefit of the visitor downstairs, "Miss Celeste, your esteemed visitor Mr Novichov awaits your pleasure."

For when Lily passed by the parlour, the barrel-chested, white-haired gentleman who'd visited Celeste every Thursday while Lily had been resident at Madame Chambon's was looming in the doorway to the parlour as he waited for her to pass.

"You're back, Mees Eustace," he said, smiling his gap-toothed leer. "How charming to see you again. I so do look forward to your leetle entertainment at Mrs Moore's."

Disconcerted, Lily asked, "Lord Lambton's seance?"

"Oh no, not Lord Lambton's seance." He raised his monocle and bent to whisper in her ear before moving on, "The other one."

CHAPTER 14

Lily's optimism was fast subsiding from the heights to which she'd allowed it to soar. Yes, she had a key and an address. These were necessary practical considerations that would help her achieve her ends.

But how could she begin to entice a gentleman she barely knew to visit her, alone, at a strange house?

Was it even wise, for who knew where it would lead?

How far was she willing to go in order to make a bargain that would depend on a priggish man's desire for her, and his honour when it came to any agreement?

Disconsolately, she tossed a crumb of bread from a stale fruit bun to a family of ducks swimming in the pond. The park was nearly deserted, and dark clouds scudded across the ashen sky. The landscape looked as bleak as she felt.

The Wednesday seances were becoming monotonous, though Lord Lambton's emotional distress at the loss of his daughter didn't seem to be abating. He happily paid Mrs Moore and Mr Montpelier a handsome sum each week so he could commune with his dead daughter.

And every week he wept more bitterly than the last.

It made Lily feel guilty, though she could rest easier in the knowledge that she wasn't about to be thrown into the street while she was still so valuable.

Lily looked about her, the hunk of stale bread heavy in her hand. Most people were probably at home, and that's where she would be if she had a home. Right now, she had as much wish to return to her tiny room in her noisy, unpleasant boarding house as she did of returning to Robert. Or even the *maison*.

There was no future for her, anywhere that she could see.

She tried to dislodge the pinprick of despair that was slowly growing in her breast. The truth was, she was frightened. Everything required of her demanded that she play a role. Survival demanded that she prop up a flimsy defence of who she really was.

Because the truth would see her catapulted right back into enslavement. True enslavement where she had not even the freedom to feed the ducks if she chose.

"Mrs Eustace, what a surprise to see you here!"

Lily turned at the pleasure in the refined young woman's voice, astonished to see Miss McTavish coming towards her.

The girl dropped her eyes and added in accents of embarrassment, "Actually, Mrs Eustace, my being here is quite deliberate, for you said you fed the ducks here most fine afternoons, and I did want to speak to you."

Lily had indicated a location where she might be found in the hope that Mr McTavish would seek her out. As the siblings were clearly fond of one another, she'd thought it not a hopeless wish that the younger McTavish might pass on something positive about her meeting with Lily. Miss McTavish did seem to regard Lily with some admiration judging by her smile and eager manner.

"Yes, happily the ducks are always pleased to see me," Lily said. "London can be lonely when one doesn't know anyone."

"What *did* bring you to the metropolis?" asked Miss McTavish, coming to stand beside her. Lily was conscious that the young woman's blue and white princess-line dress, while plain and demure, had all the trimmings that brought it right up to the minute. Unlike Lily's gown. Mr Montpelier hadn't the funds to supply her with a modest wardrobe less than two years old, and in her lodgings, and with such a modest income, it was difficult to keep her clothing properly laundered. "I imagine you'd have had dozens of suitors where you hailed from."

"You did? That's a nice compliment." Lily smiled. "But I was not interested in suitors after my mourning was finished." The lies again. But what could she do? "Not for some years, in fact. But," she shrugged, "I think that might be changing. I will admit to being lonelier in London than I had expected."

"My brother is lonely too," Lucy said artlessly, accepting a hunk of bread from Lily with which to feed the ducks.

"Is that so?" Lily tried not to sound too interested. But when Lucy didn't reply, just continued to stare thoughtfully into the pond as she tossed breadcrumbs to her noisy, squawking audience, she asked, "Has your brother ever married? Or lost someone?"

"He's never married. But there was someone, I gather, in France." Miss McTavish sent Lily a pained look. "Hamish and Papa didn't see eye to eye, so Hamish went to live in France when he was twenty-one. To be an artist."

"An artist!"

"Yes, he's a very good one, you know. You should see some of his paintings in the house. Goodness, it's starting to rain! Come back with me and take shelter. I live not far from here, and then you can see some of Hamish's landscapes."

Lily didn't need to be asked twice. And not because the heavens really did open at that moment.

They were laughing as they rushed through the front door of a dwelling only three minutes from the park, and indeed, Lily was impressed to see the walls covered in paintings. "He hasn't done all of them, of course, but he does love the Impressionists," his sister said proudly. "See, that's one of his. Isn't it good?"

Impressed, Lily nodded as she gazed up at a brooding landscape painted at dusk. "Is that where he stayed in France?"

"I imagine so. He doesn't talk about it much. I just know that as soon as he received my letter telling him that…something bad had happened to me…he left everything and caught the next boat back to England." Her voice dropped, and a deep colour suffused her cheeks. "That's when he took me to live with him. Nearly three years ago, now. But I sometimes wonder if I took him away from someone he loved, for there's a sadness in him. He never used to be serious like he is now."

Lily's interest grew like a small bud slowly unfurling in her heart. "What was he like when he was young?" Her desire to know more had nothing to do with how she might persuade him to publish a photograph or give Mrs Moore the publicity she craved.

Really, solving Mr Renquist's murder seemed a hopeless and, in fact, completely unimportant distraction right now.

"Would you really like to know?" Lucy looked delighted. "I'll show you some photographs if you like."

Happily, she led the way up the passage, saying over her shoulder, "Come into my room. I have them framed on my mantelpiece. There! Isn't he sweet? Of course, I was just a baby when Hamish went to boarding school. I'm nine years younger. And there's Mama and Papa and Hamish and me, just before Hamish went to live in France."

Lily studied the family group. Mr McTavish senior

looked a serious gentleman with a head of snowy-white hair, even though he was the father of two young children at the time. Beside the grim father figure was seated a demure, sweet-faced young woman nursing the infant, Lucy, on her lap.

"What happened to your mother?"

"She died when I was eight. I don't remember very much about her except that she was kind. Hamish was at boarding school, so it was just Papa and me."

"But then you went to the Ladies' Seminary, and that's where you met Cassandra, Lord Lambton's daughter." Lily moved the subject forward. Lucy looked like it was unpleasant dwelling on childhood memories, and she was anxious to discover what she could that might promote her Wednesday seances with Lord Lambton. Lord Lambton seemed a lost soul, his grief so very genuine as far as Lily was able to tell. "Were you friends from the beginning?"

"I suppose so, although Cassandra was always a bit… different. But we became friends because we both despised our fathers," Lucy added boldly.

"Goodness. Did you?" Lily picked up a photograph of Hamish as a young man and thought what a kind, open smile he had. "Why did Cassandra despise her father?" She thought of the Lord Lambton she knew, a kindly, harmless old man. "I believe he really is distraught at her death. Was he unkind to her?"

"Good heavens, no!"

Lucy must have realised that the vehemence of her refutation was extreme, for she coloured and bowed her head. "Theirs was one of complete harmony and her father never struck her for even the gravest misdeed. She had nothing to complain about."

Unsure whether to press this, Lily instead said mildly, "I think Lord Lambton loved his daughter more than she might ever have realised. It's the impression I get from seeing him these last few Wednesdays, as you know."

"Yes, and I wish I could attend."

"I'm sorry your brother is so disapproving."

"He's just afraid word will make it to Father's ears. Poor Hamish tries so hard to find the balance between keeping in Papa's good books and doing what I might want. Or what he wants, for he had his years of freedom in France. I truly thought that the carefree brother I once knew, and who left England, would accept that I have a right to making my own choices of the heart." She looked furtively at the door. "I have an admirer, you see. He's very poor, but I've known him since I was at the seminary. He's the older brother of one of my friends there, and he's the sweetest young man, but it'll be several years before he'll be in a position to take a wife. I don't mind. I'll wait forever. But I do wish Hamish would let me see him."

Lily was more interested in quizzing Lucy over her remark regarding her brother's increased gravity since his return from France but said instead, "He doesn't approve?"

"He knows how violently Papa would *dis*approve. That's the problem, really. Oh, but Mrs Eustace, you don't know what it is to be violently in love and to be denied even seeing your sweetheart. Sometimes we meet in the park. We have to pretend it's a coincidence in case someone passes on word to Papa, and then he'd take me back to live with him. And I'd rather be dead than have that happen," she added dramatically.

They were sitting on the edge of the bed now, the picture of Hamish lying between them. Lucy picked it up. "My brother likes you very much, Mrs Eustace," she said, smiling shyly as she traced her finger over the edge of the frame.

"And I like him very much." In a burst of bravery, Lily opened her reticule and closed her fingers round the paper and key Celeste had given her. "I don't suppose you have an envelope and writing implements so I could compose a quick note?" she asked abruptly.

Lucy was only too happy to oblige, laying everything out on her writing desk. "I'll happily pass that on to Hamish when he gets in tonight," she said, taking the sealed pale-pink envelope Lily handed to her when she'd finished scratching out a quick, artful invitation to Mr Hamish McTavish. "And perhaps, Mrs Eustace, you could persuade my brother to let me attend one of Mrs Moore's seances. I think it might be something my Arthur would be very interested in attending too." She smiled shyly, adding, "I'm sure you understand what I'm saying."

"I do," Lily reassured her. She rose. "And now I must return home and prepare myself for tonight's séance. Tomorrow will be a very different one." Nervousness clawed up her throat as she answered the young woman's questioning look. "I'm the conduit that will communicate between a dead man and his bereaved widow. You might have read it in the newspapers. Mr Renquist—"

"Of course, I know every detail of the Renquist murder! A man that rich doesn't just vanish into thin air never to be seen again. Hamish was upset because his photographer wanted to attend tonight's seance, only Hamish said he'd not buy into that mumbo jumbo, as he termed it. Not that *you're* pretending to be someone you're not, of course, Mrs Eustace! I know you're doing this to get at the truth for the benefit of society at large."

Lily sent her a wry smile. "So your brother calls it mumbo jumbo, does he? I thank you for your honesty, Lucy."

Lucy blushed. "Hamish calls me a terrible liar and quite tactless, and I know it to be true. But the truth is always best. That's one thing I remember my dear mama always telling us. Don't you think the truth is always best?"

Lily weighed up her answer. "As long as the truth is in the interests of the listener," she said, finally, hoping she'd struck the right note and that young Miss McTavish wouldn't think to unravel the finer points of her answer.

To her relief, this seemed to satisfy the young woman, for she hooked her elbow through Lily's as she led her to the door saying, "I think we are very much of the same mind, Mrs Eustace. I couldn't agree more. Harmful lies are the devil's work. That's one of Papa's favourite sayings. And there I would agree with him. Now, please borrow my umbrella for your walk home. I know the rain has stopped for the moment, but you don't want to be wet and discomposed for the event tonight. There's an old man to comfort tonight and a murderer to catch tomorrow. Goodness, we don't want you to be sick for what could be one of the most important performances of your life."

DESPITE SUFFERING no ill effects from the cold weather, Lily felt very sick as she waited in the cellar beneath Mrs Moore's parlour and listened to muted sounds of the chattering throng following another heartrending session, during which Lily had relayed the love that Cassandra, Lord Lambton's daughter, had felt for her father. And her guilt for causing him such pain.

But it was cold and damp, and when the crowds seemed disinclined to disperse, Lily decided to clamber out of the coal chute and seek warmth inside the house. Heavily veiled and wearing a dark cloak over her clothes, she made her way into the parlour.

The lamps were still dimmed, and the audience was shoulder to shoulder, many in working-class garments, some in the finery of the upper classes. Sherry was being dispensed freely, and the mood was merry.

"You are miraculous!" Lord Lambton declared to Mrs Moore. "I was a disbeliever, but when I faced my daughter tonight, I knew it could be none other than Cassandra come back to pour out her heart to me." Overcome by sentiment, he dabbed damp eyes with a snowy-white handkerchief while Mrs Moore patted his shoulder.

"That I can speak with my Cassandra is…a miracle." Lord Lambton blew his nose, loudly. "But there are others with whom you hope to communicate. I hear you are appealing to a different audience tomorrow night. Regarding the mystery of Renquist's disappearance, I gather?"

Lily watched as Mrs Moore fingered her purple velvet scarf. "I have discovered someone whom we believe may be able to communicate with the deceased Mr Renquist."

"Good lord! How did you manage that?"

Mrs Moore lowered her eyes. "I cannot divulge that, my Lord; however, we are confident we can bring some peace and comfort to the grieving widow, even if the mystery cannot be solved tomorrow."

Mrs Moore slid an enigmatic look towards her credulous client, who was stroking his bushy white beard and moustache and who looked even more intrigued as the woman added, "Communication with the spirit world has been made. We are at least in the initial stages of solving a crime that has proved beyond the capabilities of the police though it may take some weeks." She looked smug. "Indeed, performances are nearly sold out."

"Extraordinary!" Lord Lambton muttered. "In that case, if the mystery has not been solved before the end of the month, I shall reserve a place for my old friend who comes so rarely to London. Sir Robert Bradden asked me to recommend something different in terms of entertainment to please his new wife. A séance sounds ideal."

For a second, the world turned black. Lily put her hand to her veil in a convulsive act to mask her horror.

However, Mrs Moore revealed her showmanship, her duplicity revealed by neither a blink nor facial twitch as she said smoothly, "And what date did you say Sir Robert may honour us with a visit? The end of the month? Well, if we have not solved the mystery, it will be a pleasure. However, if your friend is interested in the spirit world, let me recommend Madame Barooshka's Fantastical Seances. Like me, she is a true artiste…"

Lily left at the first opportunity, slipping through the stragglers, glad that Mr Montpelier and Mrs Moore had been detained by a voluble woman in a purple turban and multiple ropes of pearls. She ignored the speaking glance Mr Montpelier threw her. Of course he'd have been rattled by Lord Lambton's information, but Lily had not the stomach to discuss it with him.

Her low-heeled lace-up boots clicked over the pavements as she walked towards home, her shadow leaping and dancing in front of her as she passed beneath the gas lamps. Once, she'd have been terrified to walk alone. She rarely did so now, in fact, but she felt safe enough. What, really, did she have to lose? She wasn't stupid, pushing out of the grasps of the occasional men who assumed her to be a lightskirt. They did not persist.

Tonight, there was a light mist, rather than the enveloping fog that she preferred. Often, as she walked, she found she rather liked the feeling of being wrapped up in the mists or fogs of anonymity. It was like a temporary blanket of comfort that put a little distance between the here and now and the worry over what was around the next corner.

Tonight, though, she felt more than just the discomfort of what the future held.

Robert was coming to London. It was bad enough to digest this horrifying piece of information.

But he had a *wife*?

Could Lord Lambton have been mistaken? How could Robert have a wife when Lily was his wife, though the Lord alone knew she'd do anything not to be his wife?

And she knew to her cost that the feeling was mutual.

But had Robert been sufficiently coldhearted to have believed Lily would cause him no further problems if he despatched her to an asylum in Brussels, meaning he could therefore do what he wanted?

Yes, he was coldhearted; that was true enough. But would he seriously commit bigamy?

And if so, who was his wife? Sir John's widow? Lady Banks? Lily had to find out. Perhaps there'd been some mistake.

"Madam, I beg your pardon."

The thick accent more than the bulk of a man blocking Lily's path made her jerk up her head.

He could have moved to the side without saying anything. Instead, the man remained as immovable as a column of stone on the wet pavement in front of Lily, doffing his hat and revealing a head of snowy-white hair above a face that was not genial like Lord Lambton's.

But cold and cynical as he eyed her with very real calculation.

Mr Novichov.

Drawing in a sharp breath, Lily took a step back, glancing over her shoulder in the hope that someone bringing up the rear should come to her aid.

A family group, chattering as they took up most of the pavement, heading towards the river, boosted her courage.

When she turned back, Mr Novichov had gone.

CHAPTER 15

It was not as if the pink notepaper could burn his fingers, though the truth was it felt exactly that as Hamish carefully placed the invitation onto his writing desk and leaned back in his chair.

The brazenness.

The boldness.

It shocked him.

Fascinated, and called to him.

She'd asked him to meet her at her lodgings at 3 p.m.

An invitation for tea, she said. There were matters to discuss.

Hamish picked up the paper once more and studied the elegant, looped handwriting.

Had she written it herself? Could she really write with such finesse, or had she farmed this out to someone who could?

Closing his eyes, the blood roared in his mind as he pictured her limpid blue eyes assessing him. Travelling over his body, considering him.

For what?

A means to an end? Or was he too inclined to judge harshly? The last visit had battered his defences like no other. She'd seemed so real. A lady with a very natural hope that he'd regretfully said he was unable to fulfil.

But a palpable sexual tension had swirled between them. Hamish felt his throat swell just to recall the way she had stood across from him, the graceful incline of her head as her beautiful eyes had said so much more than her soft, pouting lips.

Archie thought him a fool for turning her down when she'd come to the newspaper office requesting his assistance in the matter of publicity.

But now Hamish wondered if he'd be a fool if he declined her invitation to tea.

It was undecorous and unladylike to request a gentleman call on her. She must know her behaviour invited the danger of being misinterpreted, and that he might prove himself a man who took advantage where he saw it.

Uncomfortably he shifted in his chair, glancing through the window at the busy street below and worrying the paper between his fingertips.

She'd not asked for an answer, and he'd not given an RSVP. She'd merely said she hoped he might find himself free at 3 p.m., and if he were so inclined, she would like the opportunity to discuss any differences between them that may have occurred earlier.

In the privacy of her sitting room at ….

Mayfair was not so very far out of his way. A quick cup of tea and a polite discussion would reset matters between them, for he feared he had come across as tight-lipped and buttoned-up, as he was wont to do when confronted by beautiful, desirable women.

He stood up, folding the paper and putting it in his pocket, making for the stairs, determined now.

"Miniver, I'm going out," he said to the clerk working at a desk by the door as he put on his hat and coat.

"And where shall I say, sir, if Mr McTavish senior wishes to know?"

Although this was less likely these days, with the old man increasingly incapacitated, a surprise visit was not impossible. And always his father wanted a thorough accounting of Hamish's movements if he was not at his office.

"I'm seeing Sir Lionel at his club."

"Ah yes, his redemption story."

"That's right, Miniver. Now that he's retired from the Ministry, he is keen to…reminisce. I may be a while."

"Very good of you to indulge him, sir. The public likes a tale of bad come good and just rewards. Send my regards, if you will."

"Of course."

Of course, it was a blatant lie that Hamish was headed to his club, but he didn't care.

Just rewards? Truth to tell, he didn't much care to think that far.

Mrs Eustace's invitation was burning a hole in his pocket, and now he couldn't wait to see what she had to say to him.

Or what she really wanted of him.

IT WAS NOT difficult to find the house, a charming little residence nestled amidst a row of similar structures where both the respectable, and the occasional nicely set-up mistress resided, he knew. She'd chosen well, and his presence here would not be remarked upon should someone of his acquaintance recognise him.

"Afternoon, sir."

Hamish barely glanced at the young maid who relieved

him of his outerwear, though he thought vaguely she seemed familiar.

And then the door was opened for him, and he was admitted to the drawing room, a charming, light-filled chamber tastefully furnished with an admirable collection of art upon the walls. She was more of the connoisseur than he'd thought and he found himself fighting the thought that it would be nice to know her better.

That was taking matters too far.

However, he could indulge her for a short while.

"I didn't think you'd come." She rose as he entered, the light in her eyes beaming their way across the decreasing distance between them, her mouth a curve of pleasure, her tea gown falling in suggestive folds from a low neckline…he swallowed…contouring a body that sported no corsetry, he was certain of it, in the brief glance he allowed before swinging his gaze back to her lush mouth.

"Please take a seat, Mr McTavish," she murmured, angling him towards the sofa and lowering herself beside him, her fragrant bosom crossing his line of vision as she bent to adjust what he realised, shockingly, was the garter holding up a white stocking that encased the shapely leg pressed against his.

"Thank you for the invitation." He hoped he didn't croak the words as much as he felt he did. Already he was out of his depth.

"And thank you for coming."

The words sounded simple enough, but as she placed her hand over his, which was in his lap, it was as if an electric eel had just wound itself from neck to groin and discharged a volt that made him jerk into combustible awareness.

He should have known how it would be. There'd been enough warning that his defences were crumbling with every acerbic exchange; that the time would come when his every attempt to ward off the attraction he felt would come to nought.

And that time had come.

Instinctively, his hand closed over hers, and he brought it up to his lips to kiss, his eyes trained on hers, not breaking contact as with seemingly infinite slowness their lips drew nearer.

The silent, subtle connection between them had been apparent from the start, so why should he be surprised when the mere brush of her lips provoked a response like nothing he'd experienced?

"Mrs Eustace," he murmured, grazing the impossibly soft barrier between hope and hell as he responded to her kiss; incinerating the last vestige of restraint that now plunged Hamish into the lust-driven demon she knew him to be at his core.

That she was clearly requiring at this moment.

"Lily," she corrected him, softly, in that brief moment before their mouths fused and, with bodies hot with need, she gripped his hand and rose.

As if unable to draw apart, they stumbled into the passage, through the gloom, and into a dim bedroom, collapsing with soft sighs and heated breaths upon a cool pink eiderdown, her womanly curves and contours pinioned beneath him, her long, creamy limbs twining about his waist as she laced her hands behind his neck.

His initial suspicions had been correct. As he reared up above her and her tea gown fell open, he saw that she wore no underthings.

Yes, her beautiful body was his to feast upon, judging by her silent encouragement, and patent enthusiasm, as she arched into him, her fingers nimbly helping to release him from his trousers.

And when he lay naked the length of her, she made it

clear that she desired he pleasure her as he took his own pleasure.

She was a widow with experience of men.

With experience he could only begin to imagine, and any scruples he might still cling to were to protect himself, not her.

So, with the last of his reluctance and reservations now firmly tossed upon the turbulent winds of his growing and unstoppable desire, Hamish proceeded to make love to the one woman in all the world he considered the most dangerous.

And the most desirable.

He should have accepted it from the start.

THERE WAS an urgency and an elegance to his lovemaking Lily had not expected.

A passion and an enthusiasm that had taken her by surprise when, having obviously committed himself, he clearly decided on no half measures. Her breasts were laid bare as she wore no chemise or corset beneath her afternoon gown, and now he was kissing them with rapture, stroking and kneading them so that her nipples stood taut, and Lily shivered from head to foot with a rare and barely restrained excitement.

Lord, it had been a long time since her body had felt the attentions of an experienced lover. Not since Teddy had taken what Robert had forsaken had she been this in thrall.

Robert. Just the mention of his name brought back the old, familiar terror. He must never learn that she still lived, for she was still, legally, his property, her fate in his hands.

No, Lily to be on her guard. She needed to shore up all the defences she could.

And getting past the defences of this surprisingly desirable man above her was a good start.

"Oh!" she squeaked when he touched the slick, sensitive nub between her thighs. She'd not expected to be so aroused, and certainly not this early, with so few preliminaries.

Over his shoulder, the glow of the street lamps through the window punctuated the gloom; the late afternoon shouts of a newsboy selling his wares pierced the silence of the bed chamber broken only by their soft sighs.

Was this what he presumed she was? A woman selling her wares? A flicker of dismay quelled her excitement, but only briefly, for the truth was that she was enjoying Mr McTavish's ministrations like she'd never enjoyed a man's attentions.

He groaned, and she shivered with excitement and anticipation to feel him tense as she opened her legs to him a split second before he drove into her slick entrance.

"Oh, bliss," she whispered into his ear, holding him tightly as he moved within her, and she matched his movements, feeling the vicarious thrill of bringing him pleasure, and the ratcheting up of her own desire before, with a cry of triumph, he came, withdrawing at the last moment though he held her tightly against his chest when he rolled off her, his eyes closed as his breathing calmed.

She tensed, awaiting his reaction.

But when his features relaxed into the tenderest of smiles as he opened his eyes to look at her, she smiled too, gently pressing her lips to his before she nestled into the crook of his arm.

For a long time, they were silent. Then, staring at the ceiling, he murmured, "That was unexpected."

Her breath left her in a soft sigh as she whispered, "I don't think it was," and his chuckle was instantaneous.

"True," he agreed, turning to gaze at her. "I've been fighting it from the start."

She cleared her throat and reminded him, with a nervous twitch of her lips, "Not quite the start."

He blinked as if he didn't understand before realisation made him say, haltingly, "Now that…this has finally happened between us…I think you should tell me the truth about you."

The truth.

Yes, the truth was uncomfortable, but he had shown himself a man of honour. All subterfuge had been on her part, and he deserved a full accounting from her.

That is, if she could manage it, for the very utterance of Robert's name and the many painful indignities he'd inflicted upon her could not be divulged in one cosy, convenient revelatory conversation.

"I was married to a cruel man, and I ran away." She squeezed shut her eyes, and the wetness ran a crooked path down her cheek before he kissed it away.

Then they were in each other's arms once more; the passion reignited into a flame that would make words redundant until such time as their sensual urges were sated.

With kisses even more loaded with feeling, and bodily senses aquiver, Lily threw herself into their second bout of lovemaking, another surfeit of desire metamorphosing into a crystallisation of awareness that this really was a man worth cleaving to.

Not for what he could do for her in terms of survival through the material necessities of life.

But what he could be for her as their souls seemed to rise and mingle in another dance of intimacy before they became one again, mouths and bodies fused with a final thrust of ownership and openhearted sacrifice.

Yes, Lily was prepared to sacrifice all she had to give—her body, her soul—for a future with a man this good.

CHAPTER 16

"Get yerself downstairs, me girl! Newcomers for Widow Renquist's do are arrivin', an' yer at risk o' exposin' everyfink!" Mrs Moore admonished as Lily peeked out of the parlour window when she heard voices outside. A party of three women and one man was advancing purposefully up the front path.

Lily stepped back, stroking the crystal ball on the baize-topped table before heading obediently towards the passage. In front of Mrs Moore's mystical glass orb, the trapdoor to the floor below would disgorge Lily amidst a burst of swirling mist in about twenty minutes' time, though she'd not be properly seen.

She wondered if Mr McTavish would attend. His sister had made it clear she was keen, but her brother was deter-mined to uphold the appearance of sceptic and not indulge the spiritual craze that was sweeping the nation.

He'd indulged his sensual desires not long before, though; despite the fact he'd been highly resistant, initially. That should give Lily hope.

Nevertheless, she'd not heard from him since, which grew daily more troubling.

She'd thought to establish mastery over him once he'd he proved susceptible to her charms.

But it was she who'd been left wanting him. Needing him.

The raw desire that had combusted into its almost shocking culmination had ended with real intimacy.

Mr McTavish—Hamish—had left her with tenderness in his tone and in his eyes as he'd kissed her lips in parting.

He'd made no promises, but Lily had been sure she'd have heard from him by now.

She wanted to fill in the gaps in her history. She wanted to be open and truthful. It would be a relief.

In the next room, Mrs Moore greeted the first arrivals, whose working class accents resembled Mrs Moore's au naturelle. She, by contrast at this moment, was attempting to sound as refined as any duchess. "Ladies and gentlemen, welcome to our esteemed company!"

Lily could see the woman's reflection in a tall mirror near the door. Dressed in an elaborate bustle gown of black crepe with a sequin-adorned black lace bonnet over her dark hair, she was a forbidding sight. By contrast, Lily was in her usual garb, dressed to appear vulnerable and mysterious with her long golden hair, unbound, lightly covered with a black mantilla that cascaded over her shoulders, wearing a second-hand gown of black and purple purchased the day before.

Tonight, though, her role was for sound effects only. However, there was no point in augmenting Lily's wardrobe more than necessary and the gown had been a serendipitous find in a second-hand barrow, as it resembled a gown worn by Lord Lambton's daughter in one of the photographs Mrs Moore had located. Lily would be wearing this same gown tomorrow for Lord Lambton's benefit.

"Come this way and take a seat to the left. The right is reserved for fine company."

Fine company. Lily shuddered. Her husband's rank classed him as fine company in Mrs Moore's view. Did his character count for nothing?

When she thought of his impending visit, she felt ill.

What would be Hamish's reaction to learning Lily was not a widow? And that Robert might, in fact, be in this very house in several weeks?

His principles were already besieged by her daily regimen of smoke, mirrors, and subterfuge.

But she could be useful to him, she knew. It was her trump card, perhaps. He wanted to learn more about Celeste and her paramours; though not, Lily gathered, so he could publicly expose and shame the men involved—which Lily thought would be divine justice.

Hamish was a cautious, principled man who wanted to ensure no danger befell the natural order of things. This, Lily gathered, was how he regarded the whole sordid scenario regarding her former room mate. He did not want to see a scandal erupt in either the domestic or political arena if he could help it.

So Hamish's interest in this potential scandal was one of Lily's greatest weapons—if she could call it anything.

If Hamish thought Lily had information on Celeste's lovers and the possible dangerous sharing of information, then he would surely seek her out—even if he pretended that was the reason, and nothing relating to the physical.

And this was where her unsettling encounter with Mr Novichov might be in her favour. He'd want to know about that, surely?

With a final, backwards look at the festooned concealing drapery between the parlour and the passage, Lily headed towards the trapdoor in the scullery, daunted by tonight's new role.

By comparison, the Lambton seances felt safe. She felt authentic, talking to the old man as any loving daughter might, and it was easy to find the right words; words that brought him to tears, and words that clearly brought him comfort. All she had to do was pretend to repair the schism between herself and her own disinterested parent.

But the atmosphere tonight felt different and dangerous. She wasn't ready to descend to the cellar, wanting to gauge her new audience, which had been steadily growing so that the seating was now filled and it was standing room only. Concealing herself behind the tasselled drapes, she ran her gaze over the mixed gathering: working-class people in the clothes of their trade, middle-class men and women in their formal finery. There were even a couple of government ministers. With a frisson of fear, Lily recognised several from her short time at Madame Chambon's. Customers of the girls; men who had paid for Celeste's services. Although Lily didn't feel afraid of being recognised from those days, for she'd been such a poor physical specimen who had kept to the shadows for the most part, and she was veiled, she did feel afraid of the expectations of these people here tonight.

And the expectations of Mrs Moore and Mr Montpelier.

Now she was glad Mr McTavish was not coming, and unlikely to come either. She was glad she'd not entreated him, as had been her intention.

Unbidden, a memory returned, as it often did, of their afternoon together, and her body pulsed with a deep longing and desire.

And fear, for he'd been silent too long.

As she withdrew from her hiding place, she caught a glimpse of Gracie conversing with a fellow in a checked cloth jacket and trousers, who'd just removed his cap and was scratching behind his ear. Gracie looked animated, and, when the fellow turned, Lily recognised Archie the moment before Mr Montpelier took her by the arm and hustled her towards the scullery, where he pointed at the trapdoor.

"There's a man wot's brought 'is photographic equipment so yer jest be sure yer keep that veil down, yer 'ear?" he exhorted softly, stress causing him to drop the refined accent he cultivated for his clients. "We want the essence o' the spirit world published in the newspapers, not some picture o' yer that anyone can recognise." Clearly, he did not know that Lily had been photographed with Lord Elkington and Mrs Bennet.

As he raised the lid of the trapdoor with one hand while the other lay heavy on Lily's arm, his tone softened. "But yer did well persuadin' that young newspaper man ter send 'is feller ter take pictures." For a brief moment, they locked eyes, and despite the uncharacteristic kindness of Mr Montpelier's tone, Lily wondered if every move she made these days was watched.

Surely, though, Mr Montpelier would have indicated if he'd known of Lily's secret tryst with Mr McTavish at the house in Mayfair.

Downstairs, in the chill, damp cellar, Lily shivered and tried to focus her mind on all the possibilities that might be thrown at her during her convening with the so-called spirits.

With Mrs Renquist paying a handsome fee just to hold the event, Lily felt the burden of expectations. She listened as Mrs Moore attempted to glean all she could from the widow about her husband's disappearance for the benefit of the audience.

At least, that was how the woman had described the proposed prelude would proceed. Lily could only hear the indistinct murmuring of Mrs Moore, with intervals of silence punctuated by a gong which reverberated from rafters to cellar. It was at the third of these that Lily was to show herself, which she did, emerging amidst the fragrant smoke to the sound of gasps and applause.

With her head bowed, she listened as Mrs Moore intoned, "Tell us, communicator with those in the afterlife and those caught somewhere between the two, have you seen or heard anything of this man, Bernard Renquist, who vanished mysteriously eight weeks ago?"

While Lily's role was to keep Mrs Renquist and a growing and interested audience returning for several weeks, Mr Montpelier and Mrs Moore had conceded that discovering the truth was unlikely.

Lily's own brief hopes of playing investigator were, of course, little more than foolish child's play. How could she, a mere woman with no means whatsoever of learning anything valuable in her limited sphere, hope to shed light on the mystery?

Nevertheless, if she could supposedly summon the spirit to the satisfaction of those in Mrs Moore's parlour tonight, she would be assured of a roof over her head for at least another few weeks.

As she stared at her black boots peeking out from beneath the hem of her gown while Mrs Moore began chanting, her head swam with fear.

Robert was coming to London in two weeks. The thought kept returning like a spectre. Mr Montpelier knew as well as Lily did the dangers of discovery and might therefore decide she was replaceable at the first opportunity.

She went over all the avenues open to her, and her heart grasped at possible salvation. The first of these was obvious.

Mr McTavish?

"Speak, communicator!" demanded Mrs Moore, throwing

up her arms and swaying. "Speak to the dead! What can you tell us?"

With an effort, Lily trotted out her carefully curated words of mystery.

The audience gasped on cue.

They oohed and they aahed.

Once, they even shrieked, though that was because Mrs Moore's judicious thud—the cue for Lily's bloodcurdling cry —acted in concert for a response that was hardly surprising.

Yes, Mr Renquist was apparently trying to communicate from his prison in the afterlife. He was, he indicated, in torment; and only by solving the mystery of what happened to him on Earth would he be freed from the eternal condemnation of trailing the confines of his nether world, unable to find peace.

Only then would Mrs Renquist be granted her rights as a widow rather than a woman in limbo with a missing husband, enabling her to claim his fortune and remarry.

It was a fine show, and one that had bereaved Mrs Renquist, afterwards, exhorting Mrs Moore in tears not to give up until she'd found the truth; declaring that the spirit summoner clearly knew more than she was prepared to divulge about what had happened and, possibly, even, the location of her dear Bernard's body.

The lively commotion suggested that Lily's performance had been satisfactory. But it wasn't until Grace spoke to her that she learned more.

The girl had slipped away from the crowd and discovered Lily, still veiled and in hiding.

"Ooh, ma'am, but they was all enraptured an' called yer a vision. A spirit caller. They says yer can summon the dead an' that them'll be comin' back next week. Bringin' their friends too, I 'eard 'em sayin'. Archie reckons 'tis a 'front-pager' fer sure!"

Excitement fizzed through Lily. Of course, she hadn't expected Mr McTavish to attend. But Archie had come, and he would relay her success.

Not that Lily's only hopes hinged on her success in the spiritualism arena.

Warmth flooded her as she closed her eyes briefly and thought back to her illicit, stolen moments with the young newspaper editor.

Mr Montpelier and Mrs Moore weren't the only two upon whom her survival could depend for, despite his silence, Lily knew that the beginnings of something deep and serious had been established with Mr McTavish.

For the first time in her life, she believed it was love.

Possibly, even, trust and lasting love.

And if Lily could only nurture with care and honesty the seeds that had been sown between them, something might grow as a result, providing her the salvation she so desperately needed.

CHAPTER 17

Hamish leaned back in his chair and watched in amusement as his sister and Archie argued over the merits of the photographic offerings Archie had carefully laid out on his desk ten minutes before for his perusal.

"A true spiritualist! This is the one that will have the readers clamouring for more!"

"Wiv respect, Miss McTavish, I b'lieve the young woman's mystical powers are shown in greater respect when juxtaposed wiv the painted ol' crone rubbin' 'er crystal ball opposite 'er," Archie objected.

He might have been tempted to discount them all if only to light a fuse to Archie's pique, but the business side of him had to concede there was a strong case for including one of these pictures in the publication. Other serious-minded publications had covered the wealthy industrialist's disappearance, after all.

"Lor' but she's a sight fer sore eyes," Archie remarked, holding up one of the photographs to the light.

And Hamish silently agreed, though he did add mildly, "Not that you can tell what she looks like in that disguise."

"And you wouldn't have it any other way, Hamish, of course," said Lucy.

"Know 'er, do yer?" asked Archie, in a burst of egalitarian impertinence. Hamish was only glad their father was not part of the conversation. But then, if he had been, Archie's place would have been made very clear to him. He would not be part of any editorial decisions.

The fact was, Archie Benedict was something of a genius with his box camera, though Hamish would never tell him so.

Lucy straightened and stuck her nose in the air. "She's a beautiful widow fallen on hard times." With a meaningful look at Hamish, she added a trifle defensively, "The fact she's always in disguise means she can still be accepted into society."

Despite himself, Hamish smiled. "Yes, she can, Lucy."

His sister's mouth dropped open in clear surprise before her eyes lit up. It was obvious Lucy had taken to Mrs Eustace, and that she took a dim view of her brother's distrustful attitude.

Hamish would have to gently and subtly make it clear that matters had altered somewhat, and no doubt Lucy would be delighted. Their father would not be so easy to convince, but that could be navigated later.

In the meantime, Hamish would pay another visit to Mrs Eustace to reorient matters between them. They'd parted with sincerity and tenderness and promises to meet again, soon. Tingles of sensation speared him at just the thought of being alone with her. But perhaps it would be safer to meet for tea where hot-headed passion didn't skew the conversation.

Of course, there were many issues that needed to be dealt

with in practical terms; the first one being that if his father got wind of the fact that Hamish was involved with a woman, the resulting inquisition could be uncomfortable for everyone.

And while Hamish had no doubt there were aspects of Mrs Eustace's past that would not be acceptable to his father, Hamish was also very committed to helping her appear in the best light as regarded a potential romantic interest for old Fergus McTavish's son.

If Lily had fled a violent husband, a future was still salvageable. The law had changed and it was easier for women to bring redress.

Hamish knew he was getting wildly ahead of himself but the truth was, he was wildly in love. Lily Eustace had secrets and, no doubt, he would rather not know the worst of them. But, of all the women he'd met, she exerted the most fascination.

Who knew what the future held for both of them?

Hamish was very determined to find out.

"I knew you'd come around to my way of thinking about this very excellent woman," said Lucy, and would have said more except that Mr Miniver was at the door, announcing Sir Lionel, and the next moment the old man was making his rather shaky progress towards the chair offered to him while Lucy drew back and, at a nod from Hamish, Archie excused himself.

"Hope I haven't intruded," said Sir Lionel. "Fact is, I was passing your offices and thought I'd look in just in case your father was here." Wheezily, he lowered himself with a thud, carefully hooking his walking stick over the arm of the chair; then adding, after he'd been told that Mr McTavish senior rarely visited the office these days, "No matter, the old haunts of elderly gentlemen like myself are mostly in here." He tapped his skull. "Truth is," he added, "our last conversation at my club, in which I laid out some of those achievements of which I'm most proud, cannot be put into perspective without a true accounting of my youth." He glanced at Lucy. "Are you the young lady who proposed that your brother write a profile of a respected figure in public office?"

She nodded.

"A redemption story, I believe you suggested, and in a moment of weakness, I declared I had much material to contribute; however, as I was amongst company at my club, I balked at revealing some of the earlier exploits of my misspent youth." He chuckled. "Not to be repeated in front of delicate ears here, either," he said with a look at Lucy as he drew forwards several of the photographs Archie had taken the previous night. "Well, well, what's this all about then? Didn't peg you for a spiritualist, McTavish."

He held up the photograph of Mrs Eustace in which she was partly angled towards the camera, her arms raised, the merest suggestion of a beautiful face hidden by her veil. "Interesting looking creature," he remarked, and Hamish breathed a silent sigh of relief that the woman he did indeed hope might be reintroduced to the polite world under his aegis was not recognisable in her disguise.

"She's beautiful!" Lucy declared before, to his horror, she dug in the desk drawer and withdrew one of the two photographs he looked at frequently, and had no idea Lucy even knew about.

"No, Lucy!" he snapped, seizing it from her fingers, though not before Sir Lionel had raised his lorgnette, holding the photograph a moment, before releasing it to the clearly discomposed Hamish. "And now you must go, Lucy, for Sir Lionel and I have business to discuss."

Hamish busied himself with the brandy decanter to cover his embarrassment after Lucy had gone, for he'd spoken too hastily, drawing more attention to that which he'd wanted to remain hidden. "It was good of you to humour me, Sir Lionel, and subject yourself to public scrutiny at the same time," he said. "Call it a bit of whimsy on the part of my sister to whom I must give credit for wanting to inject a more... human touch. She challenged the dryness of my journalism." He sent his guest a wry smile. "She accused me of appealing primarily to a god-fearing, humourless readership, and said she'd only consider picking up an issue if I was adventurous enough to include a ripping yarn of redemption. Recalling my father's stories, you were amongst the first who came to mind."

"I've no doubt your father used me as a cautionary tale." Sir Lionel raised an eyebrow as he ran a hand through his thick snowy locks. "Well, any excuse for an old man to rake over the past and indulge in daydreams of when he was young and brave—albeit young and foolhardy—is welcomed in my twilight years." He took a sip of his brandy, relaxed back in his chair, then asked, "Where do I begin? With my first act of utter folly, when passions ran high, and I marched the requisite paces with pistols drawn before winging my opponent?" He put his monocle to his eye and regarded Hamish with a louche grin as he went on, "Just so long as I come across as the swashbuckling hero, misguided only in his youth." He patted his moustache of which Hamish gathered he was very proud. Sir Lionel was a vain man, and his moustache was truly a magnificent specimen.

"That is the intention of my article, yes." Hamish took a sip of his drink then reached across for his notebook. "One learns from the mistakes of the past, to be sure. I don't need to put words into your mouth. And I appreciate the kindness you do me of responding to my request, when I'm trading on little more than your acquaintanceship with my father and the fact we go to the same club—where I, might add, I am not often to be seen."

"The fact we go to the same club says a lot. And you have not sunk into sensationalism—rather, the contrary—so I feel safe revealing my secrets to you." Sir Lionel's mouth twitched. "And to the world? I trust a dashing photograph will accompany this? Like the one of the two beauties you keep secret in your drawer?" He winked, then lowered his voice. "I'd have done the same. Not that I can really make out the blonde nymph, but the brunette is a beauty, and one I recognise. Can't deny having visited Madame's m'self." With a glance at the door as if he feared they might be overheard, he added, "Just a word of warning. Be careful that you're not treading on Carruther's turf if you wanted to make a play." Then, before Hamish could respond, Sir Lionel leaned back, saying in a more normal tone, "Yes, a photograph of me and my moustache." He stroked it reverently. "I've not yet lost interest in winning over the ladies."

"A photograph." Hamish tried not to stammer and to keep his mind on Sir Lionel, though the old man's reference to Carruthers had thrown him for a six. "Yes, of course I'll include a picture. I'll have my photographer, Mr Benedict, set up the necessary." He drummed his fingers on his desk, anxious to understand the old man's meaning with regard to Carruthers and Madame and trying to formulate his question when Sir Lionel went on, "Yes, a good thing I only winged him, too. Now, what year are we talking? Ah yes, the year our queen ascended the throne. Thirty-seven, it was, and I was not yet twenty and fancied myself in love with the wife of my superior officer. Let me tell you, that foolhardy little episode didn't go well. My saving grace was that my injuries were far greater than his, and I was not expected to live. In fact, so long did I exist between this world and the next, I think my commander had forgotten all about me by the time I was declared out of the woods. And by that time, my light-o'-love had eyes only for her husband, once again."

Hamish let go of the question he'd really been wanting to ask as he began to take notes. It was his father who'd told him that Sir Lionel, who had recently retired from the House of Commons, had had quite a reputation in his youth.

"Youthful folly is where I wanted to start with this," Hamish agreed, "before I focus on your great contributions to society which have, naturally, redeemed those youthful excesses." He grinned.

"And youthful folly I did indeed have in excess. I was lucky to live long enough to redeem myself." Sir Lionel laughed. "But you know what it's like...when you lose your heart to a lady, one is not thinking with one's head. The power they yield can be frightening, and only a better man than I could resist that, eh?"

Hamish put down his pen. He presumed Sir Lionel didn't require a response to that. Yes, he knew the frightening power a woman could wield over a vulnerable man's heart. "How many duels did you fight, Sir Lionel?"

"Four. Never killed a man though, else I'd not be sitting here with you, talking about redemption." He looked reflective as he stroked his moustache. "Luck got in the way. Redemption is hard for those who've committed murder. And that's at the heart of duelling, eh? Bloodlust. The desire to assert superiority. Honour. It's the Young Lion testing his claws, thinking honour is about besting the other man when it's nothing of the sort. Honour is here." He tapped his heart. "It's not what you do to one's opponent in the heat of the moment. No, I was lucky. Very lucky, for it was a close shave when I was Sir John's second and facing down Lord Lambton a quarter of a century ago." He cleared his throat. "Too close, in fact, and the last time I let the heart rule the head."

Lord Lambton? Hamish paused in his writing. But Sir Lionel was running ahead with his commentary. "You said Sir John had you do his dirty work? And you accepted?"

"Yes, and a big mistake it was, too. I never held Sir John in high regard. Can't think what came over me. Feller was a bounder, and I risked my life for him!"

Hamish sensed reluctance on the part of the other man to elaborate, so waited patiently. Silence was often rewarded with a confession.

And he was in luck.

But only after Hamish dug a little deeper into the reasons behind the duel.

Sir Lionel took a sip of his drink. "It's true that Sir John was defending his honour. He did have just cause to challenge Lambton. Old Lord Lambton, you see, was having an affair with Sir John's wife." It looked as if he were about to continue. Then he sighed and put down his drink as if it were all too much to remember. "Ah well. Enough said on that. Lord Lambton has not spoken to me since. And why would he? I tried to put a bullet in him on behalf of a man I never liked and have even less respect for now. The old codger spends his days counting his money in his counting house, I hear. As for old Lambton, I don't even know if he's alive. Now, where was I? I think I'm ready to move onto my more noble achievements, if you don't mind."

"Of course." Hamish rose on the pretext of reaching for the brandy decanter. Sir Lionel had made short work of his first drink, and although it was early in the day, and Hamish would never, under normal circumstances, have dreamed of pressing brandy upon a subject for his own ends, he could not help but prod to get more on Lord Lambton.

Or rather, Lily Eustace, given the connection.

"Lord Lambton is very much alive. In fact, he's gaining an audience through the offices of a spiritualist who has supposedly been communicating with his deceased daughter on a Wednesday night at Mrs Moore's séances," he said casually as he refilled Sir Lionel's glass. "My man, Benedict, photographed one of the sessions not long ago. That's if you're interested in seeing your old foe after all these years."

"Old Lambton? Who'd have believed it? A rascal in his day, so no surprise he's been taken in by this mumbo jumbo, eh? Yes, let's see what the years have done to my old adversary."

Thoughtfully, Hamish pushed aside the photographs Archie had proposed could accompany the write-up on the séance to publicise Renquist's disappearance. Mrs Eustace featured in many of them, and although she was veiled, Hamish was still concerned to ensure she not be recognised. However, if he showed Sir Lionel a photograph that featured her with Lord Lambton, would the old man make any connections?

"This was taken last week," he said, handing his guest a photograph of Lord Lambton, seated and gazing at the spiritualist who was shrouded in a black lace mantilla.

Sir Lionel bent over it with a frown before he chuckled. "His black locks have gone white like mine. Thinner, of course."

Hamish indicated Mrs Eustace. "And that is the spiritualist who communes with the dead, namely his dear departed daughter."

"Yes, I heard his daughter had died some months ago. A troubled child, by all accounts."

However, Sir Lionel made no comment on the woman in the photograph. Conflicted, Hamish slowly withdrew the second of the photographs he'd hurriedly snatched from Lucy's innocent fingers earlier. In this picture of Lily and Celeste, the clarity was better, whereas in the other, Lily had appeared grainy and in shadow. Sir Lionel's eyesight was obviously impaired but to Hamish, the young woman was entirely recognisable in this photograph.

Casually, he placed it on the desk; not as if he were directing it towards Sir Lionel for his notice, but as if Hamish were, in fact, looking for something else.

The old man picked up the photograph and stared at it a long moment. Then his eyes widened, and he muttered, "By gad, if that's not…" Squinting, he raised his monocle and brought the photograph closer. "Surely not…" he said, under his breath, and Hamish asked quickly, 'Do you recognise the woman, Sir Lionel? The blonde woman?"

"By Jove, but if my eyesight wasn't likely to be letting me down, I'd say it was a poor mad creature I once knew. A beauty and quite sane when I met her, but from all other accounts, as mad as a March hare. Used to wander the hallways stark naked during a full moon before her husband had her locked up in a madhouse several years ago." He glanced at Hamish. "When did you say this was taken?"

"I didn't. However, my photographer took this a few weeks ago."

Sir Lionel returned the photograph to within a few inches of his nose and shook his head. "Only weeks ago, you say? Then it can't be the same woman, for right now she's baying at the moon in some lunatic asylum in Brussels. And since this glorious creature is photographed with Carruthers' fancy piece, I would be so bold as to suggest that she, too, is one of Madame Chambon's nymphs." He raked Hamish with a salacious look. "I don't wonder you keep her likeness tucked away in your drawer. Mighty uncomfortable having to explain that to your sister, eh wot?"

"I have made no judgements, Sir Lionel, for, in truth, I do not know how either woman came to be in that photograph, and the fact the blonde damsel is in dubious company may be quite coincidental." Hamish hoped he didn't sound as hot under the collar as he feared he did. "They are, after all, simply sitting at opposite ends of a sofa in a public place. I believe young women of such a calling—" He tapped Celeste's face — "are known for their brazenness."

"Yes, yes, of course, young man," Sir Lionel responded, picking up his stick and pounding it on the floor several times as if to test it preparatory to making his departure. "You can rest assured I'll say nothing to your father. You know what's what, and you keep a steady hand at the helm. His newspaper is in good hands, and that's what I'll tell him."

Discomposed, Hamish helped Sir Lionel rise, calling to Mr Miniver to assist him down the stairs.

Then he resumed his seat at his desk, pulled out all the photographs he could find of beautiful Lily Eustace and decided there was not a moment to lose before seeing her to ascertain the full truth of who and what she was.

CHAPTER 18

Making an excuse to Miniver, he snatched up his hat, shrugged on his coat, and stepped out into the street, flagging down the first passing hackney.

He should have sent her notice of his impending call, but the urge to see her this moment was all-consuming. She'd promised to tell him her story, and no doubt he was not going to like it.

It didn't matter if she was not a widow. Hamish would not condemn; he would not judge.

He would listen.

The match had been struck, and the tinder had combusted into a fiery flame of feeling between them. Hamish had no idea where it might lead, he only knew he could no longer resist the powerful force to see her.

He got the driver to set him down a few houses along. A couple of minutes' walk would give him a dose of the fresh air that he felt he needed as a preliminary to any potentially uncomfortable discussions.

So, with head bent, he trod the damp pavement, hands

thrust into his pockets, his collar up against the chill. Perhaps their talk would lead to somewhere warmer than the drawing room, he thought, feeling again the strong desire to hold her in his arms and press his face against her cool, creamy neck.

He was nearly there, stopping a few yards back as he heard a gate swing open and saw that it was Mrs Eustace's house. And that a man was coming out of the garden. He had a head of bright-red hair, clearly revealed as he repositioned his bowler hat, and Hamish had no difficulty in recognising Lord Carruthers from a distance.

With hammering heart, Hamish waited a few seconds until his lordship was out of sight before he quietly let himself into the garden, taking the steps two at a time before he rapped on the door.

"Really, darling, what have you forgotten this time?" came a feminine voice he didn't recognise until the door was swung open, and he was confronted by the lush, willowy form of Miss Celeste.

She looked surprised, frowning a moment before she said, warily, "I don't take gentlemen callers without prior arrangement." Still, she looked anything but forbidding as she leaned against the doorframe, sizing him up, perhaps recognising his shock before raising one eyebrow. "I beg your pardon for not instantly recognising you. Our editorial gentleman, of course. Do come in, sir, if you please. You're here because of Lily, aren't you?" She swayed slightly as she stifled a soft hiccup and Hamish, who'd been on the verge of excusing himself, realised she was tipsy, and that, perhaps, he really did need to hear whatever she had to say about Lily.

He waited as she went to the sideboard, silent as he heard the chink of glass on glass.

"Here's a nice brandy for you, sir. And another one for me," she added, dropping into a chair and stretching out her legs in a surprisingly abandoned fashion. Regarding him with a smile, she waved him to a chair opposite. "Lily said she'd persuade you and, truth to tell, I didn't think she had it in her. Why, you'd never seduce a gentleman to get what you want? I said to her." She put her hand to her mouth to cover another soft hiccup, adding, "But she's a dark horse, like I said." She leaned forward, her eyes suddenly bright. "When will the photograph be published? Will it be front page?"

Hamish looked about him, his eyes running over the pictures on the wall, everything so tasteful.

He felt slightly nauseated.

This was not, he realised, Mrs Eustace's normal abode, but she had pretended it was.

She'd also pretended to be someone she was not.

"What is this place?" he asked, ignoring her question. "I thought you ladies conducted your business at Madame Chambon's."

"Not every gentleman is going to be satisfied with the four walls of Madame Chambon's." Celeste pouted. "You certainly wouldn't have been, even with a discreet side entrance, as I told Lily when I gave her the key this little bower. Now, you were looking for her, were you? Well, you won't find her here, and I can't but say that it's a good thing you didn't come earlier, for Lord Carruthers mightn't have taken kindly to have had you knocking on my door."

Hamish felt trapped. He remembered how beautiful he'd thought this woman. Yet in the space of several months, her skin had lost a little of its dewy freshness, her hair a little of its lustre.

Or was it he who was simply jaded? Right now, he felt disoriented.

"Mrs Eustace said nothing to me about putting any photographs in my newspaper," he said, toying with his drink. He tried to think what Mrs Eustace had told him that was actually the truth. Even her name was a fabrication, though to be fair, she'd not hidden that fact.

"Well, maybe she hadn't got around to it yet for she said that was exactly what she was planning to do." Celeste looked put out. "She showed me the photograph your photographer took of us. She swore she'd be able to persuade you."

"And why did she think she could do that?" Hamish tried to sound measured, though there was a nasty taste at the back of his throat.

He was suddenly swamped by the sensations of their lovemaking. It had all felt so real and sincere at the time.

"Because she's clever! And it would make us famous!" Celeste shifted in her chair and sent him an irritated look. "Do you think we enjoy what we have to do to get the necessities of life, much less elevate ourselves? Lily is in desperate straits, obviously, otherwise she wouldn't have sunk all her scruples to get you to agree. I lived with her for two months. I know what she's like." She pouted. "So, are you going to put our photograph in your newspaper?"

"I haven't decided." Hamish put down his unfinished drink and rose. "Do you know where I'd find Mrs Eustace?"

"No. I thought you'd be eating out of her hand by now." The young woman sounded even more sulky as poured herself another drink.

Hamish paused at the door. "What do you know of what she was doing before she came to London?"

Celeste shrugged, her face averted. "She didn't talk much. Certainly not to me. Though I heard rumours." Sighing, she tilted her chin, but almost resentfully, as if this artful manoeuvre—clearly designed to show her profile to best effect—were a chore. "Do you promise to publish my photograph in your newspaper if I tell you everything I know about Lily Eustace and everything I've heard people say about her?"

Hamish tightened his grip on the doorknob. "No," he said, carefully. "But I promise I won't print your photograph if you don't tell me everything you know about Lily Eustace and everything you've heard people say about her."

Celeste merely smiled as she knocked back her drink. "Where do I start?" She stretched languorously, and her decolletage fell open, revealing one creamy breast as she added huskily, "There really is so much to tell you about mad, bad Lady Bradden."

CHAPTER 19

Still no word from Mr McTavish, though she'd given him Gracie's address if he needed to contact her.

Feeling deflated and dispirited, Lily made her way to Mrs Moore's for another Thursday performance.

"Dammit woman, wot's got inter yer?" Mr Montpelier appeared like a wraith, standing on the bottom step as he peered into the dimly lit cellar. "The crowd is growin' impatient."

Lily jerked into the present and wrapped her stole about her shoulders. There was nothing to say to him other than to gather whatever inner resources she still had and mount those stairs to…

What?

Another close, tightly occupied room with strangers hungering for what she could not give them.

Answers.

They all wanted answers, and Mrs Renquist wanted answers more than any of them. The pinch-faced widow had every reason to want to know what had happened to her husband, in order for his estate to be wound up and her children settled.

Stiffly, Lily mounted the stairs, her eyes adjusting to the semidarkness as she stood upon her dais and stared, unseeing, across the sea of unrecognisable faces. Some were regulars. A quick glance told her that. Some were admirers. No longer just a voice and an outline in the mist, she'd been allowed to gain more substance now.

The way the audience raked their gazes across her made it clear they were not here only for the answers Mrs Renquist desired.

At first, it was the usual preliminaries that Lily had come to expect. The soft whispering, some muted flute playing from some distant chamber to set the scene, a glowing ball.

Then the questions began.

In the past, Lily had been deliberately vague. Yes, she had it on good authority that Mr Renquist had last been seen alive in the vicinity of Shepherd Market, in Mayfair. It was not so very far from where he worked, so it wasn't a stretch to imagine it was where he'd died since he hadn't made it to his home.

And he didn't frequent taverns or drink with his peers. No, Mr Renquist was a paragon of virtue.

Except that he wasn't. Lily knew very well that he consorted with prostitutes. Or, at least, that he had had a mistress.

Celeste.

How did Lily begin to suggest that Mr Renquist was anything other than the upright, moral, loving father and husband his widow claimed? How could she hint at a truth that might in fact shed some light on what had happened to him and which, his widow hoped, would prompt someone with the knowledge to speak?

She was tired of spouting untruths, and besides, Mr

Montpelier had demanded more. She'd been threatened, and she might be afraid—but she had so much of which to be fearful.

Her husband would soon be coming to the capital. How much longer would she be of use?

She tried to assume her mantle of spiritualist, pretending she could communicate with the dead man. This was what Mrs Moore and Mr Montpelier wanted. A show. Drama. An invested audience.

"Were you threatened before the end? Did you see him? Was it a man? A big man? A cultured man?"

"A man with an accent."

Yes, that was when someone asked the question. A man with an accent.

Lily didn't want to open her eyes wide enough to see if she could identify the white-haired, bear-like Russian in the front seat who'd stared at her throughout her earlier performance, and then blocked her way in the middle of the street.

To her relief, she could see no sign of him which gave her the courage to speak.

"A man from a cold country across the sea. The Balkans, perhaps? Or Russia? He was big and bulky."

She described him in vague terms for she had little more than her own description to go by. Celeste's lover was like a bear with a big white beard and a fur hat, a heavy coat, and a monocle. Not that bears wore monocles.

My, but she was weary. Fear was making her lightheaded. She couldn't do this much longer. The anxiety over the implications of Robert's return was making her paradoxically incautious, and there was nothing she could do to alleviate her stress. In the old days, she thought the laudanum had saved her life.

Until she realised how wrong she'd been.

Now, she had only her own wits and inner resources on which to depend.

Think! Think!

Surely, if she could continue to titillate the crowds at Mrs Moore's, Mr Montpelier would continue to put a roof over her head. He'd find something else for her to do while Robert was in the capital and then he'd find another lost soul looking for a spiritualist…unless Mr McTavish—

No! These were foolish thoughts. She could depend on no man. She'd learned that to her cost.

She felt herself swaying as the room seemed to close in on her and the crowd tossed questions at her.

"Did he beat you with a club? A heavy bar? Describe the death blow…"

Their words tumbled over each other, booming, yet muted, as they jostled for primacy in her beleaguered brain.

She felt hands on her, people crowding her, her senses revolting as she remained standing, yet within herself she struggled towards the safety of her own dark little world within the deepest recesses of her mind. The same dark world that had been her sanctuary during all the dark years that had preceded her time coming here.

And then she opened her eyes with a start at the acrid smell of Mrs Moore's vinaigrette, and saw that Mrs Moore and Mr Montpelier were glaring down at her, and she was lying on the ground.

She groped about her to make sense of what was happening, relieved that she was no longer in the parlour but down in the basement, lying, it would appear, on a hessian sack upon the hard stone floor.

"Lor', will yer stop yer screamin', woman!" Mr Montpelier demanded, and with a shock, Lily closed her mouth.

"What happened?" she asked, glancing towards Mrs

Moore to discover she wasn't glaring, but that a smirk was plastered upon her face.

"Oh, my, what a fine performance that was," she said. "Your keening and crying brought the house down. I almost believed you was being murdered as you stood there."

"But 'tis time ter stop!" snapped Mr Montpelier. "The people 'ave gone 'ome. There's no need ter keep up such a racket. We'se yer only audience now."

Lily struggled to sit upright. She felt drained and ill, and her head ached. "I was screaming?" she asked. She had no recollection of anything much beyond the fear she felt upon opening her eyes to see the room so full of bright, expectant eyes.

"Screaming like a banshee. The audience loved it. They saw you as their victim as he suffered his final moments." Mrs Moore's expression was more kindly than Lily had ever seen it. "How did you manage it? You were not there, after all." She leaned in further. "Do you know what happened?"

Lily shook her head.

"I know that you know more than you let on." Her tone was conspiratorial, and Lily felt uneasy, for she really knew nothing and only wished she did.

But Mrs Moore was like a dog with a bone. "That woman, Celeste, knew him. Not that I told Mrs Renquist that, knowing as what kind of woman that Celeste was." Her nose twitched. "And that you lived with her for a time, Mrs Eustace."

"I didn't earn my living as she did."

Mrs Moore shrugged. "That's neither here nor there. Fact is, you gave the audience just what they wanted. And now they've gone home, satisfied for tonight."

"But more than eager to return for the finale," Mr Montpelier said, collecting himself and delivering his verdict with the finesse that had no doubt served him well when he was a gentleman's valet. "I wonder what you will deliver them, eh, Mrs Eustace?" He raised an eyebrow. "What can you deliver them that will top this evening's performance? When, after all, you really do know nothing. How will we keep stringing them along?"

Lily furrowed her brow, unsure what he was saying.

He held the lamp up to consider Mrs Moore, who was crooning that as long as Mrs Eustace did perform as she had, then the people would be back every week.

"And when do you suppose the penny will drop, Mrs Moore? When do you suppose they will realise Mrs Eustace is a charlatan?"

Just as you both are, thought Lily.

Mr Montpelier looked troubled. "Next week they will return, looking for satisfaction. But again, they will be fed the smoke and the wails and the mystery. That's when the dissatisfaction sets in." He gripped Lily's arm and gave her a shake. "Do you hear what I'm saying?"

Mrs Moore's crepey neck wobbled. She leered down at Lily, pulling her to her feet and dusting down her gown as if she were some concerned mother hen when, really, she was preparing Lily for the next plan they had in store for her.

"We've 'ad a little nibble, m'darlin'. Tonight, Mr and Mrs Bunting plan to call on you and discuss how you might speak to their dead little Nell from the spirit world." Exchanging a look with Mr Montpelier, she went on, "Maybe you can get a nice fat deposit out of them before we have to close down shop when your husband comes to town. Well, at home doesn't work so well when it's a boarding house that smells of burned cabbage, so Mr Montpelier did a deal with Madame Chambon." She sent Lily an expectant smile. "Yes, indeed. For the next two weeks, Madame Chambon has let you a lovely little villa in Mayfair where her girls sometimes entertain At Home." Her cheeks puffed out, and she looked enormously pleased with herself as she added, "So now you can do all your entertaining in just as much style, thanks to kind Madame Chambon."

"For the next two weeks?" Lily clarified.

"That's right," said Mr Montpelier. "For as long as the people continue to come and pay good money to see Mrs Eustace." He cleared his throat. "For as long as you can provide them with what they want to pay good money to see. And," he added again for good measure, "until your husband comes to town."

He helped Lily walk shakily to the sofa. "Get yourself in order, Mrs Eustace. You did well tonight. Tomorrow you'll do even better."

But that was the extent of his concern for her. Mr Montpelier saw that she had nearly outlived her usefulness. Lily could read between the lines. Soon he would install some other bright young thing who would dazzle the audience as a sop to them learning Mrs Eustace had been taken by a seizure, or the killer, or whatever excuse he had for why she was no longer the star attraction at Mrs Moore's seances.

While Lily would be sold on to Madame Chambon.

CHAPTER 20

They left her sleeping on a divan in the cold cellar, a blanket thrown over her.

So, that was as much concern as they would show the woman who would soon make way for someone new and fresh?

Shivering, Lily crept through the silent household and into the street outside. The snow had melted, and the cobbles were slick with the recent rain.

"Miss, yer look done in!"

It was Grace who opened the door at Madame Chambon's and led Lily up the corridor, depositing her in a small, unoccupied antechamber having hurried her through a room where several gentlemen lounged, sipping aperitifs; preludes to the sexual congress that had brought them here. One was elderly and looked as if he'd just stepped out of his club. He could have been anyone's grandfather, so benign did he look.

The other was a young blood, eager and impatient, the way he shifted in his seat.

Lily's skin tingled with revulsion as she turned back to

Grace who tutted, saying, "I'll get yer dry boots an' then yer can tell me wot brings yer 'ere."

"I would like to see Celeste if I could," Lily managed. Though what help Celeste would be, she had no idea. Still…

Grace regarded her dubiously. "I don't know as she wants ter see anyone ternight, miss," she said softly. "Celeste ain't too welcomin', at the best o' times."

"And this is not the best of times?" Lily enquired, before pressing her. "Have you noticed any change in her over the past couple of months?"

Grace's glance flickered as she looked up from lacing Lily into sturdier boots that belonged to one of the young ladies, but which she'd said Lily could return to her before they'd be missed.

"Now as yer mention it, miss, she were nevva one ter say much. But these days she says even less." She shrugged. "The uvver girls says she 'as tickets on 'erself an' finks she's better'n the rest o' em. Me, though?" She contemplated the matter. "I reckon she's scared."

"Scared?"

"Of a gennulman. Sometimes it 'appens that a gennulman 'urts a girl. Madame won't 'ave any o' that, but 'tis the kind o' look Miss Celeste gets in 'er eye when—"

"Grace! What are you doing chattering like a blackbird when I asked you to bring me a cordial more than ten minutes ago?"

It was one of the other women whom Lily recognised, though not by name. But as she went on her way with barely a glance at Lily, and as the staircase that led to the bedroom floors was empty, Lily decided to take her chances and see for herself if Celeste would speak to her.

The night had drained her; Mr Montpelier's words had rattled her, and the cold and damp of the cellar had stripped away what little was left of her resources.

But there was warmth and familiarity at Madame Chambon's.

Tapping three times upon Celeste's door, Lily opened it after a muffled invitation to do so, and then was greeted by Celeste's clear outrage as the girl rose from her dressing table, her sheer tea gown falling about her shoulders, revealing a bare breast and slender hips.

Clearly, she'd been expecting someone else, and, indeed, she was dressed to entertain a gentleman.

Lily advanced into the room. She had to get the words out before Celeste sent her away. "Tell me what you know about Mr Renquist. And what happened to him?" she asked softly, but with enough conviction that Celeste might admit to more than she'd ever revealed to Lily.

"Get out!" Celeste held herself up like a pencil, an arm outstretched and pointing towards the door. "You have no right to intrude and imperil my ability to earn a living."

"You do know what happened to Mr Renquist, and that there's a murder investigation, but you're not saying anything." Lily's mind churned as she made the accusation. She remembered seeing Mr Renquist visit Celeste when she'd shared a room. Surprisingly, Celeste had seemed fond of him. She lowered her voice. "If you have your suspicions, tell me, Celeste. I need to know for the safety of both of us."

The other young woman's look was mutinous; her mouth set in a hard line as she retained her Valkyrie-like stance. "If you don't leave this instant, I'll have you forcibly removed."

"One of your consorts was responsible, wasn't he? Was it the Russian? Why? Jealousy?" Lily tried to puzzle it out on the spot. "You weren't responsible, Celeste, but you're afraid, aren't you?"

"I'm not afraid of anything. Nor am I guilty of anything."

"I'm sure you're not. But you know who did it, didn't you?

You know who killed an innocent man. And you continue to consort with the killer."

Celeste's fury was so palpable that despite everything, Lily felt a jolt of satisfaction. She had come here on nothing more than a hunch, and certainly on the spur of the moment, but now she was about to solve the mystery.

And if she solved the mystery, she would be lauded for her discovery; not only provide peace to the grieving widow. She'd present compelling evidence to the Metropolitan Police, or a magistrate.

If nothing else, she could persuade Mr Montpelier that she could offer a grand revelation with evidence, so he could sell the event at twice the price. In addition to solving a crime, Lily would be too valuable to discard.

"Don't be afraid, Celeste." She softened her tone. "Just tell me—"

She stopped, not because Celeste had just picked up a pot of face cream with the clear intention of hurling it at her head, but because the door suddenly opened behind her, knocking her forwards.

She stumbled a few steps, shaken by the malice on Celeste's face, that was quickly followed by horror.

A sickening horror Lily shared when she gazed upon the visage of the white-haired gentleman now staring at her, seemingly with incomprehension, before his lips turned up.

"What a surprise, madam," he said in thickly accented English, his surprise having turned to satisfaction. "Our amateur sleuth who communes with the spirits has come to take me to task, in person, has she?" He was blocking the doorway, and so close Lily could smell the brandy on his beard and the fragrant tobacco he smoked. But his bulbous eyes had the greatest impact. For they gleamed at her with a strange satisfaction; and she knew that he meant to do her harm, unless she quit the room before he could wrap his meaty hands about her throat.

Ducking beneath his outstretched arm, she darted for the door, squealing when he clutched at her hair and yanked her into his clutches. Fortunately, the pounding of feet heralded the arrival of one of the brothel heavies who jerked Lily away.

She did not wait to be asked to give an account of herself.

Picking up her skirts, she dived out of the heavyweight's claws and all but tumbled down the stairs and into the street.

Would he come after her?

He knew where she lived, and if he didn't, Celeste may well tell him.

Her breath came in convulsive bursts as she dodged down an alleyway and into a courtyard. It was unfamiliar territory, amidst the rookeries of those who would slit her throat—or worse—for what they could find upon her person.

The clattering of harness and an indignant whinny heralded a hackney carriage which nearly drove over her, but she was nimble enough to escape harm, instead pulling open the door and leaping inside after shouting instructions to the driver.

It was unconventional, but surely he'd take a woman alone at night, and not consider that her unchaperoned status proclaimed her a whore—someone unlikely to pay the fare. With trembling fingers, she counted the coins in her purse, exhaling in despair to find she had only a couple of pennies.

Where else could she go for help but to Mr McTavish? He'd been absent for too long, perhaps caught up with recrimination at succumbing to her lures, but he would help her, surely?

That is, if he were at his editorial offices and not at home.

"Stop!" She rapped on the roof. "The gentleman I'm to see will pay your fare. Please wait."

The jarvey's response was as expected. He was not happy as he grumbled that he'd wait two minutes for his money before coming in himself.

The offices of McTavish & Son were dark and shuttered. There was only a small chance Hamish would still be here, but Lily knew he worked late on a regular basis. She'd often passed by and seen the lamp lit in his upper floor office.

Equally often, she'd had to resist the urge to pay her addresses.

But he was in the building, and right now, he was the best chance Lily had of escaping harm.

When he opened the door, she all but threw herself at him, beyond caring that she was begging, when she'd never begged in her life. "Please will you pay the jarvey? Please can I stay here? Just for a few hours. There is a man who is after me, and I think he wants to kill me. The Russian I told you about. He was there. At Celeste's. Madame Chambon's. He grabbed me—"

His body was warm and comforting as his arms closed around her as she sagged into him and sobbed.

Suddenly her cares and fears seemed to dissipate. He was her safe haven. During previous encounters, she'd been highly susceptible to him, physically. Their sexual encounter had taken this to surprising heights. It had been exciting and satisfying, and left her wanting more.

But right now, he represented stability, strength, and wisdom.

He'd know what to do.

He'd help her.

"Lily, come in, my dearest." He settled her in the drawing room after paying the jarvey, his hands gentle, his voice soft and calming as her tears subsided.

"I'll build up the fire and we'll get you warm. Then you can tell me all about it." He guided her down the corridor, then up the stairs to his office, talking to her as if she were paying a social call rather, which, she supposed, helped to take the edge off her terror. "It's lovely to see you, and lucky that you find me still here. I fell asleep at my desk, in fact."

But Lily needed to convey to him the urgency of her situation. To make him understand.

"Please heed me, Hamish. Mr Novochov might be following me. He knows that I know his secret. That's why I couldn't go home because he knows where I live—" She was gabbling but she didn't care. At last, she was with someone she trusted. Someone who believed her. Who wanted to help her.

"And you're quite sure he's trying to kill you?" His tone was deeply caring, as if he were comforting a child.

"I think he murdered Mr Renquist. In fact, I'm almost certain he did!" Lily clutched at his arm and jerked her head up to look at his face, suddenly unnerved by his attitude. "You do believe me, don't you?"

He led her into the small sitting room behind his office, closing the door behind them, then settled her into a chair.

"Of course I do, Lily." He knelt at her feet after he'd rested them on an ottoman, then began to wrap them in his muffler. "Now let me make up the fire so you can get warm, and then you can tell me all about it." There was no urgency in his tone.

"We have to tell the police that we know who killed Mr Renquist!" Lily put her feet on the floor as she thrust her body forward. "Now! Before he kills someone else to protect himself. Like Celeste! Or me! Tell me you believe me?"

Gently, Hamish pushed her back in the chair, cupping her chin with one hand and stroking her hair. "Lily, you've had a big fright, I can see that," he murmured. "And I want to help you in any way I can."

Lily clasped his wrist and tried to see in his expression the urgency she felt should be there. But there was no urgency and none of the briskness that usually characterised his mannerisms.

Instead there was kindness, and, surprisingly—but unnervingly, too—patience and something that looked curiously like sorrow.

He stroked her cheek, then put a finger lightly upon her lips as she opened her mouth to challenge him.

"I will help you, Lily, and I will ensure you are in no danger." He sighed, and now she could see that it really was sorrow, for as he blinked, she saw the moisture in his eyes.

"But first, my dear Lady Bradden, I need you to tell me a few things about *yourself.*"

It was nearly midnight. Lily watched as he made up the fire and found blankets and cushions and settled her.

He was tender and attentive, and Lily was quiet as he offered her all the bodily comfort she could need. He wrapped them both up warmly and held her close upon the sofa.

Not so long ago, she could never have imagined physical closeness like this.

But now she knew he would never offer what she truly craved.

Not now he knew she was Lady Bradden.

Lady Bradden had been locked up for a reason. Somehow, he'd learned her true identity, and it clearly hadn't been hard to find people who'd given an embellished account of all that had led to Lily's incarceration.

With a patience to match his, she held his hand as she protested softly, "Everything I've described about this evening was real. I visited Celeste. And then her...her Russian paramour burst into the room and threatened me. He caught hold of my hair as I tried to run."

"But you escaped. And therefore, you believe he is Renquist's murderer? With no evidence other than that he was menacing towards you?"

Lily tried to break through his scepticism. "I lived with Celeste long enough to know when she's afraid. Nothing and no one seemed to do that except this man. I think she sold Mr Novichov's secrets to Mr Renquist, and that's why Mr Novichov murdered him. And Celeste is afraid she'll be next." Lily shuddered. "And I'm afraid I will be, because of what I've found out."

He looked at the ceiling. "You say you have not reported this to any authority?"

"No. It was only tonight that he threatened me."

"Will you report it?"

She covered her face with her hands. "I must."

"But you will have to do so under a name that does not exist. There will be no real record of who you are. And you cannot do so as Lady Bradden. Either way, they will not believe you."

"Do you believe me?" It was painful to ask the question. Even more painful to see the truth in his regretful look.

"Lily, I know how much you want to believe you've found Renquist's murderer. It's worth a great deal to you. You're beholden to the people who make you perform. You need to satisfy them, and the crowds." He stroked her cheek. "I also understand that Celeste has put herself in a compromising position by consorting with gentlemen who have opposing agendas. But this sounds like fantasy. You've taken a wild leap with no evidence."

"You think I'm making it all up!"

"I think it's not true; that's all I'm saying."

Outside the window, the streets were silent. Lily felt ready to admit defeat. She rested her head on his shoulder and did not try to stop the tears. "What shall I do?"

He was silent a long time. "I don't know. But I will help you."

She gasped. "You feel you are beholden to me because of…the other day? Something you deeply regret?"

He tensed. "Lily, I never set out to take what you didn't give freely, and I would never have taken anything had I realised how…vulnerable you were. My feelings for you got the better of me. I was weak."

"We both wanted it, Hamish." Her throat felt thick with emotion to realise that the love she'd thought was about to blossom between them had withered on the vine. Now, his innate decency was making him behave towards her as he would towards a troubled friend to whom he owed some kind of reluctant duty. "I thought perhaps you…" She tapped her heart. "Felt something for me, here."

Impulsively, he gripped her more tightly. "I did. And I do. But now I know the truth, and…" He looked away, but not before she'd seen his pain and disappointment. "Too much stands in the way of…a future."

"Like my husband? Despite all he did?" Bitterly she went on, "At first I was the thief. The runaway you chased into a… brothel." Her voice faltered. "You had little reason to trust me after that, I suppose."

He looked at their interlaced hands. At least he was still being tender and understanding. She must make the most of this moment.

He sighed. "Never once did you tell me the truth, Lily."

"The truth?" She gave a short laugh. "That I was the wife of a baronet who despatched me to an asylum? No, strange I didn't mention that in such terms. Do you think you'd have believed that? Do you think you would have believed the truth when I was, to all who only looked at me, a creature from the gutter? The rookeries?"

He shook his head.

"I was abducted from a *maison* in Brussels where my husband discarded me and then threw away the key. Then I became Mr Montpelier's prisoner as effectively as I was my husband's. I had no one to turn to. And no one to turn to, now."

It was time to go. She struggled out of his arms, but he held her, soothing her panic. "Except me," he said softly. "I will help you. Somewhere there will be a place where you can get better—"

"But I am not ill!" This time she resisted his efforts to calm her, the blanket falling to her feet as she rose. "How do you propose to help me? Tell my husband my whereabouts? So he can lock me up again?"

"Wait, Lily!"

She turned at the door.

He'd risen to his feet and his arms were outstretched though he did not come after her. "My darling, there are places that will take you. Places where you can be looked after until you are well again."

"Like the *maison* in Brussels looked after me?" Her mouth twisted. "Another man I once loved promised to take me to a place where I would be looked after."

He let her speak.

"My lover!" she flung at him. "Like you, he soothed me with soft words, made me believe he had my best interests at heart. He was supposed to restore me. My husband paid him well enough to do it, and Teddy promised to take me to a place where I would be cured. I spent the next two years starved and ill-treated. I would rather die in the gutter than return to a place like that. Teddy was my doctor, and then he was my lover. There! What does that make me in your eyes? The whore you didn't want to believe?" She tried to reign in her emotions so she was not the hysterical lunatic he clearly believed her. "I believed in Teddy. Loved him. Trusted him. Now you, Hamish, promise to take care of me." She put her hands to her face, and this time allowed the tears to fall freely. "Every time a man has promised to take care of me, I become a prisoner all over again."

DESPITE HIS PROTESTS, and even her own fears, she insisted she leave, and he put her in a cab before dawn.

She could not stay, and besides, there was nowhere else for her to go.

No one visited her the next day. Or if they did, Grace did not mention it, and let Lily sleep. For what else could she do?

In the early evening, she dragged herself out of bed.

Another night, another performance.

How long would life go on like this? She could feel her tenure coming to an end; could feel that something was about to happen.

Waiting for the audience to quieten, Lily rubbed her gloved hands together and then her chilled arms. It was cold and dark in the cellar, and she looked forward to the rush of warmth that would envelop her once she stepped out of the depths through the trapdoor and into the centre of the parlour above, to confront the crowds amidst the haze.

A gong sounded, silence echoing in the aftermath of the chatter.

Lily could have heard a pin drop had the floor not been carpeted in Turkish rugs, and the occasional cry from the street vendors not filtered into Mrs Moore's very middle-class parlour.

But that woman had an eye to milking an audience to the fullest extent of its credulity, and the lace curtains and doilies that had adorned the room when Lily first arrived in London had given way to heavy drapes of purple, gold, and black, with Oriental urns and paintings in the spaces once taken up by stuffed foxes in glass boxes.

"Does his earthly being still walk the earth, or can you tell the world that Bernard Renquist has quit this mortal coil and now communicates through you his conduit to inform us of the terrible crime committed against his person?" Mrs Moore's quavering voice was heavy with drama and portent. There was only one way Lily could answer, but she did it with misgiving.

Lily let out her breath in a slow, drawn-out sigh, gathering her energy for the intonation that the widow and her audience had been waiting for.

She felt their expectation like a heavy being upon her shoulders.

"Bernard Renquist wishes to make it known from the other side that through foul play, he met his maker, and his body lies in eternal rest."

She stopped short, then let out a theatrical gasp, clutched her stomach and bent double as she cried out, "Find me! Please, find me so that my soul may be released, and my wife given her freedom. Find the perpetrator of this foul deed who followed me down a dark alley and plunged a dagger into my heart."

Lily closed her eyes as she continued to hold her stomach while waiting for the response of her listeners. Would something she'd said recall a memory? Perhaps the sight of a heavyset, white-haired man with an accent?

It was, however, a faint hope, and she didn't really think her theatricals were going to tip the balance and unmask a murderer. Mr McTavish was perfectly correct in dampening her earlier enthusiasm.

Hamish didn't even believe her suspicions regarding Mr Novichov.

Yet, he was very ready to believe the story that Robert had broadcast about his wife.

Wasn't that at the heart of it? The injured party was, too often, the one who had no power.

And Lily, as Robert's despised wife, certainly had no power.

SHE BLINKED, as if coming out of a trance, opening her eyes just long enough for her to scan the audience.

She recognised a few familiar faces, locking gazes with Mr Novichov in the front row.

But the terror was short-lived because Mrs Moore was rapping on the floor, and the smoky mist was once again being released with a hiss. It was Lily's cue to drag open the trapdoor and disappear down the steps and into her dungeon.

Her dungeon and her respite, she thought with strongly beating heart once she was safely out of the public's eye, and she could let out her breath in one thankful sigh.

For a long while, she stood with her cheek against the cool stone wall, eyes closed, listening as the burst of chatter above faded to nothing.

Then Mr Montpelier was before her, telling her she was free to go as their audience had dispersed.

It was a strange moment, that moment of quiet when her job was done, yet Mr Montpelier had released her with no claim upon her time. Nothing other than the faintest suggestion that he was satisfied with her performance.

Exhausted and frightened, she longed for warmth and

companionship. Someone who would believe her as well as comfort her.

But she had nowhere to go except the villa to which she'd been given the keys by Madame Chambon for two weeks.

She was, she realised, quite alone.

CHAPTER 22

Lily had taken a hackney home, despite the cost. She wasn't going to risk walking alone after dark these days.

Her heart was heavy, and her future felt like a leaden weight upon her shoulders, but the one compensation was that she had Grace to attend her in her new lodgings.

The young maid must have heard her tread upon the path, for she opened the door, her eyes large with worry. "Ma'am, I weren't sure wot ter do," she whispered. "There's a gennulman 'ere ter see yer but I weren't sure if I should let 'im in."

Feeling the burn of hope and excitement as Grace relieved her of her outerwear, Lily murmured, "I'm sure you were quite right to do so, Grace. You can go to bed now. I shan't need you anymore."

At the entrance to the parlour, Lily had to put her hand on the wall to support herself as relief washed through her.

Hamish had come back. His desire to be with her exceeded his reservations. He was prepared to give her the chance she needed to prove her claims.

That Mr Novichov was a villain?

Maybe not that, but that Lily could be what he needed.

Nervously, she put her hand to her heart and tried to calm herself.

"Ma'am, I should tell yer—"

But Lily had already thrown open the door, Grace's words only half attended to before she realised her error in assuming what she should not have.

For it was not Hamish who sat comfortably in the armchair by the far side of the fire, his long legs stretched in front of him, his manner as insouciant as she remembered.

"Teddy!" she gasped, as he rose, coming towards her, arms outstretched to draw her into his embrace as he touched his lips to the top of her head.

"Lily, my own precious darling!" he ground out, holding her tighter.

Shock and confusion made her submit with no words in response. Then she was enveloped by the past when the feel and smell of him was a comfort and a sanctuary, his words bearing this up as he asked, "Do you have any idea how long I've searched for you?"

But as his hold tightened, her head seemed to clear a little.

She broke away, putting her hand to her mouth, confused by both his words and her own reaction.

"Darling?" He frowned, extending both hands as if he had no idea what could have occasioned her behaviour. "Are you not glad to see me?"

"Teddy! I...I..." She barely knew what to say.

Capturing her hands once more in his, he squeezed them tightly. Behind him, the light cast his face in shadow. She tried to see into his eyes but only his voice provided the clues she needed right now.

Was Teddy really here to save and protect her? There was

a time when she never would have doubted him but too much had happened.

"Darling, I've taken you completely by surprise. I can see that. I'd have given you notice if I hadn't been so eager to find you the moment I learned you were not dead."

"Dead?" Lily shook her head. Her mouth felt dry, and a painful tattoo was playing upon her heart. "No, I'm not dead, Teddy. But you are married," she said softly.

"Married?" He looked surprised. "I'm not married. Why, Lily, I told you I'd wait for you, didn't I? I told you I'd get you out of that dreadful place. I've been trying for two years, thwarted at every turn. Until I got news that you were dead."

His arms were about her again before he released her, bending to cup her face with his sensitive, long-fingered hands. "My, but you're even more beautiful than I remembered. But Lily..." He straightened, frowning again as he obviously tried to make sense of their altered relationship. "How is it that you are here? You escaped from the *maison*, I can see that. But you did not come searching for me? I thought that after all the letters I'd sent you, it would be clear that I was on my way to whisk you to safety."

Lily covered her face with her hands. "Letters? Teddy, I received not one letter from you. The man who took me from the *maison* made me think it was at your direction. But then he told me you were married! I work for him. That's why I live here." She indicated her surroundings with a sweep of her arm, adding hurriedly to dispel the suspicion in his expression, "I mean, I work as a...a spiritualist. It's respectable, and he's never..." She swallowed, unable to finish the sentence; unable to gauge the true state of her heart.

Here was the man she'd loved, gazing at her as he had during the days of their wicked, wonderful, illicit relation-

ship when he'd promised he'd rescue her from her overbearing husband.

Now he was here to make good on that promise and,
while Lily should feel only the profoundest relief that
someone was going to help her, the truth was, she didn't
know what she felt.

"Of course! I don't doubt that your behaviour is utterly
beyond reproach. Not that I would judge," he added, hastily.
His eyes were warm as he raked his fingers through his pale
blonde hair. Then, opening his arms wide, he drew her once
more into his embrace, dropping his head and leaning in to
kiss her.

It was a light kiss upon the lips, but as his enthusiasm
grew, Lily was physically unable to draw away.

Teddy's arms were exploring her body now, his kisses
more heated as he walked her back to the sofa, his lips still
upon hers.

"Teddy, please…no!"

He tried to place her on the sofa as he loomed over her.

But she could not go there. Not again.

"Lily?" His look was more confused than reproachful as
they remained standing, looking awkwardly at one another.
He hesitated. "Is it this man…Mr Montpelier? I thought you
said—"

She shook her head. "No. Not Mr Montpelier."

"Who then?"

Lily closed her eyes. "It's…no one," she finished lamely. "I
just need time, Teddy. This is so sudden."

Time. She'd used that old excuse, but she had no choice.
She couldn't nip this in the bud and perhaps damn her
chances of rescue forever when she had no one she could
depend upon.

He sat down, slowly, his brow furrowed as he took Lily's

wrist and drew her onto his lap and rested his brow against her neck. She could feel his breathing, the steady rise and fall of his chest, the heat from his breath against her bare skin.

She tried to remember how she'd felt towards him in the past, but her heart was completely untouched.

If Teddy really were here to help her, could she change the way she felt? She had to when her survival depended on someone with influence.

After a long silence, she twisted her body and placed a kiss upon his cheek. "Thank you for rescuing me, Teddy," she whispered.

"Have I, though?" He blinked, and Lily was shocked to see the tear that had lodged at the tip of his lashes scatter into a fine mist. "God, Lily, I've waited more than two years for this, and now that I've found you at last, I don't know what to think."

Lily stopped the sob that rose in her throat. "I'm just saying that I...I'm not ready to do the things we once did, Teddy. You remember what happened last time?"

His expression warmed. "How could I forget? You were so soft to hold, so willing, so...responsive." He touched his lips to hers. "You wanted me, then, as much as I want you, now."

"I don't mean that, Teddy," she whispered. "I meant... Robert. It was Robert's rage that destroyed everything between us and sent me to that place. I can't forget that...you delivered me there."

He shook his head, his expression sorrowful. "No, Lily, it wasn't Robert's rage that sent you to that place." His voice hitched. "It was you." He hurried on. "Lily, we were both duped. I took you to a sanatorium for your health, your delicate nerves. Your..." He shrugged. "I don't like to put it into words when I know how sensitive you are. But the laudanum…those terrible bouts of frenzy. I thought I was taking you to a place where I could retrieve you when Robert's back was turned." He buried his head in her bosom, and she felt the shudder that ran through him as he whispered raggedly, "But Robert was a step ahead of both of us. He knew exactly what he was about when he had us obligingly follow his directions. You know what he was like."

"Oh, I know very well," Lily said bitterly, stroking his hair as she gazed at a picture on the wall. "After five years of his cruelty, it was little wonder I was responsive to the first kindness a man had ever shown me."

"But surely that's not the only reason you came to me?"

Teddy sounded hurt, so she added quickly, "Of course I'd grown fond of you, coming so often to the house and attending both Robert and myself. It was hardly difficult to feel myself in love with you and…and doing what we did." She pressed her lips together. "But I was wrong to have been unfaithful to him, even though I don't believe he cared. He cared for his reputation, of course, so I understand why he was so angry."

"Angry enough to cast you away from him forever and then tell the world that you were dead?" He sounded outraged.

"Dead?" Her voice sounded small to her ears. "Did he really? I heard a rumour that he had a new wife, but could find nothing in the newspapers or another source to verify it. How can it be true? When I am still very much alive?"

Teddy's eyes bored into hers. "He told me you were dead, Lily," he said slowly. "And then he told the world you were dead. You owe him nothing. Come away with me, I beg you."

His words sounded shocking when once they'd have offered her the greatest comfort. "Come away with you?" she repeated. "Where, Teddy? Where could we possibly go? What about your work? Your standing in society? Your reputation? I'd be a millstone around your neck."

"Don't you want to be with me? Don't you want the security I can offer you? A return to those wonderful days of endless loving?" He touched his heart. "I've relived those days every single moment of my life. I care nothing for society and my standing. Lily, this is what I am here to tell you. That I wish to answer a calling to make a difference in the world and exonerate our sins. With you by my side, think of the good we could do in Africa? In India? You'd be my wife in all but name only."

He was going too fast when Lily could think of only the immediate danger. "But if Robert were to find out—"

"He'd be the last to call attention to the lie. Not when he has so much at stake." He gripped her hands. "Please, Lily. Tell me that I have not come here to woo you once again…in vain."

Lily rose and began to pace before the fire. He truly was offering her the salvation she needed. Without an offer like this, what hope had she for anything other than life as one of Madame Chambon's girls? Or in an asylum, helped there through Hamish's well-meant efforts?

And Hamish?

She stifled a sob. He'd been shocked and horrified by the truth.

But Teddy knew everything about her. And he'd come looking for her. She couldn't knock back this opportunity.

She stopped and turned. "No, you've not come here in vain. I'm just in shock, that's all." She forced a smile. "I've just returned from a very strange evening trying to summon information regarding a man who may well have been murdered. My thoughts are all a jumble, and my nerves as disordered as they ever were when you saw me last, Teddy." Closing the distance between them, she stroked his cheek.

"The next time you come to me, Teddy, I shall be very much decided."

He rose with obvious reluctance. "You will?"

"I'm sure of it," she said.

Hoping against hope that the truth was as firm as the conviction with which she'd uttered the words.

CHAPTER 23

"Why so glum, Hamish?" Lucy sent him a concerned look across the breakfast table. "Until a few days ago, I thought I'd got my old, carefree brother back again. Are you missing Mrs Eustace? Maybe you should go and see her again."

He ignored her blatant dig for information, saying instead, "I have to see Father today, in case you'd forgotten."

"Oh, goodness. Do, please, keep me out of the conversation." Lucy pressed her lips together, her expression worried. "And don't say anything about my unsuitable suitor."

"If Mr Myers is worth his salt, he will be patient and win your hand by proving to me that he is worthy of you." Hamish sent her a reassuring smile. "But, of course, I'll say nothing. I have only your best interests at heart."

"Just as I have only your best interests at heart." She took another sip of tea. "That's why I think you and I should both go and see Mrs Eustace perform at Lord Lambton's séance tonight."

"I hardly think Father would approve of that, Lucy." Though it was not their father, Hamish was worried about.

Hamish had a duty to help Lily find the help she needed now he knew the truth, but his susceptibility to her stood in the way.

She had escaped from an asylum, and she was clearly unwell. How could she be otherwise if she truly believed her life was in danger from a man she identified as a murderer on the flimsiest of suspicions?

Besides, Lily Eustace—or, rather, Lady Bradden—was the antithesis of the kind of woman he needed in his life. She was a bold, desperate seductress. He knew it, yet, the moment she was within his orbit, it was his heart that ruled his head.

Or was it entirely his heart, he wondered, ruefully. Animal instincts were at play whenever he even thought of her.

He thought with shame of the afternoon he'd visited her; so recent, so carnal.

What had possessed him?

It was as if she had. She—beautiful Lady Bradden—with her ability to bend men to her will.

Isn't that what he'd learned of her past?

He didn't know what to think.

Glancing down, Lucy stirred her tea thoughtfully. He realised she'd changed the subject. She was trying, it seemed, to broach a difficult topic, for her hand shook and her mouth trembled, and she was unable to look him in the eye. "You took on your responsibilities with the business far more seriously than I expected you would, Hamish." Her mouth had hardened, but then she glanced up and he thought he'd never seen her look so vulnerable. "And you did it for me. I never thought you would agree to take up the reins. I thought you were set on going off in your own direction after you came home from France. The last thing I expected was that you'd take up the editorship. When you went to France, you seemed so…" She sought for the right words. "Well, so full of wonderful and exciting ideas that really were so different from Father's."

Hamish found it hard to meet her eye. She wanted to quiz him about his relationship with their father? He knew Lucy lived in terror of being returned to her overbearing parent.

He knew, also, that this was the time to speak of it. When Lucy was prepared to open up about her fears.

But the truth was that Hamish could barely contain his disappointment over his recent brutal discovery.

Everything stood in the way of any kind of relationship between him and Lily.

Lady Bradden. Even the social divide.

He should, of course, just bow out gracefully and leave her to her fate. He was surely not in so deep that a graceful retreat would not be excusable?

"Father said he'd pay a visit to the office." Lucy pretended unconcern as she buttered her toast. "Are you worried?"

Would he be honest with her? She was so much younger than he. Barely twenty, and yet, despite her liveliness, so full of intelligence and perception.

"Father doesn't control my every decision, Lucy. I'm not so under his thumb," he said softly.

"I think you are, more than you like to admit it," she countered. "I can't tell you how happy I am to only have to see him once a quarter in order to make a full accounting of my sins, but he makes it very clear that he is the one who cracks the whip, and that one whisper of wrongdoing would see me marched down the aisle with the first suitable offer." She looked up at Hamish, puzzled. "How does Father have so much influence when he's been mostly bedridden all these years and has so few good days?" She dropped her eyes. "It's as if his ghost is always there, hovering over us."

Hamish reached across to put his hand over hers.

"Appearances are deceptive, Lucy. Father is not as hard a man as you believe. I don't expect you to understand." In truth, Hamish was only spouting platitudes. Their father was a hard man.

"Good lord, you've never sounded so condescending, Hamish!" Lucy cried. "As if I didn't understand that nothing is as it seems, and that there's something between you and Father that I'll probably never know. And since you won't tell me, I'll naturally suspect the worst—that you've done something terrible that gives Father a hold over you, and makes you financially beholden to him." She focused troubled eyes upon him. "It all started when you came back from France. You were so happy when you left, ready to explore the world." She paused, significantly, before adding, "Now that you were free of Father, and free to go your own way; and, what's more, that he had willingly released you. Your letters home made me wonder if you would ever return. You were so filled with life and energy."

"But I did return home." Lucy's pleas that her brother protect her from a harsh and violent father had coincided with Hamish's own heartbreak. He didn't want to think too much on what had really influenced him, though of course he wanted to believe that those reasons were noble: his concerns for Lucy.

Her eyes brimmed with tears. "It was because you are too good to see someone you care for come to harm. I know you came home for me."

He couldn't look at her. Lucy was seeing the very best in him when he wasn't sure he deserved it.

Furthermore, here he was dictating to Lucy that she refrain from seeing the man she loved because Hamish knew their father would find him unsuitable.

Yet Hamish had been barely older than his sister when

he'd fallen in love with someone much more unsuitable: a Frenchwoman, a deserted farmer's wife who'd employed Hamish before her jealous husband had returned and beaten her for her faithlessness.

"I have always admired your loyalty, Hamish."

Lucy's words needled him. Hamish hadn't come home for his sister. He'd come home because after Madeleine died, there was nothing left for him in France.

He'd come home plagued by guilt. Young and naïve, he'd lost his heart, and then his pride when he'd been unable to help the woman he loved.

"Yes, you returned home, sad and changed." Lucy's expression was so full of sympathy it tugged at his conscience when she added, "Whatever happened in France —and I always suspected it was because you fell in love— made you bitter, and too ready to agree to Father's proposal that you take over the magazine, with Father retaining full editorial control." She gave an eloquent shrug. "That's not like you, Hamish! To bow down to Father without a fight."

Hamish blinked. Is that how she saw the matter? Did it appear to her like that, in such simplistic terms?

He pushed back his chair. "We all make decisions based on what seems best at the time. I'm sorry, Lucy." He rose. "But at least you share a roof with me, and not Father, now."

"I'd have run away a long time ago if that were not the case." She glanced up at him as he escorted her to the door. "Will I still have a place under your roof if I have not made a match before you, Hamish?"

He started. "Good lord, what makes you think I'll make a match anytime soon?"

"I think your heart is engaged. I think you'd like to marry Mrs Eustace. There, I said it." She looked triumphant. "She's a beautiful widow, and the two of you clearly like one another very much. What's stopping you from being happy? I hope it's not guilt, or some misguided romantic notion that you must be forever loyal to your long-lost French love."

He was glad she didn't see his face before she left him.

Otherwise she'd have read guilt written all over it, as clearly as she thought she'd correctly read the situation between their father and himself.

His visit to his father was as predictable as he'd expected. He was lambasted for allowing the tone of the publication to drop by printing the photograph Lucy and Archie had pressed him to publish.

Mrs Eustace, the spiritualist.

"Look at her! Temptress! Charlatan! And to think this filth ousted Reverend Snell's Talk at the Temperance Society's monthly meeting. You are a weak-minded young man if you think you know better than I what our readers want from this magazine." His father had tried to rise, but his legs would not support him and, in frustration, he'd snatched up his walking stick and flung it at Hamish.

It reminded Hamish of why he'd made a bad bargain to keep Lucy safe under his own roof.

"I don't want to see any more wasted inches of print devoted to this woman. Or any spiritualist."

"With due respect, Father, the public are interested. Other magazines have covered the story of Bernard Renquist's disappearance. Furthermore, Lord Lambton's séances to speak to his dead daughter are well attended. There's supposedly not a dry eye in the room."

"You've been to them, have you?"

Hamish shook his head.

"Then you have no idea what you're talking about.

Lambton has always been a tough nut to crack. Not a man I'd want to cross in business and not a fond parent. Well, if you want a story, go and print one about his crocodile tears. That's an order! Do you hear? Go and reveal that Eustace woman for the fraud she is. And old Lambton's tears for the glycerine water they no doubt are!"

CHAPTER 24

For days, Hamish had resisted, but now he was here. In Mrs Moore's parlour, attending a séance on his father's orders.

On his right sat Lucy, her eyes aglow as she gazed at the audience. Such variety, including a sprinkling of women whom he suspected hailed from Madame Chambon's.

What would Lily think when she saw him in the front row next to Lucy?

They'd parted on strained terms; he, exhorting her to seek help if she would not accept it from him.

She claimed she'd been wrongfully incarcerated. That nothing ailed her.

Was it only her exposure to the world of the supernatural that caused her to believe in mystery sightings of so-called murderers? Did she suffer no ailment of the mind, as she declared?

Hamish put his hand to his head which ached—and that was not due to the hocus pocus smoke that was swirling about the place.

Lady Bradden was married. She was from the upper

classes. She claimed she had no one to turn to, but Hamish had done his due diligence in the days since he'd learned the truth from Celeste.

The former Miss Taverner—before she had become Lady Bradden—had lived with an aunt. Both the aunt, and Lily's father, were not deceased, as Lily would have him believe.

If Hamish were to aid Lily in any way, perhaps it would be to inform either of these relatives of her whereabouts.

His mind warred with his heart over how best to help her. Any possibility of romance between them was doomed, but the feelings he'd developed for her would not be shed so easily.

A thumping noise and the clash of a cymbal diverted his line of thought. When he blinked open his eyes, there was Mrs Eustace, dressed in a flowing black gown that contrasted magnificently with her golden tresses and ivory skin, her eyes closed and her plump, rosebud mouth pursed as she hummed tunelessly.

Helpless, Hamish stared. He'd plundered those lips just days before; had run his fingers through those golden tresses. He swallowed down the lump in his throat. Had she indeed resorted to sorcery to bewitch him? For bewitched he certainly was.

Though when he glanced at the white-haired old man who sat in a chair a little distance from her, his bushy eyebrows and moustache twitching as he stared, mesmerised at her, Hamish thought that a great many in this room were under the same spell.

When she began to speak, he could understand why.

She was gentle, but compelling. Passionate, yet wholly believable and deeply empathetic.

The old man, who was, of course, Lord Lambton, asked questions about his daughter, and the spiritualist communing with the lamented departed answered with compassion and insight.

What were Cassandra's true feelings regarding her father, Lord Lambton asked? Had his attempts to keep her safe been misconstrued as controlling? What of his deep love for her which she'd thrown back at him as less than his fondness for his cat?

Mrs Eustace communed with the dead to bring comfort to the living. She did it in a way that was believable, and when Hamish saw what it did for Lord Lambton, he began to question his scepticism.

Mrs Eustace's fame had spread, not because she was a charlatan, but because she was sincere. Others here tonight had come to mend their broken hearts, showing her photographs of their dead loved ones, and speaking of their regrets that rifts had not been healed before it was too late, or of their final harsh words which could never be taken back.

It was a much noisier gathering than Hamish had expected. Certainly, it had started in silence and with a hushed reverence, but by the end of the evening, a buzz of excitement had infected everyone.

Even Lucy, it seemed, whose eyes were shining as she rose, saying, "I daresay it's not the done thing to speak to Mrs Eustace when all these people are gathered, but perhaps you could send her a note asking if she'd like to avail herself of a lift home in our carriage."

Hamish stiffened. "I don't know, Lucy—"

"It would be rude not to. Why, I'll ask her."

He wasn't sure what he felt when she accepted, and now he and Lucy sat in the carriage, his sister leaning across the small space to declare, "Mrs Eustace, I remember Lord Lambton as an ogre, not the tenderhearted man you've revealed. Cassandra spoke of him as if he were a monster.

But then, Cassandra had some strange ideas, I will admit. As for tonight, I didn't know what to expect. But I certainly wasn't expecting this."

Hamish had certainly not been expecting this. He caught Lily's eye, and the communication was like the thrust of a spear through the heart.

He owed her something. It was true. But it was not his place to encourage her to return to an institution where others would decide the kind of treatment she needed.

Right now, Lily seemed as far removed as possible from all the rumours he'd heard of crazed Lady Bradden.

"Lord Lambton is a kind man, Lucy." The beautiful young woman patted his sister's hand, adding with a smile, "I think he'd seen it as his duty to protect Cassandra from fortune hunters, but she saw it differently. I think that with age, he has mellowed. But he has lost his daughter. And he realises he will never get her back. It must be hard for a man to realise too late that he has lost forever something so precious."

Hamish shifted in his seat, and felt the heat rise in his cheeks. For she'd been looking at him when she said this.

It was a moment of clarity.

It was also the moment he realised he'd lost the fight between his heart and the rational part of his nature, just as had happened all those years ago in France.

BACK IN HER OWN LODGINGS, Lily sat alone in her sitting room, with the lamp turned down, and only the fire for company. It had been a successful evening, but like every evening, it took a while for the energy pulsing through her to subside.

She'd have liked company. She had so little of it. There

was no one to speak to of her fears for the future. To talk to about their day.

To ask if they thought she really was mad.

She tensed at the sound of light rapping upon the front door.

Surely Teddy would not seek her out at midnight?

Grace was asleep, and when she found the courage to open the door, relief had the blood fizzing through her veins, thrumming in her ears, and her breath coursing through her lungs, fast and shallow.

"Hamish! You came!"

In the dim light, his expression was serious. He looked diffident as he held his hat in his hands, his jaw tense, his eyes boring into hers. "How could I not? After tonight?"

So, it wasn't only she who felt the connection between them?

"Come in." She stepped aside, the eagerness in her voice and her discomposure making no secret of her pleasure at seeing him. And her hope. "Grace is asleep, and I'm very glad to receive you."

She led him up the passage, pausing by the drawing room. How she so longed to take him further. Up the stairs to her bedchamber.

He clearly understood her feelings, and, with no words needed, she put her hands on his shoulders to steady herself against him as his lips came down upon hers.

Pressed between the wall and his chest, she could feel the hammering of his heart. Hers seemed almost ready to leap out of her chest cavity as his arms tightened about her, skimming her waist, contouring her breasts.

She felt herself responding to him even more readily than the last time.

"Come upstairs," she managed between kisses, cupping his face as he continued to kiss her, not breaking the contact as they clumsily negotiated their way to the next level.

"Have you forgiven me?" he asked, drawing back as the paused on the landing. "I said some cruel things. And you are married, Lily—"

"Hush." She put a finger to his lips. "I've waited in hope for this moment. Now, come."

She took his hand and together they entered her bedchamber.

They were about to commit an immoral act, but what was one more sin when her entire life was based on sin?

At the foot of the bed, he paused, bringing her fingertips to his lips. "I didn't come for this. I could have stayed in the drawing room."

"Where we would have been so less comfortable?" Lily smiled, drawing away her hands and hooking her fingers in the waistband of his breeches. "Now, get these off. There'll be plenty of time to talk afterwards."

When finally skirt, basque, and breeches had been discarded, they clung to each other on the bed, Lily in her linen chemise, and Hamish in only his shirt.

"I adore you, Lily," Hamish whispered as, afterwards, they lay side by side, staring up into the darkness. He reached for her hand, raising it to his mouth as he kissed each finger.

"I've come to love you, too, Hamish. And that's so much better than the impulsive love of lust and misguided passion," Lily whispered, the sting of tears like a catharsis for the years she'd not known him. When she found the courage, she asked, "Why did you come here this evening?"

"Because I realised I was wrong to let you go as I did the other night. I don't know what the future holds for us beyond tonight. But I had to see you again."

She inched her body closer, in the inky blackness more than ever aware of the sensation of touch: the heated moistness of his skin against hers, and the curdling in her belly that longing and hope combined to create.

Could there be more to tonight than simply the physical union? She was not the virtuous embodiment of womanhood he esteemed, but he knew that.

"There is so much that is a mystery about you, Lily," he murmured, placing her hand upon his heart. "And I know you face many trials in the coming weeks. I thought I could abandon you to your fate. And then I thought I could direct your fate—until I realised I have no right. All I know is that my life feels incomplete without you in it."

CHAPTER 25

For a long time, Lily stared at the door that had just shut behind Mr McTavish, listening to his footsteps as he took the front steps, then the creak of harness and whinny of a horse as a hackney slowed to a stop on the cobbles.

Closing her eyes, she slumped against the wall.

He might be leaving now but he'd come back to her.

Yes, he'd come back to her, and he would again.

"Ma'am."

She jerked open her eyes and swung round at Grace's whisper, shocked to think that her maid may have witnessed her recent intimacy.

"Ma'am, yer doctor gennulman friend is waitin' fer yer in the drawin' room." Grace came forward, her bed cap awry on her head and her little pinched face bleary from disturbed sleep.

"How long has he been waiting?" Lily exhaled on a fearful breath. She hadn't expected Teddy to return. Certainly, not so soon. "Did he…?

"I don't fink he 'eard Mr McTavish," Grace whispered,

though she looked frightened. "He were already in the drawin' room when yer came down."

Lily looked down at her bare feet, her creased chemise, and ran her hands through her untidy hair. "Tell him I'm sleeping."

"Lily, is that you?" His voice sounded from the next room before there was the sound of a chair scraping on the floorboards, and then Teddy was standing in the doorway to the passage, looking at her with interest.

"My dear, how...delightful that you were so anxious to see me. You shouldn't have got up if you were already abed." He stepped back for her to enter the drawing room, and with guilt and fear robbing her of speech, she obeyed.

"I didn't think you'd come back so soon, Teddy?" To distract herself, so she wouldn't have to look at him, or take the seat beside him that he was patting, she stroked a marble bust of Beethoven that stood upon the mantelpiece.

Teddy rose and came towards her. He put his finger beneath her chin and tipped her face to look at him. "Why would I wait a moment longer when you know my feelings for you, my love?"

She dropped her eyes from the tenderness she saw in his look. "Teddy, I—"

"It's very late, I know, and you must have only just fallen asleep. I understand you had a performance tonight." He hesitated. "Do you sleep well these days?"

She nodded, uncomfortable at his close proximity, unable to look him in the eye.

"You aren't visited by the demons that plagued you when I knew you?"

Lily swallowed. "I have been so very well, Teddy," she whispered. "And so much stronger."

"Why, Lily, that is wonderful to hear! It's not often

patients report such improvement. Perhaps Brussels did you good, after all."

Lily stepped backwards, turning her head and encountering Grace's wide-eyed look as the little maid crouched, tending to the fire. No, there had been nothing improving about her time in Brussels, but she had not the energy to tell him that. Or anything that reminded her of those dark days.

"You must take good care of your mistress," Teddy said, directing his words towards Grace. "She has been through a great deal, and we must ensure she remains strong."

"Please, Teddy," Lily whispered, embarrassed. "I'm very well these days."

"But that has not always been the case; you must admit that, my love. You can't wonder why I'm so anxious to reassure myself that you stay healthy."

Lily dropped her eyes from his furrowed brow as he said to Grace, "I trust your mistress does not suffer from the fitful sleep and nightmares that plagued her in the old days?"

Grace fiddled with the poker. "No, sir." She seemed awed by the doctor.

"I'm glad to hear it," said Teddy. "Laudanum is not a cureall, as you know, Lily. I trust you—"

"I haven't touched a drop in more than two years, Teddy." She closed her eyes, shame stinging the back of her lids as she pulled away from him and went to stand behind the sofa. She wasn't going to add that the torment of her first months at the asylum had been exacerbated by the fact she wasn't able to rely on her old crutch.

It was her incarceration which had made her realise it for what it had been. A drug that had done her more harm than good.

He rested an elbow on the mantelpiece, looking very much at home, and very disinclined to leave. "I am comforted by this understanding. Grace, take it from a doctor that there are too many hocus pocus potions to be wary of, sold by every apothecary who wants to profit from human misery. Isn't that so, Lily?"

Lily nodded, unable to say more.

After another silence, he sighed. "I have timed my visit too late and you are tired." He straightened. "My apologies. I shall leave you now, my dearest, and come back tomorrow."

He moved towards the door and put his hand on the knob. Unable to meet his eye, Lily tried to think of something to say. Had he come back because he loved her? Because he wanted to help her? Such a short time ago he'd seemed her only salvation.

And then Hamish had come back to her. After tonight in his arms, she truly believed a future was possible.

Hamish knew the best of her.

And the worst of her.

Yet still he'd come back.

She didn't want to hurt Teddy, but he was a painful reminder of the past. She wanted him gone.

When she glanced up, his brow was creased, as if he were trying to make sense of the Lily, Lady Bradden, he'd once known and loved.

But she was no longer that woman.

"Good night, Lily. It's good that you seem so much better. I'd hate to think you may ever be tempted back to your old ways." He cleared his voice, adding, "And please understand that I'm speaking as your doctor with your health a much greater concern. Of everything sold over the counter, laudanum is the most dangerous and overused by society ladies. You've done well to wean yourself off it, Lily. You certainly look well on whatever it is that sustains you these days. I'll let you go back to your slumber, but please see me out."

As the door closed behind them, leaving them a moment

of privacy in the passage, he put a hand upon the small of her back and whispered, "Can you tell me anything to put me out of suspense…or misery, Lily? Will I be welcome if I come back here again?"

She tensed at his touch, but said with more energy than she'd intended, "You'll always be welcome, Teddy!"

Mostly because she was trying to cover up just how little she wanted to see him again.

He reminded her of days she would rather forget.

CHAPTER 26

Despite Teddy's interruption the previous night, Lily woke feeling refreshed. With no performances that night, the day had been hers. She'd shopped and walked by the river. A weak sun had shone, and she'd felt nourished with hope.

Even the thought of Robert's imminent return didn't fill her with the fear it had. Now she had Hamish to support and protect her.

She didn't have to perform at another séance for two days, and that would be her last, for soon it would be time for her to leave before Robert arrived in the capital.

All her thoughts centred on Hamish these days, and although she tempered the expectation, it charged her nerve endings as she imagined a future where the two of them faced shared hopes and dreams together.

Mr Montpelier and Mrs Moore thought they could continue to profit from the woman they had kidnapped by sending her to Madame Chambon's, but Hamish would step in to save Lily from her uncertain future.

Their last loving encounter had reaffirmed his love and loyalty.

A smiling Grace opened the door at the end of Lily's day in town, and the girl's cheerful prattle added an extra layer of brightness to Lily's mood, especially when Grace told her she'd sent her most recent visitor on his way.

"I told Dr Swithins yer would'na be in 'til midnight an' he said he 'ad ter go away fer a few days and to pass on 'is respects."

So, it was with relief that Lily walked into the drawing room, before shock stopped her in her tracks, which obviously caused Grace some alarm, for she darted forwards, picking up a copy of *Manners & Morals* that lay untidily on the table. She darted a guilty look at Lily. "I'll get these cleared away right now, ma'am. Dr Swithins left not long ago an' I gave 'im some tea, but then the butcher's boy were visitin'." She broke off, blushing. "'E didn't stay long, ma'am. Promise."

Lily couldn't care less about the butcher's boy. She was looking dumbly at the letter on the table. It lay half under a copy of The Times, the name of its intended recipient proclaiming Lily's lie for all the world to see. It wasn't the use of her correct titles, however, which caused her heart to lurch, but the familiar handwriting.

Grace saw the direction of Lily's look and snatched up the cream envelope.

"I'd 'ave gived that letter right back ter the postman if there'd bin a return address on the back, but..." She gave an eloquent shrug, "There weren't. An' I 'ave no idea who Lady Bradden might be. Wot should I do wiv it, ma'am?"

"Give it to me," Lily said faintly, swallowing with difficulty, and slipping the letter into her pocket. Then, unable to bear the suspense, tearing the seal and scanning the few lines while Grace busied herself with tidying the room.

. . .

Dear Lily,

Your fame has spread. It was indeed a shock to learn of your escape from your house of care, and of your unusual profession in London, if sorcery and hocus-pocus deserves such a title.

The truth is, that while it would be more comfortable for both of us to pretend the reality is otherwise, the law is the law, and this precarious existence of yours, combined with your notoriety, puts me in a difficult position.

I am still legally responsible for you, and I have a reputation to protect.

I do not know with whom you have been associating while you have adopted this false identity, but I trust you have been discreet, for the taint of scandal would be ruinous to all.

I shall call on you at my earliest convenience.

Yours,

Robert

"YER LOOK DONE IN, MA'AM," Grace said, sympathetically, looking up from shaking out an antimacassar. "Why don't yer sit down, an' I'll fetch yer summat ter eat an' a nice soothin' drink ter calm yer nerves?"

Unable to speak as she tried to hide her shaking, Lily allowed herself to be fussed over.

"You are good to me, Grace," she murmured, barely knowing what she said.

"Jest lookin' afta yer, ma'am. Now, put yer feet up on the ottoman. Yer do look pale an' wan. I 'ope yer not sickenin' fer sumfink."

Lily pushed from her mind the niggling fear that naturally would intrude at such an observation. She'd not conceived after five years of marriage, which included her shameful affair with Teddy.

The thought was one of mixed emotions: relief at the probability she was barren, and therefore that her wan looks weren't symptomatic of pregnancy, and sadness that she could never enjoy a proper relationship with Hamish that included marriage and children.

Overriding all was this new horror.

Robert had returned to claim her. Not to look after her as a husband should.

But to punish her, as he always had.

She must have put her head in her hands to sob the anguish her thoughts caused her, for a few minutes later, Grace was at her side with a plate of steak and kidney pie and a mug of steaming warm milk.

"It'll 'elp settle yer nerves, ma'am," she said, when Lily wrinkled her nose at the faint aftertaste. "'Elp yer get a good sleep, which I fink is jest wot yer need, if I says so meself."

Lily closed her eyes as she sipped her milk and thought of Hamish.

Should she tell him of Robert's letter? Of his threats?

She hiccupped on another sob. Robert would never allow her to love Hamish. He might be married, but he'd find a way to destroy whatever happiness Lily had found. She knew it.

"Now, now, ma'am, it surely ain't as bad as all that." Grace stood awkwardly at her side.

"It is as bad as all that, Grace." Lily wept. "I don't know what to do. I really don't."

"Then that nice feller wot were 'ere will know wot ter do. 'E'll know how ter make yer better."

"Dr Swithins?" Lily sat up with a start, but Grace shook her head.

"No, a'course not, ma'am. Doctors are only good wiv prescribin' medicines fer the body but yer need someone ter fix yer heart. I were referrin' ter Mr McTavish. Now, drink up yer milk an' then I can 'elp put yer ter bed. An early night, mayhaps, ma'am."

Lily felt the trickle of tears down her cheeks, and the warmth of her drink sliding down her throat, the precursor to the welcome dulling of her senses as Grace's soothing tones washed over her: "Yer need a good night's sleep, ma'am. That yer do."

"I'll stay here a little longer, Grace," she said. "I need to think. I'll call you when I'm going to bed."

Lily rested her head on the side of the chair. She should rise before the effects took hold. She knew how sleeping draughts worked. She should be in a darkened room where she'd slip into oblivion as the medicine did its magic.

In the morning, Robert's letter wouldn't seem so ominous. She'd show it to Hamish. He loved her. He'd know what to do.

She closed her eyes. She'd rise in a minute. Usually, her eyelids would feel heavy and her body lethargic. Tonight, though, the sleeping draught was having the opposite effect. Strange colours in the form of shooting stars were exploding in the back of her head, and she was pulsing with nervous energy.

"Let me 'elp yer up, ma'am." Lily felt Grace's gentle hands exerting pressure on her upper arms.

"In a moment, Grace," she murmured. She felt captive, unable to stir.

A kaleidoscope of colour was metamorphosing into strange, contorted objects.

She blinked open her eyes. And then found she couldn't stop blinking.

It was as if the whole world was blinking with her.

Gasping, she gripped the arms of the chair as she stared at the blue wallpaper.

What were the flowers doing? Were they looking at her? She closed her eyes again, but the colour pulsing at the back of her head made her open them again. The flowers were beckoning to her. Not only did they appear more vibrant, but the very walls appeared as if they were breathing.

In and out, their pursed mouths pulsed air, like trumpet players at first before the breaths became words. Taunting, threatening, unkind.

Lily screamed, curling into her seat as she put her hands over her eyes, squeezing them tight.

This couldn't be happening to her. Not again.

Vaguely aware of another presence in the room, she reached out her hand and grasped at it, crying out, "Look at the walls! Do you see what they're doing!"

"Wot 'tis it, ma'am? Please, ma'am, are yer 'oright?" The faint, frightened voice of her maid was swept away by the ominous tones of the flowers themselves, booming at her in unison, "Evil woman! God will punish you! Bigamist! You deserve to die for your sins! Hamish will be ruined because of you!"

Lily shook her head vigorously and opened her eyes to try and clear her vision. But the flowers all had faces that glared at her with spite and malevolence, their words searing her brain.

"The flowers! Tell them to stop! Tell them to leave me alone!" she cried, feeling the wetness on her cheeks as she thrashed in her chair until someone tried to restrain her.

"Liar! Liar! Lily's a liar!" shouted the flowers. "If you love Hamish, you must give him up!"

Swaying on their long stems, they threatened to burst from the walls and devour her.

Lily thrust out of her chair, disregarding the pain when

she crashed to the floor, banging her knees on the bare floorboards.

Scrambling to her feet, she dashed to the far wall where she cowered, covering her eyes.

"I'm not evil! Please, don't hurt me!" she pleaded. "It was never my intention to hurt anyone. Not Robert. Not Hamish. No, not Hamish!"

"Ma'am! Ma'am! Wot are yer sayin'? Ma'am! Yer need 'elp! Listen ter me, ma'am!"

But Lily was beyond listening to anyone. With a cry of despair, she picked up the cut-glass decanter from the sideboard and hurled it at the grinning, malevolent faces of the flowers on the wallpaper, then stared hopefully at the stain and the shards of glass.

Weeping uncontrollably when that didn't stop the flowers' cruel taunts at all.

CHAPTER 27

"Your father is here to see you, sir." Miniver put his head around the door, just before the old man pushed through.

How was it that Hamish hadn't even heard his laboured tread upon the stairs?

He supposed, quite simply, that love had a habit of obliterating everything else in one's world.

"How are you, Father?"

"Not well, and even more unwell after the rumours I've been hearing of your conduct."

At first, Hamish assumed with a shock that he was referring to Lily, until the old man began a long and precise criticism of every editorial decision Hamish had made in the past month.

Well, Hamish's tenure at the newspaper might just have reached its natural course. If he had to decide between the family business and the woman he loved, he knew which one would win.

When he despatched his father with soothing words, for

he would fight the real fight another day, he was pleasantly surprised to receive a visit from his sister.

"Mr Myers wishes to take me to a piano recital tomorrow night," she said, thrusting out her chin as if she were expecting opposition. But Hamish merely smiled. "I'm glad to hear he sounds a cultured young man. I'd hate to see you spend your future with a philistine, Lucy."

She frowned. "Why, Hamish, that almost sounded like you're ready to give your consent."

Hamish couldn't stop the grin that stretched his face. "If he remains faithful to you and hardworking, then it will be a relief not to have to worry about having you live with us when I cut my ties with the newspaper."

"You and Mrs Eustace?" Lucy squealed, coming round to give him a hug. "Why, Hamish, I'm so happy for you."

"I haven't made any firm decisions, but my thoughts are taking me in directions I'd not expected lately," he said, still unable to stop smiling. "Now, if you'll excuse me, I have a few calls to make."

"An' I 'ave a picture ter buy, sir," said Archie, coming into the office at that moment, doffing his cap and putting down his satchel. "I met Sir Lionel in the street, an' 'e said 'e wanted ter buy a copy o' me picture I took o' the blonde beauty yer like ter keep in yer desk. Reckoned it t'would solve some age-ol' mystery that 'ad bin troublin' 'im."

Hamish opened the drawer and drew out the picture of Lily sitting on the bench next to Celeste. He gazed at it lovingly. "Sorry! You'll have to make another copy," he told Archie, tucking it into his breast pocket before putting on his bowler hat and picking up his umbrella. "Now, good day to both of you. I have much more important business than labouring here all day."

At the gate to the quiet house where Lily would live for just another week at most, Hamish paused to look up the path to the windows of the front parlour. They were half drawn, which was surprising. Sloppy housekeeping? The little maid was sweet but very young, and there was only her to attend to her lovely mistress.

He saw a flash of colour and a stirring of movement within, so he knew someone was at home.

Taking the steps two at a time, he knocked, and to his surprise, the door was flung open, revealing the little maid looking wild-eyed.

"I 'oped yer'd be the doctor come back!" she cried, twisting her hands in her apron and staring at him. "I dunno wot ter do, Mr McTavish, but mayhaps yer can 'elp me, sir. Come this way, quickly!"

Struck dumb, Hamish followed her a few steps down the passage before she thrust open the door of the parlour.

Lily was ill? He'd thought this with a lurch of his heart when the girl had greeted him, but what met his eye was infinitely worse than anything he could have conjured up on his grimmest of days.

"Lily?" He took a tentative step forward. "Lily, what is it?" Then, when there was no indication she even recognised him, he crossed the room to take her elbow and help her up from the ground where she was curled up, he now realised, apparently in fear.

Of him? Of someone else?

"Lily, tell me what's happened?"

To his horror, his touch occasioned a shrill cry of anguish, and she made a tremendous effort to remove herself from his orbit, hampered by her skirts though she did manage to put an overstuffed chair between herself and him, almost tipping it over in the process.

"I dunno wot's got inter 'er, Mr McTavish," Grace whimpered. "One minute she were right as rain, then she walks inter this room, an' next 'fing she's...like this." The confusion on Grace's face must mirror his, he thought. He glanced back at Lily, whose hair was in disarray as she raked her fingers through it, disregarding the effort she must have made that morning to fashion it into the stylish ringlets that tumbled down her back.

"Lily, you need to lie down. Rest," he soothed. "Take my hand and let me help you up." She seemed insensible to him, but he couldn't leave her cowering on the floor like some wild creature. He was frightened, but clearly not as much as she was. Her eyes were glazed with fear, and she looked at him as if he were the devil himself.

"Make them go away!" she screamed, covering her face with her hands, and hunkering into herself, swatting away his hand when he tried to help her a second time.

"Make what go away? What is it, Lily? What are you frightened of?" he tried again, his desperation rising, unable to make sense of the situation.

"The flowers!" she shrieked. "They're evil! They want to punish me! Kill me! If you don't get rid of them this instant, they're going to kill me; I know it!"

"Flowers? What flowers?" he asked, inching forwards so that he might be ready to seize her and draw her to her feet to comfort her, or at least help her to bed or somewhere she could lie down. There was nothing else to be done except call the doctor. And he couldn't do that until Lily was properly restrained.

"There!" With her eyes averted, she stabbed a finger at the walls. Hamish and Grace exchanged glances, for the floral-covered wallpaper seemed to present the only flowers he could see.

He put his head close to her ear and murmured, "Darling, there are no evil flowers that would do you harm. Only the flowers on the wallpaper."

"They're the ones!" she shrieked, becoming more agitated.

"The flowers on the wallpaper." She ventured a look at him before hunching back into herself, covering her eyes again as if unable to confront the horror of the spectacle before her and sobbing, "They've come to kill me! To punish me!"

"To punish you? To begin with, they are inanimate. They are drawings. You must try to calm yourself."

He felt helpless. Nothing he said was getting through to her. Her sobbing had grown louder, and she was now lying in a heap, her hair a tangled mess after she'd torn at it in her attempts to ward off whatever it was that was threatening her.

"And no one is going to punish you. You're a good, honest woman who has never done any harm to anyone." He had to reassure her where he could.

"I'm not, I'm not!" she wailed. "And now he's sent the flowers to kill me! I knew he'd find me. I knew he'd never let me be happy!" The pain of her distress was equally painful to Hamish, he was sure. This was the woman he realised only recently that he loved, though he'd been drawn to her for much longer. He crouched down beside her, indicating with a nod to Grace to move slowly to her other side so that she could help him.

The hand he put on her arm was reassuring and soothing. He didn't want to use force if he could help it. Surely his words would get through to her.

"No one wants to kill you, Lily. I won't let them. And I'm here now, to protect you. Who is it you're afraid of?"

"My husband! He wants to kill me! He wants me dead, and now he's sent his soldiers!"

Hamish put his mouth to her ear as he snaked an arm about her, trying to get the leverage to draw her up sufficiently so he could carry her to her bed if he had to.

"Tell me the name of your husband, Lily?" he whispered. "Just so that I know who you are afraid of."

"Robert! Sir Robert! He has always been angry with me. Especially when I became sick. He hates me, and now he's sent his soldier flowers to kill me!"

"Sir Robert Bradden is not a murderer, Lily, dearest. Even if he is you husband," Hamish reassured her as she stared at him with eyes burning with fear.

"You know Robert?" she asked. "I didn't know you knew my husband? Has he sent you to kill me?"

With another shriek, she hurled herself out of his arms, heedless of the broken glass beneath the windowsill.

Picking up the lamp that sat upon a low table, blood dripping from a cut she'd just sustained to her hand, she hurled it across the room—at his head.

Hamish ducked, the lamp shattering, just as there was a loud banging on the doorway.

"Lily!" Hamish cried more urgently as he made another attempt to comfort her. "I'm here. It's all right, my love." It didn't matter what she'd just done. She hadn't tried to injure him out of malice. All Hamish wanted was to help her.

"Sir! The doctor's 'ere, praise the lord!"

Then Hamish was being edged aside as a young man crouched beside Lily, opening his leather bag and selecting a vial of powder. "Grace. Fetch water!" he demanded with a cursory look at Hamish. "We need to get this into your mistress before she does herself any more harm."

Helplessly, Hamish gave the doctor room so he could tend to his patient. "Will she be all right?" His throat felt thick with fear.

The young man raked him with a considering look. He was in his shirtsleeves, as if he'd been summoned from a sporting match, for his light blonde hair was slicked back, and there were sweat marks beneath his armpits. "I was playing tennis, but I came as quickly as I could," he explained, following Hamish's gaze. "As to how the patient will fare, it depends." He weighed up his words. "If she's kept sedated, she will be unlikely to harm herself or others." He nodded at Grace. "You'll do everything that needs to be done, won't you, Grace? You're a good girl."

"Yes, Dr Swithins. 'Fank yer, Dr Swithins," she whispered.

Turning back to Hamish, the doctor sighed. "Sometimes patients in such a situation enjoy a year or two of relative stability. But when the insanity is upon them once more, there's no telling if they'll ever recover."

Hamish glanced from the doctor to Gracie, who sent him a stricken look. "Is there anything I can do?" he asked.

The doctor paused in the midst of administering a draught of medicine to his patient.

"The kindest thing you can do, sir, is to leave the patient to sleep out her torments in a darkened room," he replied. "If you think that the sight of you might be in the slightest bit agitating to her—even if you think she'll be pleased to see you—I strongly urge that you keep away for the next forty-eight hours."

Hamish wasn't sure he could comply. How could he stay away when Lily had never needed him more?

"I'll wait in the drawing room. I won't disturb her," he said, but the doctor shook his head.

"It's best that you remove your presence or she'll sense it. Grace will keep you informed, won't you, my girl?"

CHAPTER 28

Lily came out of the dark sludge, crawling on her hands and knees through the tunnel as she strove to reach the light. But at each turn, the light disappeared, and darkness descended once again.

Until, with a gasp, she opened her eyes and…

Found herself in her bed, staring up into the frightened face of Grace.

"Oh, ma'am, yer…yer awake. Oh, ma'am…" The young maid wrung her hands, stepping forward, then back, as if she didn't know what to do.

Lily stared about her, trying to make sense of the feelings that she was struggling to discard: the heaviness and fear. Such conflicting emotions juxtaposed with the familiarity of her surroundings—the iron bed with its pink satin eiderdown, the walls covered in pictures of dancing nymphs.

And the floral wallpaper. So ordinary. So benign.

"What happened?" she whispered, steeling herself for the answer. Grace's expression and the wave of sensation that had engulfed Lily—with its residue still lingering—were answer enough.

She had sunk back into her old ways.

The black fog had, once again, sucked her into its maw.

And now Grace had witnessed her shame. She sat up, a terrifying thought assailing her. No, she could not think of it. Of anyone else having witnessed her in the grip of her attack of...

Of insanity?

With a moan, she put her hands over her face and sank back into the pillow.

"Yer was afeared, somethin' terrible," Grace whispered, dipping a flannel into a bowl of warm water, and gently dabbing at Lily's face.

"I vaguely remember." Lily did not move. Her limbs felt leaden, and her mind was making a slumberous journey towards understanding. Sucking in a breath, she added, "But I'm fine now. It won't happen again."

Until the next time.

Yes, she knew how it would go. These attacks that enveloped her with no warning at all could happen day upon day, or she might remain unafflicted for weeks.

But they were back.

Tears of despair spilled from her eyes and dampened the pillow.

For two years, incarcerated within the *maison*—the Lunatic Asylum, she must not forget what it really was— she had been unaffected. Perhaps the cruel medications they'd imposed upon her really had worked, though she'd railed against them at the time as being torturous, not restorative.

She'd been strapped to the bed; the soles of her feet had been whipped to 'beat out the devil'. She'd been forced to drink foul concoctions.

Yes, she'd railed against all this at the time.

But at least she'd been well. The terrifying waves of

insanity that had plagued her in the year before she'd been incarcerated had been held at bay.

In the months since she'd been abducted from the *maison*, she'd remained in good physical and mental health.

But now the disease had come back to haunt her.

She truly was insane.

Struggling up, she managed a wan smile for Grace. "Thank you for looking after me," she said. "I'm sorry if I frightened you."

"Oh, yer did that, ma'am. Yer 'fought the walls was breathin' an' the flowers was devils."

Wincing, Lily glanced down at her hand, wrinkling her brow to see the bandage on her left hand.

In answer to her confusion, Grace explained, "Yer cut yerself on the broken decanter, ma'am, when yer threw the lamp at Mr McTavish's 'ead…if yer recall."

"No!" It was too much. Sobbing, Lily sank back into the pillows. It took a while for her to gain sufficient strength to even open her eyes and ask Grace, "Is he injured?"

"Not 'is person, no, ma'am."

It was little wonder that the poor maid looked as uncomfortable as she did, hovering in the doorway. Lily was a madwoman. Not only had her actions confirmed it, but perhaps the rumours of her past had caught up with her.

"I…don't know what came over me, Grace," she whispered. "I'm sure it won't happen again."

What else could she say to reassure the girl? Grace had lost her trust.

And what would Hamish think? The woman he'd professed to love such a short time before had turned into a mad creature and tried to kill him.

With another sob, she turned to look out of the window. What future was there for her? For Hamish, who said he loved her? How could she ruin his life?

Robert was coming back to claim her. She was his responsibility in the eyes of the law. He obviously found her an inconvenience, but he always did know what would benefit him. And 'dealing' with Lily would be his first priority once he reached London.

Hearing the clock chime the hour, she threw back the bedclothes and slid to the floor.

"Wot are yer doin', ma'am! Yer need ter rest!" Grace exclaimed, hurrying forward to take Grace's arm, then dropping her hand, as if she were afraid.

How could Grace blame her?

"I have a performance tonight." Lily avoided her maid and began to rummage through her wardrobe.

"Yer ain't well 'nuff, ma'am," Grace protested, but Lily ignored her.

"Mrs Renquist is waiting for me. She believes there will be answers forthcoming tonight. Yes, my green dress will do. Help me with the buttons, Grace? Grrr, I'll do them myself. Oh, Teddy!"

There he was in the doorway, a buffer blocking her as she prepared to step out into the passage, for she couldn't stay a moment longer in this torment. Robert might arrive at any moment.

And, no, she was not going to succumb to his directives and his tyranny once more. She was stronger than she had been ten minutes ago.

A pang of despair at the thought of Hamish assailed her, but she thrust it away. If anything proved her love, it would be this.

She would not inflict herself and her torments upon him and blight his life.

That is, if he even still wanted her, which was unlikely.

"My dear girl, you're not crying, are you?" Leading her back to the bed, Teddy took her hand in one of his, stroking her cheek with his other. "Come, now, my sweet thing, everything is going to be all right. You'll see. Come back to bed and rest some more, and I'll stay and comfort you. You look like you need some bolstering."

Lily stared rather stupidly at the teardrop that had splashed onto the front of her dress, staining the green fabric. She really should put a stop to these useless tears. She'd made her decision and, after Hamish had witnessed her in the very grip of an episode, he'd be only too thankful to be spared a lifetime of it.

She shouldn't feel sorrow.

But Teddy knew exactly the risks she posed. He'd come to London to claim her, despite that.

And having someone…anyone…offer comfort was a rare treat. She rested her head against his hand and closed her eyes. If she could just let her body float into oblivion. Her mind, too. But know that sometime in the future, she could open her eyes knowing everything would be all right again.

Perhaps she did drift off to sleep, for she was awoken by a tug and Teddy whispering, "Would you like that, Lily? Did you hear what I said?"

Shaking herself, she realised she was tucked up in bed again, and Teddy was sitting at her side. Close up, the years had taken their toll. He'd had such a pale, unlined skin, and such blue, blue eyes, but now there were little red veins about his nose. From a distance, he was still the same young Teddy, but up close, he had a slightly dissipated look about him.

How must she appear to him? At twenty-six, she was nearly past her bloom.

Two years in a lunatic asylum had done her no favours. She'd enjoyed a brief resurgence of her former glory when she'd been nourished back to health at Madame Chambon's, but now she knew the lines about her mouth and eyes would only get deeper. And quickly.

Madame Chambon.

Yes, that's where Mr Montpelier and Mrs Moore intended to despatch her unless someone else stepped in.

Yesterday, Hamish was going to take on that role and champion her.

She must have whimpered, for Teddy tightened his arm about her shoulders and said softly, "Yes, I will look after you, Lily. I can't bear to see you like this. Frightened. Defenceless." Tenderly, he traced the bridge of her nose before kissing its tip. "But I know how to keep you as well as you can be. It can be like the old days. Just you and me." He touched his lips to her brow, still murmuring. "Tell me that you'll let me help you. I'll find you a lovely cottage in the country where you can be quiet and undisturbed. A cottage that only you and I will know about. It'll be our secret and we can live there together. I'll protect you from the big, bad world. And from Robert who wants to send you back to the *maison*. You'd like that, wouldn't you? It would be so much better than here."

So much better than here.

Oh, yes...

"You'd really do that for me, Teddy?" She put her hand over his and tried to move closer. "Even though you know what will happen to me?" Convulsing just at the thought, she squeezed her eyes tightly shut. "Now that the madness has returned? But...you do remember how it was last time, don't you?" Panicked, she went on, "It wasn't immediate. It was slow and...only sometimes. You remember?"

"I remember, my love," he said softly. "We still have a long time to go before we need to worry. A long time. And there are new medicines to try. I'll look after you. I promise."

Relief washed over her. Teddy was going to look after

her. How she wished it was Hamish, but Hamish didn't understand how thoroughly she would ruin his life.

Despite everything, Teddy still loved her. He knew exactly what he was getting himself into, yet he still wanted to help her.

She struggled up and pushed back the covers. "I'll pack some things."

He looked surprised. "You want to go now?"

"Yes. Now. And I don't want anyone to know. I think that's best."

If Robert came to the house looking for her, he'd think she was coming back and not pursue her.

Nor would Mr Montpelier or the Russian pose such an immediate threat, either.

For the first time, Lily felt safe. And without a conscience, for she was putting no one in harm's way who didn't know the risks.

Yes, she was going to be with Teddy. He would protect her.

Later, she would send a message to Grace.

CHAPTER 29

Feeling numb and disoriented, Hamish took a hackney to Oxford Circus. He had some shopping to do which he'd been putting off for some days. A pair of shoes for himself. He'd also long planned to buy Lily some gloves; a fancy that had visited him through the observation of her hands—a poignant transformation from those of a laundry woman's into those of a lady.

But he couldn't shop. Couldn't keep his mind on anything.

Of course, he'd accepted that life with Lily was never going to be easy. She was not free to marry. Old McTavish senior would probably deny him the financial compensation he was due.

But Hamish had fallen in love, and nothing was going to stand in the way of that.

Seeing her today had been heartbreaking.

He'd been so helpless.

But what about the future?

Really, he had no idea what course her illness would take.

He just knew he wanted to be with her.

Instead of treading the pavements of Oxford Street, he decided to go to his club.

With a newspaper and a whisky to occupy himself, he settled himself in a corner of White's, and went over everything that had happened during the past couple of hours.

When he lowered the newspaper to take a sip of his drink, he was accosted by a friend who invited himself to join Hamish, ordering a whisky from the waiter.

"Everyone is talking of the Ned Kelly Gang in the colonies," remarked his companion, Freddy Styles, glancing at the headlines. "No doubt I shall read something about it in your own sermonising periodical that reminds us lesser mortals that only the righteous shall prosper." The corners of his mouth turned up, but Hamish didn't respond, and he went on, "I was speaking to Sir Lionel over there. Told me you'd interviewed him for an upcoming piece. Apparently, Sir Lionel was a bit of a brigand in his day—though not in the fashion of Mr Kelly. I look forward to reading it. When will it be published?"

Hamish rose at his words, glad of the excuse and distraction. "Over there, you say? Then I must catch him, as there are some finer details I need to clarify with him before it goes to print. Excuse me."

He'd intended this as a ruse to avoid Styles but, in fact, as Hamish crossed the room, Sir Lionel looked up and hailed him.

Hamish had no choice but to go over.

"Was talking about you not long ago, m'boy. About that woman your man photographed. Dash it if she hasn't plagued me these past few days?"

"Mrs Eustace? The spiritualist?" Hamish prompted.

"You see, I thought it was Lady Bradden. Such a likeness."

Hamish stilled. He had to nip this in the bud. "And then

you realised it wasn't," he said, as if it was a fact, sinking into an overstuffed chair by the fire.

"Couldn't be, I realised. Poor woman died six months ago after being incarcerated in a lunatic asylum on the Continent."

Hamish's scalp felt tight, and his chest constricted. "Really?"

"Yes, saw her obituary in The Times." Sir Lionel took a contemplative sip of his whisky and raised one eyebrow, adding, "written by her grieving husband."

Before Hamish could respond, he went, "My daughter met her once, when we visited them. Seemed uncommonly intrigued, though I tried to temper her interest. Not the sort of thing to expose your daughter to."

Hamish looked at him enquiringly.

"Lady Bradden's affair. Talk of the town it was. Or, rather, after guilt sent her mad. But now she's dead."

"She had an affair?" Hamish realised he'd spoken too loudly. A crackling of newspapers broke the silence of the hushed atmosphere at the club as various members sent disapproving glances in his direction.

"Ah well," Hamish said dismissively. "I daresay that's of no account now, if the lady is no longer with us."

In the midday light, there was a greyish pallor to the old man's complexion. He didn't look as robust as he had when he'd taken whisky with Hamish not so long ago.

"Dash it if I didn't do some investigating." Sir Lionel leaned down and picked up a satchel at his feet. From it, he withdrew a photographic plate. He clearly wasn't about to let the matter drop. "I found this taken of a house party I attended at Sir Bradden's in Norfolk three years ago. That's when my daughter met the woman."

Hamish took the photograph and held it to the light.

About ten people were clustered together by the portico

of a gracious manor house. Hamish squinted, recognising Sir Lionel in the front row before his gaze ran the length of the visitors, and then found the host and hostess seated a little to the right.

His breath hitched. The petite woman next to Sir Lionel was staring with fierce intensity at the camera, a jaunty bonnet upon her curled hair. On her striped skirts, she nursed a small dog. Beside her, a much older man scowled, a proprietorial hand upon her arm.

Lily.

Hamish cleared his throat. "This is Lady Bradden?" he clarified.

Hamish could not draw his gaze from the photograph. There was a wildness to the woman's eyes that reminded him of Lily as he'd seen her just now. She wore her beauty like a disguise. It was there if he looked closely enough, but the grimness of her expression and the wildness in her eyes was more arresting than anything else.

Sir Lionel nodded. "She came to London once, perhaps twice, but she was very much under her husband's thumb being so very young and he, so much older and disinterested."

Hamish peered closer. "Yes, her husband… does appear a good deal older." He tried to puzzle it out.

"It was the unhappiest marriage I ever witnessed, but little wonder for her father allowed her no say in the matter, and was as anxious as any I ever knew to despatch his daughter to the first taker."

Was Sir Lionel touched in the head to speak in such a frank manner to Hamish? Were his faculties deserting him? Hamish had not thought so a week ago.

Now, when he looked closer at the old man, he discerned a pent-up passion that also had been absent during their convivial conversation about Sir Lionel's claims to the fame and notoriety he was so willing to boast about.

Embarrassed, Hamish cleared his throat. "I'm sure many marriages are so," he dissembled. He knew his parents' union had fallen into that category.

"This one was particularly... cruel." Sir Lionel twisted his head to look at him with rheumy eyes. "There was talk at the time that her father, old Tavener, conducted matters with particular disregard for the feelings of his only child." He cleared his throat. "I think I told you that, after my own experiences with the fellow, I didn't hold him in high regard." He reached down and withdrew another photograph from his satchel. "Do you know this young woman?" he asked, passing it across.

Uncertain what was expected of him, Hamish held the photograph to the light. It was of a couple he had never seen. An older, bewhiskered gentleman, and a girl of perhaps sixteen, for she was still in short skirts and her hair was braided.

He squinted, for the shadow of the photograph made it difficult to discern her features properly; however, the strong resemblance made him ask, "Is this Lady Bradden as a girl? With her father, perhaps?" He could see the shape of her jaw was the same as was the set of her eyes.

"This is Lord Lambton's late daughter, Miss Cassandra."

Hamish gave a start. "Lord Lambton's daughter?" She was, of course, the woman whom Lily was supposedly speaking to, from 'the other side'.

Sir Lionel considered Hamish's obvious surprise. "You knew her?"

"My sister did," said Hamish. "They went to school together." He paused, then said, carefully, "I believe her father has taken the death of his only child very hard."

Sir Lionel appeared agitated. He shifted in his seat, and his mouth worked as if words eluded him. Finally, he muttered, "That's the thing. I couldn't get it out of my mind after I saw the photograph you showed me of the woman who so greatly resembled Lady Bradden. I'd had my doubts long before, but then dismissed them. Then, of course, you dug up the past with your questions when I came to your office to be interviewed. What you said, and the picture you showed me, aroused my suspicions. So I asked my daughter to locate a photograph of Cassandra."

At Hamish's raised eyebrows, he elucidated, "My daughter has a friend who was godmother to the young lady, and she supplied this." He held up the image. "And the time frame fits. I'd wager my suspicions are right on the money."

"What suspicions?" Despite himself, Hamish was becoming as agitated as Sir Lionel, though trying not to show it. He took a breath, and forced himself to remain seated, calmly, as Sir Lionel went on, "Fact is, I think I've hit upon the root of the mystery." He gave a satisfied nod. "I don't believe Cassandra was Lord Lambton's only child."

Hamish waited tensely, afraid to prompt the old man when he paused as if he couldn't find the words he wanted to say.

Finally, he went on. "The duel I mentioned between Lord Lambton and Sir John Taverner? The duel where I stepped up as second?"

"Sir John... Taverner?" Hamish repeated, his mind running round in circles. Tavener? Surely not... Lily's father?

Sir Lionel worried at his lower lip. "I had given little thought to it for years. Then, seeing that photograph of the woman I took to be Lady Bradden, well... I realised two things."

"Two things?"

The old man didn't hesitate. In fact, Sir Lionel seemed very eager to respond.

"First, it is my belief that Lady Bradden was, in fact, Lord Lambton's love child. The timing fits. I did some investigation and learned that Sir John Taverner's wife died in childbirth eight months after the duel between himself and Lord Lambton. Lambton, you see, had been having an affair with Sir John's wife. Of course, when the brat was born so soon afterwards, Sir John would have nothing to do with the infant. The girl, Lily, was brought up by a spinster aunt, and then her father—or supposed father—married her off to Bradden."

Hamish stared. What response could he give to this?

Sir Lionel believed that Lily was Lord Lambton's illegitimate daughter?

He swallowed, and then because he didn't know what else to say, asked—though it was more of a croak, "And the second thing?"

Sir Lionel's agitation grew. "I believe young Cassandra didn't die of fever in her bed, or in the insane hospital, or anywhere else that people care to speculate." He shook his head. "No, I believe she ran away. Yes, ran away! Only Lord Lambton would rather the world thought she was dead. Don't ask me how she ran away. But that photograph that you showed me—"

"This one?" Hamish asked, sliding his hand into his breast pocket and producing the photograph of Celeste and Lily.

Sir Lionel nodded, clearly not thinking it strange that Hamish should keep the photograph so close to his heart. "That's the one. I believe it is her." Triumphantly, he finished, "I believe Lord Lambton's daughter, Cassandra, is this woman, Mrs Eustace. Only no one knows it, what with her being veiled and mysterious." He winked. "Mystery solved.

Rumour had it that Miss Cassandra was a little touched in the head. I think she's milking her father's grief, supposedly from the other side. Just you wait, though—" He chuckled— "The grand reveal will come soon enough, only I've already solved the mystery."

Hamish was silent.

A waiter came by to offer them more drinks, but Sir Lionel declined. "I should get home before it gets dark," he said. "Not as steady on my pins as I used to be." He stretched. "As for Lambton's love child... well, sad story, that one. Her father never gave her the time of day. Nor did that husband of hers. Can't imagine why old Bradden didn't appreciate his good fortune at having such a beautiful wife, though of course the fellow already had a mistress. He was well looked after. But the girl—Lady Bradden—was not just a beauty; she was a kind soul. Kind to me, who was already an old man. Kind to those in service to her, so I heard. Ah, but I'm just being sentimental. I recall the night she sat and talked with me when my only daughter was sick with the scarlet fever, and I thought I might lose her. She could have been making merry, but instead she was reassuring a querulous old father when she was no older than my Dottie." He dabbed at his eyes with a snowy handkerchief.

"I hope your daughter —?"

"She survived the fever and is now mother to three, happily married. I have no concerns on her behalf. A fond and doting daughter with a fond and doting husband. But Lady Bradden never had anyone to see to her." He lifted a shoulder. "Why do I think of it now? There was always a sense of sadness clinging to her, despite her beauty. I remember the visit I paid to Norfolk and the sense I had that —Lady Bradden had no one. Well, except that personal physician who got his claws into her through her husband's conniving. Now, he was a charlatan," he muttered. "Lady Bradden's personal physician, my foot. Bah!"

"A charlatan?" Hamish prompted, clutching at anything to detain Sir Lionel, who looked ready to depart.

Fortunately, Sir Lionel obviously enjoyed an excuse to gossip.

"Fellow used his influence for all the advantage he could squeeze out of the situation. Saw it with my own eyes over several visits. He took a healthy, virtuous woman, and twisted her into something that was poisonous in her husband's eye. Became her lover to do the job. Well, she's dead now and more's the pity. Helped greatly to her end by that bounder of a doctor. Sir Robert Bradden and I have little to say to one another these days, so I'll tell it like it is." He gave a short laugh. "I always thought he and old Taverner had something going on there, but what would I know? Full of conspiracies, my daughter likes to tell me."

Hamish was not ready to let Sir Lionel go. The urgency to detain him so he could answer more of Hamish's burning questions precluded finesse. "So this doctor was Lady Bradden's lover?" he asked as Sir Lionel struggled to his feet. Lily had confessed as much, of course. "But, you say, Sir Robert also had a mistress?"

"Yes. For years. Local squire's wife. Widow, now. Married her last month. They're coming to London in a few days, in fact. Bumped into that toad-eater, Dr Swithins, and he told me." With a groan, Sir Lionel stretched each leg and shook a foot in turn, before reaching for the photograph he'd left on the table.

"Dr Swithins?"

The name echoed round Hamish's brain. Dr Swithins? It was disturbingly familiar.

"Yes, the late Lady Bradden's personal physician?" A look of confusion flitted across Sir Lionel's face. "You recall him, surely? In that photograph? Blonde, smarmy-looking fellow." He held up the photograph, tapping the face of a young man with fair hair and the distinct look of a lady's man. Standing in the back row, partially concealed, it only took one glance for Hamish to recognise him as Sir Lionel said with a sneer, "Smarmy Swithins. That's the feller. Thought I'd told you."

CHAPTER 30

There was no time to lose. Hamish had to get to Shepherd Market as fast as he could. Dr Swithins was not the caring physician Lily believed him to be. While he might have some knowledge of how to ease Lily's anguish and ameliorate, if not shorten her episodes of insanity, Sir Lionel clearly thought he was an unhealthy influence on her.

Hamish was just trying to piece together the many strands of Sir Lionel's rather disjointed series of fact, fantasy, and conspiracy, when he saw Miniver hurrying along the pavement near the offices of McTavish & Son as Hamish was about to flag down a hackney.

"Sir, there's a constable waiting for you in your office," the young man told him. "Apparently, it's important. I've come looking for you, as I knew you were at your club."

A policeman? Hamish's hand went to his temple. Something had happened. But then, of course, what did anyone know of his involvement with Lady Bradden? Lily.

"Lucy?" This was his next fear.

"Your sister went to visit a friend," said Miniver, and with that reassurance, Hamish hurried up the steps to his office where the policeman, who introduced himself as Inspector Webb, was seated in the chair across from his desk.

"If you'd be so good as to answer some questions of a private nature, sir. Hopefully, I won't take up too much of your time."

Hamish nodded, hiding his impatience for he was burning to locate Lily. Even if she were still in the grip of her anguish, Hamish would find her proper medical care. He would dispense with Dr Swithins's services, that was certain.

Hamish was now in charge. He would look after Lily and, perhaps, under his tender ministrations, she would find greater periods of peace and tranquility.

"Can I then ask you, sir, to what extent you are a regular at Madame Chambon's?"

Hamish jerked his head up. Unexpectedly, blood burned his cheeks. Surreptitiously, he gripped the edge of the table. "I am not even a casual visitor, Inspector."

"Do you deny that you have visited the establishment, sir?"

"I don't deny it, but I had a good reason for going there. One that was not connected to," he hesitated, "the usual reason a gentleman might visit." Disliking the look in the other man's eye, Hamish added defensively, "I do not consort with the women of Madame Chambon's establishment, and I have no idea why you should accuse me of anything in relation to—"

"I am not accusing you of anything." The inspector scratched his jaw. "I am conducting an investigation into why your name should be mentioned in a letter found in the bedchamber of one of Madame Chambon's girls, now, unfortunately, deceased."

"Dear God, no!" With a start, he could only imagine it was

Lily, given his current fears, but then, she was at home, in Shepherd Market. No, it could not be her.

The inspector studied him with interest and, when Hamish had calmed himself, asked, with as little emotion as the man before him, "Dead? Please elaborate, Inspector. Who is dead?"

"A woman known simply as Celeste, though we are searching for her full identity. None of the girls with whom she… er… worked… knew where she came from or, indeed, what her real name was."

"Celeste?" Hamish ran a hand across his brow.

Dead? Did she take her own life? Die of any number of medical complications?

"The young woman was murdered sometime last night."

"Murdered?" he repeated. "Good God! And my name was in a letter in her possession? Do you have a suspect?" The questions tumbled out before he even realised that he may indeed be the suspect. "What did the letter say?" His throat felt dry. "Has she accused me of something?"

"Your name was mentioned in her diary, in fact. And no, she has not accused you of anything. It appears that she had intended to seek your assistance over some matter involving another woman by the name of Lily Eustace." The inspector cocked his head at Hamish's reaction and asked in a tone that indicated he already knew the answer. "You are acquainted with this woman?"

Hamish nodded. "I am." Then, "What did Celeste say with regard to my… interest in Mrs Eustace?"

"Interest, was it?" He looked interested himself. "She doesn't mention that, sir, but she does indicate concern regarding this Mrs Eustace. A certain disdain for her, also, but ultimately, a concern."

So, Celeste had witnessed Lily's wild moods, perhaps, and was afraid? Hamish knew they'd shared a room for some weeks. Had Lily exhibited the kind of wild, erratic moods that had frightened Celeste?

He was almost too afraid to ask the question. "You believe Mrs Eustace had something to do with Celeste's murder?"

"Mrs Eustace? Where did you get that idea, sir? No, Celeste was throttled by a very powerful pair of hands. Not a woman's hands. Celeste was afraid of one of her particular gentleman friends who had indicated a desire to harm Mrs Eustace."

Before he could stop himself, Hamish burst out, "Not the Russian?"

"Mr Igor Novichov sounds a very Russian name, doesn't it, then, sir? And this is the man who the late Celeste thought intended harm to her friend, Mrs Eustace. Apparently, he'd threatened Mrs Eustace in the street, and then, in company with Miss Celeste, elaborated upon a most specific form of injury, and Miss Celeste was in two minds whether to warn her. Sadly, she ended up losing her own life." He hesitated, looking at Hamish as if suggesting he might know more than he was giving away.

Hamish, meanwhile, remembered the night he'd dismissed Lily's fears and suspicions over Mr Novichov. Yes, dismissed them. He'd thought she was overreacting. Later, he'd assumed this paranoia was part of her illness.

Now Celeste was dead? He felt ill.

"Mrs Eustace must be warned," Hamish said.

"We are not concerned with Mrs Eustace right now. But many of Miss Celeste's diary entries mention the Russian and a certain Mr Montpelier. We would like to direct our enquiries there."

"I am not a suspect?" Hamish needed to leave but couldn't show his agitation.

Celeste was dead.

Lily was in danger.

A sudden horror occurred to him. Miniver had said Lucy was visiting a friend. Lucy had declared her intention to visit Mrs Eustace. But no, she'd not know her address.

That said, Lucy was cunning. There was every chance that Lucy had found the note that included Lily's address and had made her way to Mayfair. He needed to terminate the discussion.

"Not at this stage, sir. We hoped you might shed some light on the whereabouts of these other two gentlemen."

Hamish shook his head and, finally, with the inspector taking his leave, snatched up his hat and, hastily buttoning up his coat, hurried into the cold winter air to find a conveyance to take him to Mrs Eustace's house.

Lily might be in danger from unknown forces, but Lucy was equally at risk.

TELLING the cab driver to wait for him when he drew up outside Lily's house, he leapt out and strode up the pathway to the front door.

The parlour was dim, with the heavy curtains allowing just a chink of light to spill out onto the pavement outside.

Hamish knocked loudly. The drumming of his heart was loud in his ears, and his anxiety was at fever pitch.

He heard running footsteps and then the maid threw open the door, her face a mask of terror as she cried, "Sir, come quickly, sir! She's gone mad! Quite mad an' I don't know wot ter do."

He closed his eyes briefly. He could hear the noise. Lily was in the grip of another episode.

"Where is the doctor?" he asked, striding up the passage, but Grace shook her head wildly, saying only, "He's gone, sir!

But suddenly she came over all queer. Jest like me mistress. I don't know wot ter do, sir!"

Hamish could hear the cries of a woman issuing from the parlour to his left, and then the sound of breaking glass. Lily, his poor beloved, was obviously in there. He'd go to her shortly. But first, he needed to locate his sister.

"Where is Lucy?" he asked, more urgently now, for Lucy was not in the scullery. "She's not in the parlour with Mrs Eustace, surely?" No, the maid would not have locked his own sister in a room with a madwoman.

"She's in the parlour, sir—"

"Dear god! You mean she is with Mrs Eustace?"

"No, sir. Only 'er!"

"But who in God's name is making all that racket? Surely not my sister?"

"Yes, sir! 'Tis Miss Lucy. I dunno know wot got inter 'er. She came visitin', but Mrs Eustace 'ad already left."

"What do you mean, Mrs Eustace had already left? Lucy wouldn't simply behave like this for no reason, and—"

He didn't finish, turning to stride up the passage once more and to throw open the door, stepping back in horror as he confronted his sister with her hair in disarray and her eyes wild, clawing at some unknown adversary.

"What has happened to her? What have you done to her?" Hamish swung round, and the maid shrank back.

"Nuffink sir. Nuffink at all. I dunno wot's come over 'er."

"The same thing that came over Mrs Eustace it would appear," Hamish said over his shoulder as he ventured cautiously towards Lucy, his tone soft and soothing. "Lucy, my love, what is it? Why are you like this?"

She tried to focus on him, but what he was to her was clearly so horrific that she crumpled into a ball on the floor and covered her head with her arms. "Don't let them get to me!" she shrieked. "Save me, please! The flowers have knives. Little daggers."

"Hush, Lucy." Hamish went down on his haunches and attempted to put a hand on her back, but she lurched at the contact, shrieking as if he were one of those who would do her harm.

Hamish leaned protectively over her, twisting his head to demand of the maid, who was clearly as frightened as he, "What has come over her? She didn't arrive like this, surely?"

"No sir, she were quite calm." Grace held her apron to her face and wailed. "I cannot 'xplain it. She were disappointed that Mrs Eustace 'ad left, so I offered 'er some tea."

Lucy clawed at him. Hamish was barely attending to the maid's explanation, but he repeated, "Tea? So she took tea and then went... mad?"

"No, sir. I suggested warm milk, as it were so cold out an' wiv Mrs Eustace out, I 'ad a little left over."

"So, simply warm milk?"

"Yes, sir. Jest warm milk wiv some o' the soothin' powders the doctor give me ter calm Mrs Eustace."

Hamish snapped his head up. "Dr Swithins?"

"Yes, sir."

"And where is Dr Swithins now?"

"He already took me mistress wiv 'im afore Miss McTavish arrived, sir."

Hamish rose, casting a final glance at Lucy, who was crouched by the chair, her unfocused gaze fixed upon the flock wallpaper. "Show me these powders." A fearful thought assailed him as he added, "Presuming you did not give the last to my sister."

"No, sir. Dr Swithins give me 'nuff ter last a good long while," said Grace, leading the way through to the scullery. "'E said she'd need 'em wheneva she were feelin' poorly or, ev'ry few days if she didn't complain o' anythin'. 'E said the powders would build up 'er constitution."

"Did he?" replied Hamish with bitter irony as he took the bag of powders Grace handed him.

He tried to think clearly, distracted by another shriek from the parlour.

Obviously, he had to get Lucy home and looked after, but in her current state, he didn't know that was possible.

But, in view of everything Sir Lionel had told him, he realised his greatest urgency was to find Lily.

One woman was dead already.

"Where did the doctor say he was taking Mrs Eustace?"

"'E didn't say, sir."

"Did he take her forcibly?"

Grace shook her head. "No, sir. 'Tis in the note," she said, handing a piece of paper to Hamish. "Me mistress went wiv 'im 'cos she said it were the kindest fing ter do fer ev'ryone, unda the circumstances."

CHAPTER 31

Lily awoke in a rather chilly chamber of a dwelling which, based on the strong smell of beer, she took to be a tavern.

The fire had been allowed to die, and the light was dim.

Shivering, she drew the counterpane about her shoulders as she sat up, looking for something with which to orient herself.

By the window was a writing desk, covered with some correspondence which, she knew, wasn't hers.

She looked about to find Teddy, but the room was empty.

Her eyes felt gritty, and her head throbbed. That, of course, was due to her recent attack.

Despair washed over her once more. Once the insanity took hold, there was no saying when it would strike. She was completely at its mercy, and it was only because Teddy loved her he was prepared to look after her.

But for how long? He'd taken her to the *maison* in Brussels, after all.

Climbing out of bed, she went to the desk. She needed to write to Hamish and apologise properly. A small sob made her shudder, and she put her head in her hands. She'd have given her soul to have been with him.

A letter half out of its envelope fell to the floor, and when she reached for it, the sheets fell loose upon her lap, the salutation and an endearment making her gasp, just as the door opened and Teddy stepped in.

"Lily—" He stopped when he saw what she had in her hands, and the pleasure drained from his face.

"You told me you weren't married," Lily whispered. Hadn't he insinuated as much, if not said so in as many words?

The realisation went to the core of her being. So...he wasn't free to help Lily? Not truly. Not if he had a wife and perhaps children.

"It doesn't change what I feel for you," he said quickly, crossing the room to take her in his arms. "I was afraid you'd not come with me if you knew."

"Of course, I wouldn't have," she whispered, drawing away to stare into the dying embers. "How could you possibly have thought you could help me if your obligations are naturally with your wife?"

She felt quite clearheaded right now. It was as if the illness had completely fallen away, like a cloak, from her shoulders, and she could see Teddy for what he really was.

"Lily, don't be angry. It's because I love you so much that I was afraid to tell you." He went to stand behind her, wrapping his arms about her, and kissing the top of her head. "I was afraid you wouldn't come with me."

"You're taking me to the *maison*, aren't you?" She jerked around to look at him, her tone accusing.

"You were well at the *maison*, Lily. They cured you, didn't they?" He put his hands on her shoulders. "Don't you see? I want what's best for you. That's all I've ever wanted. Think back to how I loved you. Cared for you."

Lily bit her lip as she dropped her gaze. He did look tortured and sincere. And he had been there for her, caring for her, loving her, when Robert had been so cold and distant.

But... he had a wife.

He was still talking, she realised, his tone caressing and cajoling, like the old days. "You never had another bout like the ones that had caused you such distress before I took you to the *maison*. But I know how much you hated it there. I wouldn't take you if you didn't want to go. I want to do whatever makes you happy."

Lily broke away and went to the window to stare out at the docks.

"You don't really love me, Teddy," she whispered. "How could you—" her voice broke—"if you've married someone else."

"Oh, my darling, don't be like that!" He looked frightened for a moment. "It's always been you. I...I just thought I'd lost you before, but now...Now we are together again, at last. And if you don't believe I love you, then look what I bought you!" He smiled as he thrust a hand into his right pocket, withdrawing a small box which he held before her.

Lily waited, resting against the window as she watched him cautiously.

"Don't you want to see what it is?" He took a step closer, opening the box and then removing a ring with a large diamond that twinkled in the light.

Lily gasped, for it truly was beautiful.

"Give me your hand."

Obediently, she held it out while he slipped it onto her left ring finger, where it sat loosely.

"I was afraid it would be too big, but... here, let's put it on a ribbon. We'll take one from your hair. You can wear it next to your heart until—"

"Until what?" she prompted in a whisper.

"Until it can be resized," said Teddy, as he worked, before slipping the ring on its pink ribbon over her head. Taking her into his arms, he gave her a squeeze. "Don't worry, my love. I won't let them take you to another sanitarium, for I shall look after you and make sure you get all the care you need."

She wavered. Teddy really did look as if he would do anything for her, and it was true that, for all its evil, the *maison* had wrought some kind of cure.

She closed her eyes, listening to the sound of seagulls through the window. "I don't know what to do, Teddy?" she whispered as she fingered the ring which nestled against her breast. She hadn't thanked him properly, and she knew he'd be out of sorts. She wondered if the ring had belonged to someone else and was just a sop.

Regardless of the truth, she was in his hands now. Once again, her fate was in the hands of others.

"I think you need to comb your hair, and then go for a bracing long walk with me."

Despite herself, she smiled at the encouragement in his voice.

"And what will a walk achieve?"

"Hopefully, some enthusiasm for the future." He drew her against him once more and gently stroked her cheek as she put her head on his shoulder. "There's a brisk wind coming over the sea, and the fresh salty air will be a tonic in itself. You've not seen this part of the country before. We've travelled quite some distance north. But it's very beautiful with its majestic cliffs and all manner of sea birds." Putting his face close to hers, he smiled. "Come for a walk with me, Lily, and we can discuss the future. Our future. You can have faith in me to do only what's best for you. I won't send you to the *maison* if you don't want to go."

"If I don't go to a *maison* to cure me, where will I go, Teddy?" she asked, determined not to cry. "And you are married now. It changes everything. We can't be as we were."

For a long time, he gazed into her eyes. She wanted to think he cared for her, but really, the truth didn't matter. She just needed someone to love her. To have her best interests at heart, for once.

And maybe she'd misjudged Teddy.

When he lowered his face to kiss her lightly on the mouth, she let him, though her mind conjured up Hamish and all the sweet memories of what it had felt like to be in his arms.

But Hamish deserved so much more.

"Come for a walk by the cliff with me, Lily. I may be married, but so are you. And I want to discuss a way that we truly can be together. Forever."

CHAPTER 32

I t had been one of the hardest decisions of Hamish's life to leave Lucy wailing and moaning, locked up in the parlour, albeit in Grace's care and waiting for Dr Makim while he hurried back to the waiting cab and continued his journey.

He'd experienced doubt and fear, wondering what he should and could do. Feelings that were very similar to when he'd concluded that there could be no future between himself and Lily because she was married. And mad.

Now, he strongly suspected that only one of these was true.

Lily may well not be mad, and an analysis of the powder in the bag Grace had given him would prove, he feared, that Lucy also was a victim.

But if Dr Swithins had committed evil acts in the past, he may well be on his way to committing the most evil of all unless Hamish discovered Lily in time.

Though where would he even begin looking?

Inspector Ryan would, under no circumstances, allow

Hamish access to Celeste's diary, he was told when he was shown into his office. That had been his first idea. Not that Hamish thought Igor Novichov had any link with the doctor.

No, Dr Swithins was a man from Lily's more distant past, and the only person Hamish could think of who might wield some influence and who possibly might suggest other avenues lived in a handsome residence in Hampstead.

Hamish leapt out of the hackney when it came to a stop. Although the hour was late and Lord Lambton may already be in bed, the urgency for action was too great.

At first, there was no response to his loud knocking, but finally he was admitted by the butler and, after a lengthy negotiation, Lord Lambton himself appeared in the drawing room where Hamish had been led to wait.

The old man looked distinctly out of sorts as he shuffled in wearing a brightly patterned silk dressing gown and tasseled cap, and his first words after Hamish had done his best to explain his visit indicated his scepticism. Nevertheless, his curiosity was piqued.

"What is this information you have for me that it can't wait until the morning? You might not be as bad as the grubby newspaper reporter after a story, but that's your trade, isn't it?"

"*Manners & Morals* is hardly hack journalism," Hamish protested as he glanced at the canvases upon the wall. The man had an art collection the like of which he'd never seen, and he wondered if his wealth and privilege would make him insensible to reason as he added, "No, I'm here about your daughter."

Hamish saw him wince. "Cassandra died eight months ago. There's nothing more to be said on the matter."

"I'm not talking about that daughter," Hamish said, trying to contain his agitation and to keep his voice calm. "I'm talking about your daughter by—" He sought for a name. "I'm talking about your daughter by Sir John Taverner's wife."

Indignation left Lord Lambton's body like a deflating balloon. The strength also seemed to leave his legs, for he collapsed suddenly upon the nearest chair. "Susan?"

Carefully Hamish clarified, "Sir John Taverner's wife was called Susan? Yes, Susan. She bore her husband a child eight months after the duel you fought with Sir John."

Lord Lambton blinked rapidly. "Susan said nothing to me…" He trailed off, looking bewildered. "She went to the Continent where I learned she'd died." Jerking his head round to face Hamish, he added sharply, "If this is a ploy to extract money from me—"

"No, my lord, please hear me out." Hamish knew he had to tread carefully, but time was of the essence. Reaching into his pocket, he pulled out the photograph of Lily and Celeste. "Look carefully at the blonde woman."

"But that's Mrs Eustace. Yes, the likeness is extraordinary." His expression softened. "It gives me pleasure to look upon her face and imagine it is my own Cassandra communicating with me from beyond the grave."

"It's more than a likeness, my lord." Hamish leaned in and tapped the photograph. "This woman may go by the name Mrs Eustace, but in truth, she is the daughter of Susan, Lady Taverner—"

"That is not possible!"

Hamish nodded. "Sir Lionel told me of the duel in which he was your second. It was he who voiced his suspicions about Mrs Eustace's parentage when he came to my office with a photograph of Cassandra." He waited, watching the confusion flit across the old man's face. Slowly and clearly, he repeated, "Mrs Eustace is the daughter who was born eight months after that duel, and I've only just learned the truth of it."

Of course, it was difficult for Lord Lambton to grasp the entirety of it all.

He shook his head, then fell back into his chair by the fire, his hand to his heart. "And if she is my daughter, why knock so urgently on my door at such a late hour?" He sent Hamish a narrow look as he added perspicaciously, "Unless you had a very good reason for doing so."

So, Hamish explained the police inspector's visit, investigating the murder of a young woman whose diary had outlined the threat one of her male consorts had made against Lily.

"But why now? Why tonight?" he asked peevishly. "This does sound rather far-fetched, Mr McTavish. Normally, I would send you away. But knowing your father and the periodical of which you are highly esteemed as its editor, a god-fearing man of moderated impulses, I will indulge you. Why do you suppose this young woman, who may or may not be my daughter, is in danger?"

It was only through repeating to Lord Lambton all that he'd learnt this afternoon, that Hamish had pieced together the possibilities that might outline crime and motive.

"Because your daughter married Lord Bradden, who, believing her dead, has now married his long-time mistress." Hamish realised his foot was tapping a rapid tattoo in his agitation and forced himself to stop. If he was to be of any help to Lily, he needed to remain calm. "And I suspect that the doctor who cared for Lady Bradden during her marriage, and who himself delivered her to a lunatic asylum in Brussels, has a vested interest in ensuring that the fiction of her death becomes fact."

The old man adjusted his tasseled cap and regarded Hamish from beneath his beetling brows.

"It's nearly midnight, McTavish, and you've ensured I won't sleep a wink now that you've stirred up not only memories but the fear of God with your talk of threats to what might be my last remaining daughter." He's started off crossly but now he spoke in plaintive tones as he asked, "If my daughter has left with the man you believe intends to harm her and you have no idea where they've gone, I don't know what you expect me to do."

Hamish, too, had agonised over exactly the same thing.

Now, all he could say was, "If, by the grace of God, she manages to escape the fiendish clutches of this villain, Swithins, then I hoped you might know of the one place she might seek sanctuary when everyone else has failed her."

For Lily would surely not run from Dr Swithin's arms back to Madame Chambon's so soon after Celeste's murder?

Lord Lambton hesitated, then said slowly, "You are suggesting that I furnish you with Sir John Taverner's address?"

Hamish nodded. "I believe it's the only place she has left to go."

Lord Lambton rose upon a harrumph of disgust. "I'll need time to change and to send a boy to rouse my coachman."

"I'm not asking you to accompany me, Lord Lambton."

The elderly gentleman sent a grim look over he shoulder as he headed towards the door. "If even half of what you have told me is true, then I need to settle some matters with Sir John that should have been settled a long time ago." Flicking aside the tassel of his cap, he wiped the back of his hand across his rheumy eyes, then added, pointing, "There's the bell pull. Organise some refreshment for the journey. We'll be some hours on the road but my coach is comfortable. We should manage to get some sleep before we surprise the miserly old hermit." He gave a grim laugh and Hamish was surprised at the sudden energy as the old man muttered, "Sir John never expected he'd ever see me again, I don't doubt. Well, he's done enough damage and caused me enough pain.

You've not said what your particular interest is in this young lady, and if half of what you've said about who she really is is true, I'll need you to give a full accounting of yourself. But now," he finished with a curl of his lip as he put his hand on the doorknob, "it's time Sir John Taverner got his reckoning."

CHAPTER 33

Lily had decided she did not want to go walking by the cliff with Teddy, and now she was standing her ground in the tavern bedchamber. She felt frail and emotionally exhausted. And his insistence was grating on her.

Yes, he'd rescued her and declared he was going to look after her into the future, but he'd said that before.

So many men in her life had reneged on their obligations or their promises to look after her.

"Please, let me sleep a little, Teddy." She sank down upon the window seat by the open casement. "I'll walk with you when I've regained my strength a little." She tried for an ameliorating smile, but he seemed anxious.

"It's not sleep you need; it's exercise," he said peevishly. "I'm the doctor; I know what's good for you. Come, you're wearing a walking dress and sensible boots. Come for a walk with me. It's getting late and the light will fade soon. Tomorrow, we'll buy new clothes for you. You'd like that, wouldn't you? A nice new hat with ribbons and flowers?"

He spoke as if she were a child with limited faculties. But

then, that's how people spoke to a madwoman. That's how he viewed her.

She covered her face with her hands and glimpsed the bed through her interlaced fingers. That's where she'd spend the night. With Teddy.

Once, it would have been a dream come true. Teddy's comforting arms round her, his tenderness at such odds with Robert's callous disregard for her feelings.

But Teddy's insistence was too much. She was too weak to resist.

Too weak to do anything except what the next man wanted, she thought with part resignation and part bitterness, as she let Teddy tie her bonnet beneath her chin as if she were an invalid.

"There! Don't you look ravishing?" he declared, his smile bolstering, which did a little to improve her spirits.

Raising the back of her hand to his lips, he murmured, "Have faith, my darling, our happiness will prevail. Remember, I am the only man who has ever truly cared for you. I thought I'd lost you once, but now I have come back. Doesn't my return prove how much I would sacrifice to be with you? There now, you are safe with me." He patted her hand once he'd tucked it into the crook of his elbow, and they walked to the door.

Lily tried to think clearly.

She'd thought Hamish had loved her; and maybe he had. But he hadn't believed her. Hadn't believed *in* her.

And he wasn't here. Not like Teddy.

Perhaps it was time to resign herself to continuing to live life in the shadows as Teddy's mistress. She would never regain her former status in society, and the sooner she accepted that, the easier it would be.

Robert had gone to elaborate lengths to discard her, but Teddy had returned and declared his love.

Even if he was encumbered with a wife, Lily knew that, without a protector, she would be living on the streets.

They stepped into the corridor of the bustling inn. She wished she could think more clearly, but the effects of her recent episode seemed to come in bouts that left her vague and shaking.

"Pardon, ma'am."

She had to step back to let two young manservants who were heaving a heavy trunk pass by.

A ship had recently docked, and in the corridors and main reception room, ladies and gentlemen rubbed shoulders with the publican, his wife, and their many minions, all hurrying to carry out instructions.

In such a bustling hive of activity, Lily had never felt more bereft and alone.

"Dr Swithins! A word about how many for the dinner you ordered tonight!"

It was the publican hailing Teddy from across the room as they headed towards the front doors, and Teddy disengaged her hand, smiling reassuringly as he patted her arm.

"Stay here a moment, my love. I have organised a very special dinner for the two of us tonight."

He wove his way through the crowded room while Lily shrank into a shadowed corner.

She felt claustrophobic, and suddenly the grey skies that she glimpsed as the front doors opened to admit more guests, seemed very appealing after all.

"Of course I couldn't carry on another minute! Not even to the next inn, in my condition!"

The plaintive wail of a heavily pregnant young woman cut through the protests of the newly arrived guest's lady's maid who was remonstrating with her, saying, "But m'lady, the master was most particular that we were staying at the inn just up the road."

"And so we are, but—did you not hear?—I cannot wait even two minutes longer! Now go and fetch someone to take me to a chamber where I can have privacy for just two minutes before we continue. Two minutes is hardly going to inconvenience, Lord Bradden!"

Lily, who had been staring at her clasped hands and her neat kid boots while she waited for Teddy to finish speaking with the publican, jerked her head up.

And as she peeked around the corner alcove where she waited, she briefly locked eyes with the pretty, dark-haired young woman who'd been speaking. A second of confusion seemed to register in the other woman's gaze before her the publican's wife appeared at her elbow, and, distracted, the young woman allowed herself to be led away, plaintively explaining her needs.

"Ah, my dear, are you ready?" Teddy hailed her as he waited for a group of guests to pass.

A group which included on the periphery, Lily was quite certain, Robert's mistress.

No, Robert's wife.

Or was she still deluded? The woman hadn't seemed to recognise her.

But, yes, surely there had been the glint of some confused recognition in her eyes before she'd been ushered towards the stairs?

"Teddy, I don't think I want to go walking after all." Lily tried to extract her hand, which he was now caging on his arm as her vague fear coalesced into something greater.

"A nice brisk will have you feeling clear-headed and up to the mark in no time!" Teddy replied cheerfully as he steered her towards the door. "My dear, I am the doctor and I won't hear no for an answer!"

What could she do?

If she screamed and tried to pull away, Teddy would just

declare that he was a physician and that Lily was his insane patient.

He'd either force her outdoors or bundle her upstairs and lock her in a bedchamber.

Dry-mouthed with terror, she allowed him to walk her outdoors and onto the cobblestones while she tried to order her thoughts. They were as frenetic as the activity all around her.

But soon, they were away from the docks and on a narrow pathway that skirted the cliff face.

"There! Doesn't the fresh air and the fact we are all alone make you feel so much better, my darling?"

It did not. In fact, her heart was thundering so hard she feared she might be sick.

Teddy halted, his hand lightly on her shoulder. They were high on the cliff and there was not a soul in sight. And he was smiling at her while she could feel the wind behind her, and hear the savage waves hurling themselves on the rocks a hundred feet below.

"Yes, it does. I feel much better," she lied, while her legs refused to move, though her mind told her to run.

But what use would that be?

Teddy would catch her. He'd tussle with her and then... when it was all over, he would declare it a terrible tragedy. And everyone would agree because everyone knew Lily was mad.

"And...do you like the ring I gave you?" he asked, hooking his finger in the ribbon and raising it up to the light so that the stone twinkled in the brightness of the cloud-laden sky. "It's a real diamond. Do you know how valuable it is?"

She wondered why he was prevaricating when she knew why he had brought her up here.

To die, of course.

He would simply exert a small burst of pressure and

seconds later, her body would be smashed upon the rocks below the cliff face.

It was all too easy.

But then, of course, if it was a real diamond ring, he'd want that back first. That's why he was holding it up to the light, supposedly to admire it, but really so he could whip it off from around her neck before her pushed her to her death.

Or, perhaps it was because there was a farmer in a horse and cart trundling down the hill and he needed to wait for him to pass.

For a moment, Lily contemplated tearing herself out of Teddy's arms so that she could fling herself upon the mercy of the farmer.

But what would that achieve? Nothing more than a few minutes' reprieve.

"I adore the ring you gave me, Teddy." Her mind seemed clearer than it was a few seconds before, even. "It's the nicest piece of jewellery I've ever been given." She swallowed, forcing herself to smile as she whispered, "Oh, do kiss me, Teddy. Please."

For the farmer's cart had just passed them by and, as Teddy was in the process of taking the ribbon with its ring over her head, she gripped the ring and whispered, "Let me see it in the light once more. Yes, please kiss me, Teddy. To show you love me."

She had possession of the ring; and she had a split second in which to act.

As he half closed his eyes to accede to her final wish, Lily stepped back quickly. "Go fetch your diamond, Teddy!" she cried, flinging the ring which, attached to its pink ribbon, soared in an arc, over his shoulder, a few feet up the hill.

He turned, frowning, and distracted, his first instinct to try and reclaim the precious token he was no doubt going to give his wife and that had never been intended for Lily.

That's all she needed. A second to be in control, for by the time Teddy's second instinct had reasserted itself, Lily was some yards down the hill, her skirts bunched in her hands, her bonnet trailing behind her as she ran as fast as she could to catch up with the farmer and his cart.

"Lily! Come back!"

She'd thought the farmer, who was now only a couple of yards ahead of her, would turn at Teddy's wild cries, but perhaps the old man was deaf.

And if he was deaf, he certainly was equally unresponsive when, with one final, super-human effort, Lily managed to launch herself into the back of his cart and burrow under a bale of hay.

CHAPTER 34

Adistance of roughly a hundred miles separated Lily from the estate where she'd grown up. It might as well have been a thousand.

After her long journey on foot and by pony cart came to an end, she knew she looked as bedraggled as she felt. She'd bartered what she could in order to feed herself along the way, but by the time she'd walked the last mile to the house, she couldn't remember when she'd been so hungry.

Well, of course, that was at the *maison*. Living on thin gruel and very little else had meant she was perpetually hungry. The last four months had seen the flesh return to her bones, however, and the lustre to her hair. She'd been called beautiful again.

She stopped and gripped the wrought-iron railings of the large gates to the entrance of the driveway that wound through parklands to the familiar stone pile in the distance, and took in the familiar sight through tear-filled eyes.

Nostalgia was not behind her emotion. Instead, she felt exhaustion and fear. She'd barely been alone in her father's company her entire life. How would he receive her now?

If she had anywhere else in the world she could go, she'd turn around and seek a reception less icy than the one she knew awaited her.

But her father owed her some obligation, if not to house and protect her, then to provide some means of succour.

Not surprisingly, Edgeworth, the butler, didn't recognise her in her bedraggled state, though she greeted him warmly as he tried to send her to the servants' entrance.

His mouth dropped open, and he could only gape at her like a flounder when she identified herself.

Still shocked and unable to speak, he left her standing in the lobby while the stately retainer turned on his heel and disappeared into the nether regions of the house.

After a while, he came back and bade her follow him to the drawing room where she was left to wait for what seemed an interminable length of time.

Time to stew. Wonder what her reception would be. Question her sanity by choosing to petition her father, of all people, to come to her aid.

Unable to stay still, Lily got up and began to pace the large expanse of expensively carpeted floor. She drew aside the heavily tasselled curtains and gazed at the expanse of sweeping parkland.

Who would inherit all this when her father died? she wondered. His nephew, Lawrence, she supposed. A lad she had met only once. It barely mattered.

Or maybe he lived here now. She hadn't thought to enquire if her father had, in fact, passed away while she was in Brussels, though surely Edgeworth would have mentioned it.

Maybe she'd receive a kinder reception from Lawrence who had been quiet and withdrawn, and nothing like the cold, hard man her father was.

A heavy footstep in the passage outside made her heart

clench with fear, and she had no reserves left to pretend the bravado she'd summoned up when, as a younger person, she'd been the frequent recipient of his cold contempt.

"Lily."

She inclined her head when he addressed her, saying softly, "Hello Father." There really was little else to say.

"This is a surprise."

And, clearly, not a pleasant one.

For a long time, he stared at her as if unsure what to say. "Forgive me," he said, finally. "I had thought you dead."

She shrugged. "As you can see, I am not."

"Sit down, then." He waved her towards the drawing room, sighing as he added, "I'll order tea. You don't look well. But then, you haven't been well for a long time, I hear."

So, he was going to go with the insanity card and have her committed. It didn't take more than a brief look at his face to know that he had not mellowed with age. That he was no more disposed towards treating her with kindness than he had been in all the twenty-five years she'd known him.

"I'm perfectly fine, thank you, Father. Just tired."

"Your husband will not think you perfectly fine, I suspect. Though what the actual status is between you is a matter of conjecture." His nostrils twitched, and he looked pained, as well he might, she supposed. Lily was about to create a scandal of immense proportions just for being alive.

But it wasn't her fault that Robert had thought her dead. Or that he'd married someone else.

"So, you ran away, did you?" Sir John looked at her as if all this were her fault. But then, it always had been her fault. It had been her fault she'd killed his wife by being born. Everything stemmed from that, Lily supposed.

"I didn't run away. I was taken," she said. "I had no say in the matter."

"Indeed." The familiar scepticism was there. "Now there's just the question of what to do with you."

The iron in his expression and the lack of compassion were enough to make her want to crumple at his feet. Instead, she said softly, as she took a seat, "I don't need to tell anyone where I am."

He gave a harsh laugh. "Don't think you're going to live here with me."

Of course, she should have known he'd not take her in. Of course, she should have known that coming here was a terrible idea.

"I didn't know where else to go, Father."

A loud knock on the front door made her jump. Sir John's eyebrows rose, and he turned on her and said quietly, "What have you unleashed upon this house, Lily? I never receive visitors."

She raised her shoulders. What could she say? She had as little idea as he.

In dread, she listened to the tread of several pairs of feet upon the floorboards, and her mind explored the myriad possibilities.

It was the police come to lock her up.

It was a doctor, and several assistants from the insane asylum come to lock her up.

It was the Russian diplomat come to end what he had begun.

Whoever it was, it was not going to end well for her.

She stood up abruptly, glancing at the window as if it offered her a means of escape.

Then the door opened, and Edgeworth said in a strained voice, "Sir, Lord Lambton and Mr McTavish are here to see you."

❄

LILY DROPPED BACK onto the sofa with a thud, holding the cushion in her lap as if it might protect her.

She expected the two men would see her sitting there and immediately direct their... what... Questions? Entreaties? Incriminations? towards her. But she was many yards away on the other side of the enormous, stately drawing room with a cluster of heavyset, overstuffed furniture and potted plants obscuring her.

They were too caught up in whatever drama had propelled them to confront Sir John Taverner to think to look for Lily in his drawing room.

Huddled in her corner, Lily stared at Lord Lambton, looking far less frail than she remembered him, his voice firm and, she realised, recriminatory as he spoke of some crime committed. Some terrible injustice—she caught the word *murder*—which had prompted them to make this visit without prior warning.

Of course, before Lord Lambton had even finished speaking, her father had assumed his own daughter was the perpetrator of the crime, cutting into their explanation with, "What can you expect of a madwoman?"

In another environment, Lily might have bristled. But this was her father. Her entire experience in this household was as a victim, enduring a continual barrage of belittlement. Not that she had spent much time here, it was true. He'd always made clear how little he relished her presence.

Her father's words were like a lash.

No doubt there would be endorsement from the others. Sympathy for Sir John Taverner for being saddled with such a creature as Lily.

Instead, after a short pause, she heard Hamish ask with real curiosity in his tone, "Do you really believe that? Did she show symptoms of lunacy in the past? As a child?"

Warmth flooded her. Regardless of why Hamish was here —and it truly was extraordinary—he was championing her.

What was even more extraordinary than the fact he obviously still thought well of her was that he was in her father's house. She would have leapt up to greet him, except that their conversation was so intense, and having heard of some crime, she was terrified that she may in fact be responsible for having perpetrated it while out of her mind.

She had, after all, thrown a lamp at his head. Who knew what else she may have done when the insanity had visited her?

It was this which tempered her joy at seeing Hamish, let alone declaring herself. If she heard an account which painted too hideous a picture of her behaviour, she might manage to slip out of the room and make her escape.

But the lovely man really was putting his support behind Lily. As if he believed she could be redeemed; that she was worth championing. Perhaps her crime—of which she was still waiting to hear the details—was not so terrible. Surely she must have misunderstood and that it was not murder, otherwise Hamish wouldn't be defending her.

Lily didn't hear what her father said; however, Lord Lambton's response was quite distinct. And adamant.

"I've made enquiries, Tavener. Insanity, madness, whatever you choose to call it. Not one of the servants in this household, or acquaintances with any connection to Lily, can recall any incident that would corroborate the claim that this poor young woman suffers from lunacy."

With fascination, Lily watched the colour flood the old man's cheeks, and his agitation as he stroked his side-whiskers. Had he really come all this way, with Hamish, to champion her sanity?

The idea of having anyone champion her was heartwarming, but any accompanying glow was short-lived. Lily knew the truth. She lived the experience, and had done too many times, to question the fact that she was every bit the madwoman her husband painted her.

Lord Lambton was not content to leave it at that, for he went on fiercely, "No, indeed, Sir John. I do not believe this fabrication of lunacy when the likelier story is that Sir Robert saw it in his best interests to broadcast to all and sundry the assertion that his wife suffered from insanity."

Her father, as stately as ever, stared with beetling brows at Lord Lambton, and then spoke in a low hiss. "You've said enough, Lambton. Indeed, I consider it prodigious effrontery to show your face in my house after what you have done to me. Get out!"

Lily was as taken aback as Hamish appeared to be. She saw the colour drain from her beloved's face before he opened his mouth to perhaps try and calm the situation.

It would be like Hamish. He was a peacemaker. He'd have made a good husband, she thought sadly.

However, before Hamish could speak, Lord Lambton interjected, his voice clear and passionate. "What *I* have done?" he repeated. "I fought a duel with you over the love of the most beautiful woman in all of England. And then, even though you no longer wanted her, you stole her away from me. Took her to the Continent and severed all contact between us. Then proceeded to let everyone believe the lie that the daughter she bore was yours. That she was, in fact, born eleven months later so you'd not be shamed as a cuckolded husband. That's the truth of it. Answer me! That's what happened, isn't it? Susan gave birth to *my* daughter, yet you said nothing! I had no idea of the truth until this man, Hamish McTavish, laid out the pieces. Lily Bradden is, in fact, my daughter. Is that not so?"

Lily was Lord Lambton's daughter? What could Lord Lambton mean?

Heat burned her skin, and her heart skittered about in her chest as she waited for her father's response. But Lord Lambton was continuing with accusations so uncharacteristic from the tender tone Lily was used to hearing at their Wednesday séances. "Why did you say nothing, Taverner? If you hated her so much, why give her no reason for you clearly wishing to have nothing to do with her?"

Her father drew himself up. "What was the point? She was a girl. She'd not inherit. I had no proof of my wife's duplicity until I saw in her *your* features when she was but a few months old. From a legal standpoint, I was saddled with the bastard Susan bore."

"You fought a duel on account of your wife's duplicity," said Lambton. "And then you dragged her out of the country. She was not allowed to communicate with me, was she? Why did you then visit such cruelty on her daughter?" Lord Lambton's voice cracked.

"Do you think I'd let her sully what good name was left?"

Lily watched her father's mouth twist into the familiar, cruel, hard line that characterised his expression when he addressed her. "Of course, I gave Susan no chance to communicate with you."

"Did she try?" There was a querulous note in Lord Lambton's tone.

By now, an understanding of what Lord Lambton was saying was beginning to breach her shock. Still confused, but with her faculties finally clearing, Lily stared between the harsh, grey-haired man she'd grown up believing was her father, and the white-haired, gentler man she'd come to know as the bereaved Lord Lambton who'd lost his only child.

"Did Sarah ever try to leave?"

"What would have been the point, Lambton?" Her father sighed as if he were suddenly weary. "She was married to me and, if you recall, you were married to someone else. Well, she paid for her sins, didn't she? The bastard you and she created killed her when she was brought screaming into this world. And I've had to feed and clothe her ever since."

Lily's mouth dropped open. She might have then said something but Hamish was speaking, his words ringing out with crisp clarity, "But with due respect, you discharged that expense as quickly as you could, for you arranged her marriage to Sir Robert Bradden as soon as she was out of the schoolroom."

Lily focused her eyes on her father—well, the man she'd believed was her father—as she waited for his response. When it came, it was quite in character. "Sir Robert? And didn't he wash his hands of her as quickly as he could, then derided me into the bargain for foisting a tainted changeling upon him?" He let out a bitter laugh. "Like mother, like daughter, he told me, when she did as her mother did and began an affair with her doctor. The man he'd trusted to look after his delicate wife."

Lily bristled with indignation. That was not how it was at all.

"Sir Robert already had a mistress when he married me!" she cried, leaping to her feet and tossing the cushion back onto the sofa to put her hands on her hips. "In all our married years together, he spoke not one kind word to me. It was clear he wanted nothing to do with me—except a child, and when that did not happen, he was forever pushing Teddy —Dr Swithins—to attend me! Do not blame me for everything, Father!" She glared at the man who had cowed her for her entire life. Yet with the clear support of Hamish and Lord Lambton, she felt sufficiently emboldened to make her case.

The three men turned, astonishment written on all their faces.

"You!" her father all but spat. "Just like you to be hiding

away, eavesdropping. Well, young woman, you got only what you deserved. Madness? Yes, you became deranged. I admit I was both horrified, but morbidly delighted that such a just punishment should be visited upon you."

"Except that Lady Bradden was never mad." It was darling Hamish who said this with such misguided conviction.

"Good lord, and what would you know about that?" Sir John said derisively. "What would you know about anything? Why are you even here?"

Lily wondered the same thing. Yes, he obviously cared for her, and it was truly astonishing that he'd made this long journey to confront her father with what, so far, had been unfounded support for her mental state. But why was he here with Lord Lambton? Her father? *Could Lord Lambton really believe such a thing? That Lily was his daughter?*

Could it really be true?

And how could Hamish contradict the undeniable fact that she was prone to debilitating bouts of madness? Madness so acute that she believed the walls were breathing, closing in on her, and that she was about to burst out of herself?

"I came here," Hamish announced crisply, "because I needed to find your daughter to tell her—and everyone else who believes the lie—that she is not mad. And that I have proof."

Darling Hamish. If only it were true. Lord, if anyone knew she was mad, then Lily knew it, herself. She wanted to run to him and throw his arms about him.

"Proof, eh?

"Yes, conclusive proof in the form of the powders that charlatan Dr Swithins has been administering to her."

He swung round and looked at Lily, his expression softening, but his words clear and businesslike as he asked, "Did you suffer any spells of madness before you met Dr Swithins?"

Lily tried to think. The past seemed to roll past her eyes like a slow-moving river. Her unhappy childhood, a few tears, mostly silence, boredom, a sense of abandonment. But no episodes like she'd had after…

She had met Teddy.

"No." She shook her head.

Hamish went on, "So, after you met Dr Swithins, he started prescribing treatments for your mood, no doubt. And these moods then became quite extreme? To the point it was decided you must go to a sanitorium for your health. Only, Dr Swithins took you to the *maison* in Brussels, am I correct?"

Lily didn't even have to think about *that*. It was all just as he said.

She nodded, her mind running on, past the point which Hamish described. "They cured me when I was there," she said softly, bowing her head. "At the *maison*, they were cruel, but… at least I suffered no madness there."

"That's because you were not being fed the *Amanita muscaria* that Dr Swithins was in the habit of putting into your warm milk." Hamish's lip curled.

He swung back to the two men. Her father—Sir John— was blinking rapidly as if finding this hard to digest, and didn't know whether to deride Hamish's words out of hand, or seek somewhere to sit down, for they were all still standing near the doorway. Clearly, he wanted to be rid of them as soon as he could.

On Lord Lambton's face was an expression of satisfaction. He must have heard all this during his journey here with Hamish.

How Lily wished his belief in all this was founded. But

Lily had lived with her spiralling bouts of mania for too long to disbelieve the truth of them.

She ventured a few steps forward as Hamish went on, "Several nights ago, my sister Lucy went to visit Lady Bradden at her home."

Lily raised her eyebrows. She had not known this. Lucy McTavish must have arrived shortly after Lily had left with Teddy. She hesitated. Something in Hamish's tone suggested something of great import was to come.

"When she arrived, Lady Bradden had left, but some of the warm milk remained, and this was offered by the maid to my sister."

Lily stilled. She felt as if she were on the cusp of something. On the ledge of a very steep cliff and that, if she were not careful, she would plunge into the deep, dark depths. Only by taking short, careful breaths, could she hold herself back from this death spiral.

Sir John made a noise, but Lord Lambton turned on him, his tone sharp. "Listen to what Mr McTavish has to say, and then I think you'll change your tune." He cleared his throat and again, his voice sounded suddenly on the verge of breaking as he went on, "The greatest travesty of justice has been dealt your daughter—ha! My daughter! You need to hear it!"

Hamish, who had been looking at Sir John, shifted position, his gaze seeking Lily's. He smiled, and the tenderness in his look struck at the very core of her. She reached for the back of a sofa to steady herself as he turned back to Sir John.

"The maid said she'd made the milk using the powder Dr Swithins prescribed as a calming tonic. When I arrived at Lady Bradden's house, it was to find my sister suffering hallucinations of a kind terrifyingly similar to those suffered by Lady Bradden. I will not go into the violence of this episode. Suffice to say I had a chemist analyse the powder while I journeyed here. It was only when we reached the station, and I was able to telegraph from the village, that I received the results." He swung round to look at Lily. "Lady Bradden isn't insane," he declared in a tone that brooked no argument. "For whatever reason, Dr Swithins, perhaps with the collusion of her husband, *made* the world believe that Lady Bradden was insane."

CHAPTER 35

Lily watched the moon make its appearance over the half-frozen pond of her father, Lord Lambton's estate and shivered. Not from the cold, for with her hand encased in Hamish's large warm one, and his arm about her shoulders, she'd never felt warmer.

It was like a glow that radiated outwards, enveloping every part of her in a mantle of safety and security. Not a feeling she was used to enjoying.

"The moon reminds me of Celeste," she murmured, resting her head on Hamish's shoulder as he stroked her cheek. "Cold and beautiful. I feel so terrible about what happened to her."

Hamish sighed. "Poor woman. The police never did learn who she was or where she came from. It could have been a place like this..." he made a sweeping motion of the acres of rolling pasture lands that belonged to Lord Lambton "...or the gutter. But she lived dangerously, and her efforts at garnishing her wages at Madame Chambon's by selling secrets cost her her life." He drew Lily closer against him. "Or worse… they nearly cost you yours."

"Poor Mr Renquist," said Lily with a sigh. "If he'd not had red hair, he'd likely be sitting in front of his drawing fire right now."

"With his harpy of a wife," murmured Hamish, adding quickly, "though you're right. Igor Novichov killed the wrong red-headed lover when he learned that Celeste was channelling his Russian master's sensitive information to the British Government."

A family of ducks glided over the surface of the pond, bringing to mind the afternoon Hamish's sister had stood by Lily's side and tossed hunks of bread to the birdlife in Regent's Park. Lucy had been Lily's champion before Hamish had finally succumbed to the tension between them that Lily had felt so palpably before anything had actually happened.

"I'm so delighted your sister has found love, too," she said, glad to change the subject to something happier.

"Oh, she's been desperate to become Mrs Myers for years," said Hamish. "That young man of hers just never earned enough to keep a wife. Well, not someone like my sister. Lucy would be miserable if she didn't have a new bonnet or pair of gloves every two weeks."

"So, you only said yes when his wages increased?"

"Did I not tell you, sweetheart?" Hamish looked into her eyes, his own creased with amusement. How different the composition of his features was these days. There was nothing repressed or buttoned-up about her new husband in the six weeks since they'd said their vows at St Mary's in a small, intimate ceremony.

Lord Lambton had given her away, and her new sister-in-law had wept buckets of tears, telling Lily at the reception that she, too, would soon enjoy her own happy day now that she'd received her brother's blessing.

"No, you did not tell me, Hamish! Which makes me wonder what else you've neglected to mention."

"I've neglected nothing important, I assure you, since my every waking thought has been devoted to mitigating the damage done by your cold and callous late husband." He kissed her hand. "I was proud of you for refusing to don widow's weeds and to agree to marry me before a twelvemonth was up."

"Hamish! Did you think I wouldn't?" she began before realising Hamish was teasing her. Hamish teased her often these days. Gone was the seriousness she'd thought was ingrained in his character. Gone, too, was the intensity and distrust she'd thought were ingrained in hers. Feeling lighthearted and looking forward to the day ahead was a thrilling novelty.

"No one expected you to," Hamish said, sobering. "Not after the scandal broke when your late husband launched his violent assault upon Teddy, and the truth about everything else came out."

Lily and Hamish only learned some time later that Lily's escape from the pathway above the cliffs of Dover had occurred just in time. For Sir Robert had arrived that evening, having expected Teddy to have fixed the inconvenient problem that inadvertently made Sir Robert a bigamist.

Teddy had done Sir Robert's bidding for years, dosing Lily with the potions that gave Robert the excuse to incarcerate her when her supposed madness became so public and extreme.

But when Mr Montpelier had kidnapped Lily, the Mother Superior at the *maison* in Brussels had, in terror for the reputation of the asylum, declared that Lily had died, and then provided false supporting documentation.

Lily's arrival on the London spiritualist scene made it clear that the problem of Sir Robert's wife had just assumed epic proportions now that Sir Robert had remarried, and his new wife was expecting the child for which he so longed. Teddy had panicked when Sir Robert had threatened him, ordering him to fix the problem *any way he chose.*

"Poor Robert," reflected Lily. "What a horrible way to die."

"That's remarkably charitable of you since you know that it was *you* who was supposed to be lying dead at the bottom of Dover's lovely white cliffs." There was no sympathy in Hamish's tone when he added, "And if Teddy isn't paying for the crimes he committed against you, at least he's been locked up for a very long time for instigating the fight that led to the death of the terrible man whose bidding he did. The husband who tried to destroy you. Then what would I have done?" He put his hands on her shoulders and looked into her face. "How would I have survived without you?" He sounded quite emotional, Lily was delighted to note. "You truly are my sun and my moon and my stars."

"Oh Hamish, that's so poetic." She cupped his cheeks and kissed him on the mouth. "It sounds like something Mr Myers would say, if everything Lucy gushes about him is true."

Hamish looked embarrassed. "Actually, it is very similar to a line in a poem that Mr Myers has written for the magazine."

"What? He's writing for *Manners and Morals?*"

"Didn't I tell you that, either? Yes, I was moving onto the subject before I got distracted by how lucky I am to have you by my side, against all odds. Anything other than telling you how I intend to make you the happiest wife in England seems unimportant these days." With a twinkle in his eye, he lightly pinched her cheek. "Mr Myers is my newest staff member, now earning a salary sufficient to keep my sister in bonnets and gloves, which was, as I mentioned, the prerequisite I felt was necessary to my giving consent to their marriage." He smiled at Lily's delight, adding, "And provided I've not made a grave miscalculation with regard to the new direction I've taken the newspaper, Mr Myers will have ever more editorial responsibilities as he covers the pleasurable aspects of London life, while still keeping our loyal readers happy."

"Like Mrs Moore's and Mr Montpelier's séances," said Lily, raising one eyebrow.

Hamish shrugged. "It was you who didn't press for a conviction," he reminded her.

"That's because, the way I look at it, Mr Montpelier saved my life," said Lily. "And although what he did was terrible, he did provide me with a roof over my head and enough freedom to meet you."

"And an entertainment that reunited you with your real father." The memory of that final séance was so moving that both Lily and Hamish were silent as they paused to reflect.

Slowly, Hamish went on, "When Archie got that scoop and took those heartbreakingly tender photographs of Lord Lambton being reunited with his long-lost daughter at Mrs Moore's séance, which I published against father's wishes, *Manners & Morals* was given a new lease of life. We never sold so many copies." He tightened his grip on her hand, and they turned in the direction of the house, Hamish's mood elated. "And our readers are clamouring for more. Why, my dearest, as long as you continue to write your columns, and answer their letters with your own good advice, sprinkled with snippets from your incredible experiences, *Manners & Morals* will continue to outsell its competition, and Father won't offer a word of complaint. He is, after all, a businessman at heart."

"He'd be a much happier businessman if he'd realised a long time ago that there's as much money to be made covering the more joyous aspects of life than just ramming down people's throats how important it is to be good."

"And that's where my competitive streak comes in." Hamish tightened his grip on Lily's hand as he guided her along the narrowing path as it skirted the river towards the gracious, mellow building that Lily now called her second home.

"I always thought you *were* competitive and driven, Hamish," said Lily. "With not a pleasure-loving bone in your body."

Hamish shrugged. "You've been a good influence on me then, haven't you?" he said, lightly. "And you haven't asked what my latest competitive project is."

"Tell me?" Happily, she gazed up at him as the path widened and, side by side, they strolled towards the lights spilling in welcome rays from the windows of the house.

"Well, not only am I going to prove to father that *Morals & Manners* can make more money by offering the public stories of hope, rather than dire warnings and moralising, I'm going to make the magazine an agent for change."

"An agent for change? That's a strange term."

"But it sounds very serious, don't you think? Yes, now, I'm not sure if the public is ready for it. I very much doubt my father is. But I'm going to feature one lost soul each month."

Lily loved the way Hamish's eyes lit up when he grew excited. It always made her feel he could achieve anything. "Go on," she encouraged.

His smile broadened. "Archie is going to help find these people and photograph them. People whom society has written off. But by writing their story, and promoting a reader's fund for them, I hope to do what society won't—provide them with a means of achieving their dreams, whether that's getting an apprenticeship or a fruit barrow if they're from the gutter." His excitement grew. "Or a milliner's business, or…a fashion empire! Even if they're one of Madame Chambon's girls."

"My goodness, Hamish! I had no idea! How did you come up with such ideas!"

"It was all because of you, my love!" He stopped, clasped her hands in his and brought them up to his lips. For a long time, he simply gazed at her as if she truly were the most wondrous creature to grace his world. "Your courage, your ability to survive, your strength and forgiveness through all that's happened."

"Why, Hamish, you're making me blush," Lily whispered, feeling the burn of emotion that echoed in her own heart every sentiment he was uttering.

"It's true, my own sweet love." He cleared his throat, and in the moonlight, Lily saw the moisture in his eyes, though his voice was firm and strong again as he went on, "You've made me realise that no matter where you come from, Lily McTavish…and no matter how far you fall, and however dire the future seems…a shining new life really *is* possible—"

He would have gone on only she gripped his hand to stop him, putting a forefinger to his lips so she could add, "*If* such a person is fortunate enough to meet someone who believes in them."

Faintly, in the distance, the sound of the dinner gong echoed across the frozen lawn.

Hamish raised his face to look at the house. "We should hurry, my love," he said. "We don't want to keep your father waiting." Gently, he rested his hand on her belly, adding, "And you must be starving if, as the doctor believes, you're eating for two."

THE END

When Lily opens an agency to find respectable employment for the fallen women at Madame Chambon's, one of her first customers is Evelina Tarot, newly arrived from Paris to marry wealthy Lord Dunstable.

Evelina, who is looking to employ a lady's maid after the death of her French maid in a train crash, has no idea that her mother is London's most notorious brothel-keeper, Madame Chambon.

But when Lord Dunstable is murdered in Madame Chambon's private sitting room, it is Lily, former Lady Bradden, who begins to piece together the puzzle and to realise that Evelina's life is suddenly under threat.

Read **Murder at Madame Chambon's**, next in the thrilling **London Ladies in Peril** series.

MURDER AT MADAME CHAMBON'S

The seductive new historical mystery that will leave you breathless...

A murdered lord in a brothel. An innocent debutante in

love. And a killer who threatens to expose the secret that could destroy her.

When Miss Evelina Tarot's fiancé is found dead in London's most notorious pleasure house, William, Lord Bellingham steps forward to protect her. But even as love blooms between them, he discovers a devastating truth— Evelina is the daughter of infamous brothel keeper Madame Chambon, a secret that would ruin her forever in the eyes of society.

Joining forces with Lily, Lady Bradden—whose employment bureau offers a future to fallen women—Lord Bellingham races to unmask a killer bent on exposing Madame Chambon's darkest secrets.

For only by understanding the murderer's true motives can he protect the woman he loves from becoming the next victim, and find a way to make her his bride without society discovering the truth of her birth.

Murder at Madame Chambon's is the latest installment in this riveting historical mystery series, perfect for readers who love their romance tinged with danger and their mysteries laced with passion.

MURDER AT MADAME CHAMBON'S PROLOGUE

ENGLAND, 1880

Evelina glanced out of the train window at the dusky haze of the fading afternoon and tried to temper her excitement. The rhythmic clatter of wheels had put her maid, Mimi, to sleep, but Evelina was hurtling towards her future—at last!—with lightning speed.

Not only was she finally leaving France to return to the land of her birth, but she had all the backing needed by a young woman determined to make the most glittering marriage of the season and to secure the future *she* chose for herself.

"One scarlet and blue polonaise with blue velvet swathes and bows for Lady Gilray's ball, and the brown and green checked walking dress for the first promenade in Hyde Park..."

Mimi and she had spent hours deciding which of her vast couture wardrobe she'd wear for the events for which Lady Perry had secured an invitation for Evelina.

There'd be more to come, Evelina's mama had written, once word had spread of Evelina's beauty and accomplishments.

Not to mention, her dowry.

Then she'd wear the rose-pink princess-line polonaise with fan-shaped train to Lady Marchant's soiree...

She had hoped to have a ball or soiree lined up for every night of the week. At nearly twenty-one and with her beauty at its peak, Evelina didn't want to wait too long to find a suitable husband. In fact, she was determined to do so during her first London season. A brilliant match was what she wanted, though a good one would do if it happened sooner rather than later. She wasn't looking to fall in love. The nuns at the convent had made clear *that* was only in fairytales.

She rather thought she'd make a good political hostess in view of the education the nuns had given her, followed by her finishing school in Switzerland, complicated by her illness, which had held her back nearly two years.

But now she was in the best of health and her enthusiasm for becoming mistress of a large, impressive landholding, or similar as befitted her value, was at its zenith.

Then, for the Duchess of Kintyre's weekend house party, she'd have to take two trunks to fit—

Evelina was just doing a mental inventory of what to pack for the penultimate event of the season four weeks hence, when a bone-rattling jolt thrust her book out of her hands and sent her maid sprawling to the compartment floor.

"*Mon Dieu*! What's happening?" Evelina shielded her face as metal shrieked, the luggage from overhead tumbled to the floor, and passengers screamed in the surrounding compartments.

"Mimi! Mimi! Are you alright?"

A shuddering jolt propelled Evelina against the window with force, her head hitting the glass and her vision blurring.

She was vaguely aware of the commotion around her, but the urgency had dimmed, and suddenly everything seemed muted and very far away. She thought she could see Mimi bobbing about in the corner, and closed her eyes, for she didn't like the way her elegant French lady's maid looked right now, and—

"Miss! Madam!" The voice that jerked her into consciousness made her aware of the cold water seeping through her clothing and Evelina opened her eyes to a scene of horror, overlaid by the insistent calling of a male voice whom it took her a moment to locate.

A handsome young face loomed above her.

This seemed very odd, for she was in a train carriage on her way from Dover to London and no-one was supposed to be on the roof.

But then she realized the carriage in which she and Mimi had been traveling from the docks was on its side, the plush seats torn from the wood paneling, and water was now rising from the broken window at her feet.

"Please, miss! Quickly! Take my hand! There's not much time."

Evelina struggled to sit up, her sodden skirts heavy and confining about her ankles as she tried to regain her balance.

She realized that the face above her belonged to a young man who was crouched by the open door of the compartment which was on its side. He'd extended his arm and, judging by the look on his face and the urgency in his voice, matters were serious, and time was critical.

She managed to stand and to reach up, her hand curling around strong fingers before another violent lurch broke her grip.

With a scream, Evelina fell back against the window beneath her, and the young man's face grew distant.

"Take my wrist. I've got you!"

He hadn't, but his words were the reassurance she needed before she remembered her companion.

"Mimi?" She swung round, screaming again as she saw that the older woman's head was at an odd angle and her eyes were open and sightless.

"You can't do anything for her! Take my hand. We're running out of time!"

His urgency galvanized Evelina into action, but she had to jump to bridge the growing distance between the hand he held out as he now lay flat upon the upturned compartment which Evelina realized had slid down the embankment and into the river below.

And which was sinking fast.

He was strong. Strong enough to haul her entire body weight the distance needed before he had sufficient purchase to reach out his other hand and drag her through the broken window.

With a mighty heave, he pulled her free from the wreckage just as the carriage, burdened by its own weight and the pull of the river, slid into the water with a deafening splash.

Breathing heavily, Evelina collapsed against a pair of supporting arms and listened to the cries and screams of passengers amidst the turmoil and confusion.

But she was safe.

The thickness of her skirts and bodice had shielded her from the worst of potential injuries, though she saw her left hand was bloodied. Or perhaps it was a head wound, she wondered, as she withdrew her hand from wiping the hair from her eyes.

"Monsieur?" She cast around for her rescuer, her panic, at discovering she was alone again, increasing as she registered the carnage.

Not that she could see much until a gust of wind cleared the smoke sufficiently for her to realize that hers was one of two carriages that had derailed and slipped into the river, while the front few carriages remained on the track at the top of the embankment.

She was alone again, but alive, and all she needed to do was to negotiate the muddy climb to the top.

If she had the energy.

Evelina sank down upon the metal side of their compartment which separated her from Mimi. She wouldn't leave her friend, for Mimi had been with her since she'd gone to Switzerland. The young man would have to come back so he could get the older woman out when he'd finished saving other lives.

Her dazed thoughts were running in discombobulated loops before she was roused by the insistent screams of a woman some yards away, she saw, as the smoke once again cleared.

"William! My son William is still inside!"

Evelina sat up sharply. Then, scrunching up her skirts so she could move, she struggled through the mangled metal and mud towards the woman who was kneeling on the upturned carriage, dangling her arm through the gaping window.

"He's too small to reach! Help me! The water's rising!"

Evelina stared helplessly into the void. She couldn't see

the child, but she could hear his frightened whimpers. The woman's cries grew louder in relation to Evelina's desperation.

"Please, sir! Help me!"

Evelina saw she'd thrust out her arm to grip a checked trouser leg, and she looked up into the face of the young man who had dragged her to safety a few minutes earlier. There was a cut above his eye and a smear of mud on his cheek, but nothing else marred his obvious good looks.

Unless it was the bleakness in his eye which was directed now towards the sound of the young boy in the far depths of the carriage. Even Evelina could see it was hopeless for him to help, for the distance was too great for his seeking arm to help a small child.

Unless—

"Hold me while I reach for him! You're strong enough!" Evelina burst out, unbuttoning her tight-fitting bodice, and unclasping her skirt as she spoke, closing the distance between them. The thick heavy swathes of embellishment slithered over the bustle cage which she untied with trembling fingers and tossed aside, unembarrassed as she wriggled into a sitting position with the help of the young man who hauled her into position. The glass of the window had completely fallen away, so at least no jagged edges impeded her rescue attempt.

Only the strength and willingness of the young man, but he was already gripping her wrist while she gripped his as he carefully lowered her into the compartment.

The claustrophobic darkness hit Evelina with force and momentarily dashed her bravado as she dangled helplessly into the void, completely dependent upon the strength of her rescuer. "William?" she called.

But when small fingers almost instantly tickled her palm, relief and purpose galvanized her courage once more.

"William, take my hand and don't struggle!" she said, shouting back up to the light, "I've got him! Bring me up now!"

The little boy's eyes were wide with terror as he was drawn into the afternoon haze, before his mother threw herself upon him and Evelina fell back, her strength and courage drained.

"My name's William, too."

She blinked open her eyes as her handsome rescuer supported her into a sitting position, his warm, open smile revealing strong while teeth, his dark blue eyes seeming to connect to something deep inside her, causing a flowering sensation to bloom in her heart.

Then he was straightening at a distant cry for help, while a billow of smoke obscured him from view.

When Evelina tried to find him again so she could thank him properly, he'd gone.

"Miss! Are you all right?" Another team of rescuers, obviously from the nearby town, swarmed over the wreckage and Evelina was soon covered in a blanket before they carried her towards a line-up of carriages parked at the top of the embankment.

She twisted her head, searching for the young man—the older of the two Williams. But now the muddy slope and mangled carriages were overrun by strangers.

"Miss, let me tend to that nasty cut upon your forehead." They were motherly words and the soft hands of a woman who'd come to help were soothing. "Poor child, is someone looking for you? Let me clean you up so your loved ones can recognize you. Your poor mama, for a start, wouldn't begin to know who you were."

She was a farmer's wife by the look of her, and she'd seated herself next to Evelina in one of the carriages, cleaning Evelina's face as she spoke.

Evelina didn't answer. Her mama wouldn't know her, either way, for she'd not seen Evelina since her daughter was fourteen years old.

As for any other loved ones, that was why she'd come to London.

If not to love, then to establish a life.

The life she'd grown up believing was her due.

The one in which she finally would be mistress of her own destiny and no longer beholden to the mother who had farmed her off to the nuns when she was six because she'd said Evelina's wild and stubborn ways was the reason her papa had removed himself from the family home.

FAIR CYPRIANS OF LONDON
SERIES

The *London Ladies in Peril* series is a spin-off to the *Fair Cyprians of London* series.

These romances with mystery and intrigue follow a group of Madame Chambon's 'Fallen Angels', women who are determined to find happiness—using inventive methods —after they were ruined or betrayed.

HERE ARE THE BOOKS IN THE SERIES

Grace Fortune trusts no one after she was betrayed by the man she once loved.

Now, she's the most popular 'Cyprian' at Madame Chambon's high-class London House of Assignation, consort of aristocrats and princes.

As Faith prepares for her next job as the special initiation 'gift' procured by a mother in fashionable Mayfair for her son's twenty-first birthday, she plans her revenge.

But revenge has a strange habit of turning the tables.

Heartfelt, sizzling and with a note of redemption that'll please even the cynics.

FORSAKING HOPE (Book 2)

Honour? Or her heart's desire?

When Felix discovers the divine "Miss Hope" in his bed, his betrayal is acute.

Two years ago, he'd been on the verge of proposing to the beautiful governess who had taught his neighbour's children. Ignoring his family's objections, he'd been determined to make her an honourable offer.

But Hope had suddenly vanished.

Now, to Felix's shock and dismay, Hope is the surprise gift his friends have sourced from London's most exclusive House of Assignation in the hopes of lifting his dark depression.

Despite the pain of the past, Felix can't bear to lose her again.

But Hope Merriweather is bound to her new life by a dark secret. She sacrificed Felix two years before.

Now, she must choose again: Honour or her heart's desire?

Here's what reviewers are saying:

"So very different from most of the historical romance books I've read. Well written with plot twists and hinting but not quite divulging what is the behind cause. Truly enjoyed this book."

"Oh, I like this series! ...I started reading a bit late in the evening and had to read late into the night as I did not want to stop. Lots of tension. Good balance of dialog and action, some of it steamy."

KEEPING FAITH (Book 3)

Revenge is sweet until it breaks your heart.

Falsely accused of stealing, Faith is given two choices: Fend for herself on the streets of London, or become indentured to Madame Chambon, the ruthless proprietor of London's most exclusive brothel.

In order to survive, Faith submits to the machinations of a mysterious benefactress and begins a new life under Madame Chambon's roof. However, she does not live like the other girls.

Rather, she's taught the theory of how to entrance London's noble gentlemen with her learning in philosophy, politics and art.

Her body is to be saved for the greatest enticement of all: revenge.

Faith doesn't care what she has to do. She lives only to fulfil a bargain that will set her free.

But when Faith is recruited as the muse of a talented, sensitive painter whose victory in a prestigious art competition turns them both into celebrities overnight, she discovers the reasons behind her mission are very different from what she'd been led to believe.

Now she is complicit in something dark and dangerous while riches, adulation and freedom are hers for the taking.

But what value are these if her heart has become a slave to the honorable man she is required to destroy?

Keeping Faith is book 3 in the Fair Cyprians of London series but can be read as a stand-alone.

Here's what the readers say about the books in the series:

"This is one of the most interesting stories on why a girl might become an escort. The twists and turns are breathtaking...I couldn't put this down."

"Oh my! This story just makes you fall in love! It's exciting. It never lags. And what a most satisfying ending!"

WEDDING VIOLET (Book 4)

Abandoned at the altar, Max, Lord Belvedere believes he's evaded family obligation in favour of a life of adventuring in Africa. But his ailing Aunt Euphemia has other ideas.

When Max finds himself in the delightfully diverting arms of Violet Lilywhite while visiting London's most prestigious House of Assignation, he happens upon the perfect plan. A sham wedding to a 'penniless shop girl' should fulfil Aunt Euphemia's romantic dreams without losing him his newfound liberty.

Violet agrees to the deception with no hesitation. Lord Belvedere is certainly the most charming and surprising of all her male consorts but she has no illusions about a shared future. She wants only to escape the clutches of infamous Madame Chambon.

The plan appears perfect until Max and Violet find themselves falling in love.

Can Max give up his plans for freedom in an exciting new land? Or is freedom to be found in the arms of the woman he loves?

What the readers are saying:

"Wedding Violet is the delightful story of Max and Violet. They meet by chance when Max darkens the door of Madame Chambon's establishment after he is left at the altar. Although Max's inner and outer dialogue spout of his virtue and strong morals, he never-the-less can't leave Violet alone after their first encounter…The ending of this story took me completely by surprise! A wonderful surprise with a happy ending for Max, Violet, and Aunt Euphemia."

CHRISTMAS CHARITY (Book 5)

Reluctant courtesan, Charity, has found true love with Hugo, her first and only client.

But when poet and artist, Hugo, is tricked into gambling away his impending inheritance, Charity finds herself at the mercy of Madam Chambon and her infamous house of ill-repute.

Can the two young lovers thwart the conspiracy between Hugo's social-climbing father, and slippery cousin Cyril, so Hugo can make Charity his Christmas bride?

Get it from all retailers here
Or buy direct here

THE BENEFITS OF BUYING DIRECT

Did you know that when you download an eBook directly from an author's store, you can read it on your Kindle?

Your direct purchase also supports the author more fully and gives you the satisfaction of a direct connection with the creator of the works you love.

And it's always so appreciated!

DAUGHTERS OF SIN SERIES

THE DAUGHTERS OF SIN SERIES

Two nobly born sisters and their illegitimate half-sister — an actress and a governess — compete for love as they bring to justice a dangerous (but very charismatic villain) during several London Seasons.

With Hetty and Araminta both falling for men on opposing sides of a dastardly plot that is being investigated by Stephen Cranborne, a secret agent in the Foreign Office, there's lashings of skullduggery and intrigue bound up in the central romance.

What Readers are Saying About the Series

"...lies, misdeeds, treachery, and romance. What an impressive story! Ms. Oakley has a unique way of telling her stories, bringing unknown heroes/ heroines into the spotlight, as they navigate a world of espionage, and intrigue, all while trying to survive and find their HEA. Magnificent and mesmerizing!" ~ **Reader**

"Full of secrets, murders, intrigues and you feel you know the characters and want to strangle some of them, especially Araminta!!! I have since read all in the series and can't wait for Book 5... This is a series I will read again and again." ~ **Reader**

Below is the order of the books:

Her Gilded Prison (Book #1)
Dangerous Gentlemen (Book #2)
The Mysterious Governess (Book #3)
Beyond Rubies (Book #4)
Lady Unveiled: The Cuckold's Conspiracy (Book #5)
Prequel: Scandal of the Season

DAUGHTERS OF SIN ~ BOOKS 1-3

Read now

READING LIST ORDER

Daughters of Sin series

BUY DIRECT

**Two nobly born debutantes and their illegitimate half-sisters—
an actress and a governess—unite to bring a
dangerous (handsome!) traitor to justice.**

"These books are the best-written timepieces I've ever
read." ~ **Goodreads.**

1. Her Gilded Prison

2. Dangerous Gentlemen

3. The Mysterious Governess

4. Beyond Rubies

5. Lady Unveiled: The Cuckold Conspiracy

6. *Prequel: The Scandal of the Season*

Fair Cyprians of London

BUY DIRECT

Ruined vicar's daughters and kidnapped countesses are amongst
the courtesans feted by the aristocrats who frequent Madame
Chambon's Pleasure House.

But each woman has one desire in common: revenge...and their own
"happy ever after".

1. Saving Grace

2. Forsaking Hope

3. Keeping Faith

4. Wedding Violet

5. Christmas Charity

London Ladies in Peril

1. A Fatal Rendezvous in Mayfair

2. Murder at Madame Chambon's

Hearts in Hiding series

Heroines who must hide their identity for the protection of their hearts - or their lives.

1. The Duchess and the Highwayman (steamy suspense)

2. The Bluestocking and the Rake (sweet suspense)

3. Duchess of Seduction (steamy second chance love)

4. The Countess and the Cavalier (steamy suspense)

Scandalous Miss Brightwells series

A series of delightful romantic comedies!

Two daring sisters cause scandal and mayhem as they storm London's Regency ballrooms in search of husbands to please their mama.

Once successful, they are keen to put their husband-hunting skills to good use as they set about matchmaking—with hilarious results!

1. Rake's Honour

2. Rogue's Kiss

3. The Wedding Wager

4. The Accidental Elopement

5. The Honourable Fortune Hunter

6. The Courtship Caper

7. The Wilful Widow

8. The Gypsy and the Gentleman

9. The Actress and the Aristocrat

(Box sets available: Books 1-3 and Books 1-4)

Books 4-7)

Georgian Mystery/Romance series

BUY DIRECT

1. Wicked Wager

2. Her Valentine's Secret

Scandalous: Three Daring Charades

BUY DIRECT

1. Lady Olivia's Butterfly

2. Lady Sarah's Redemption

3. Lady Rose's Secret

The Governess and Lowly Companion series

BUY DIRECT

Three Regency-set Cinderella retellings

1. The Governess's Secret Love

2. Hazard's Mistress

3. A Scandalous Reunion

Dutiful Wives

BUY DIRECT

1. The Reluctant Bride

2. An Unsuitable Alliance

3. Passion Fever

Wings over Africa series (writing as B. G. Nettelton)

BUY DIRECT

(Prequel novella) Twilight over the Okavango

Whispers over the Kalahari

Diamond Mountain

Botswana-set novella

Okavango Angel

BUYING DIRECT

When you buy books directly from the author's Shopify store, you support them more fully while also receiving a personalized experience, exclusive offers, and the satisfaction of a direct connection with the creator of the works you love.

GET A FREE BOOK

Would you like to know when I have new releases as well as get the romantic start to my Regency-set 'Dynasty'-inspired *Daughters of Sin* series?

Visit: www.beverleyoakley.com

ABOUT THE AUTHOR

Beverley Oakley is an Australian author of more than 35 Victorian and Georgian-set romances laced with mystery and intrigue, and Regency Rom-coms.

Under her other pen names—Beverley Eikli and B.G. Nettelton—she writes Africa-set romantic suspense and Women's Fiction.

Born in the African mountain kingdom of Lesotho, Beverley married the dashing Norwegian bush pilot she met in Botswana's beautiful Okavango Delta while managing a safari lodge.

She began her writing career as a journalist, but it was during long aerial survey contracts around the world—often as the sole woman among the crew—that she began to write romance novels, finding in them an escape from the isolation.

Beverley lives just north of Melbourne with the same wonderful husband she whisked away from Botswana thirty years ago, together with their youngest daughter (the oldest lives in Norway), and a gorgeous, dopey Rhodesian Ridgeback who weighs more than she does.

When she's not writing, she runs a Wuthering Heights Bed & Breakfast & Farmstay in South Australia's beautiful wine growing Clare Valley with her two sisters, and teaches Writing.

You can visit her websites at: www.beverleyoakley.com or www.beverleysbooks.com

Visit Beverley's Shopify store:
www.beverleysbooks.com
Or her website: www.beverleyoakley.com

Join Beverley's reader group on Facebook

Follow Beverley
On Bookbub
On Goodreads
On Facebook